Honour The Sun

(Extracted and revised from the diary of the Owl)

Ruby Slipperjack

PEMMICAN
PUBLICATIONS
INC.

Cover Design by Grandesign Ltd.

Pemmican Publications Inc. gratefully acknowledges the assistance accorded to its publishing program by the **Manitoba Arts Council** and **Canada Council**.

Printed and Bound in Canada

First Printing, 1987
Second Printing, 1989
Third Printing, 1990
Fourth Printing, 1992
Fifth Printing, 1994

Canadian Cataloguing in Publication Data

Slipperjack, Ruby, 1952 -
Honour the Sun

ISBN: 0-919143-44-X

I. Title.
PS8587.L57H6 1987 C813'.54 C87-098105-6
PR9199.3.S54H6 1987

Unit 2-1635 Burrows Avenue/Winnipeg, Manitoba, Canada/R2X 0T1

CONTENTS

DEDICATED

to My Family

Ruby Slipperjack

1

FIRST ENTRY

Summer 1962

Small poplar trees surround us, their leaves swish and flutter in the gentle breeze. I hum a lullaby to my doll cradled in my arms. The waves lap against the shoreline beside me. Rocking my doll back and forth and listening to Sarah's constant chatter, I'm drowsy. My friend, Sarah, is sitting at the other end of the blanket. She puts her doll aside and leans over her big, protruding belly to stand up. Suddenly, her big belly moves down beneath her dress and a rolled up blanket falls out at her feet. We glance at each other before we burst out laughing. She kicks it. I'm holding my sides from laughing so hard. Bobby, her big brother, comes down the path by the shoreline, ducking low-hanging branches. Sarah is rolling up the blanket again when I nudge her. She smiles up at Bobby, who is now standing over us.

"What are you guys laughing at?" he asks.

Sarah giggles and shakes her head. "Nothing."

His black hair is long and stringy at the front where it hangs over his dark, beady eyes. He looks at us and our dolls before he digs in his pants pocket and pulls out a snuff box. He pops the lid off and offers the snuff to his sister.

'Oh, thanks," Sarah says.

"Want some?" The box is shoved almost under my nose.

"N-n-n-no…" I start to say.

"Here! What's the matter? You're supposed to be a mother with your baby there. Here, take some."

I look up at his tall skinny body bending toward me and his eyes dare me. Again, he pushes the box at me. My hand goes up and I take a small pinch.

"Hey! Take more. You need more than that. Use your middle finger, too. Go on, take lots!" he demands. His low voice growls in annoyance.

I take a deep breath and plunge my hand into the soft brown powder. His eyes follow my hand, so if I thought of dropping some, I cannot. His voice comes again: "Pull your lip out with your other hand. What's the matter with you?"

Obediently, I pull my bottom lip out and shove the messy wad of stinky powder in. My lip barely reaches my bottom teeth when I let it go and there I sit with my enormous, fat lip sticking out over my chin. I start to giggle, but then my mouth stings, burns. But I continue to grin. My mouth is flooded with the snuff juice. I swallow. My eyes start to water.

Bobby commands, "Don't swallow your spit. Spit it out like this." He shoots a brown stream of spit over my head as he passes by me. Laughing, he runs down the path. I spit out all my saliva, again and again, but by that time, the snuff is washing between my teeth, into my mouth and over my tongue. My throat burns. Still I stay.

Pretending I'm having fun, I listen to Sarah's endless chatter, broken occasionally by an effortless spurt of spit from her lips. I'm getting dizzy. I make excuses as I gather my doll and blanket, wave good-bye, and dash down the path, scratching my face and hands on the branches that whip by me. Spitting out the snuff and gagging, I emerge by the sandy beach behind our cabin. My little brother, Brian, and Tony are there playing by the water. I run by them so fast, they're curious. Their feet pound on the path behind me.

At the woodpile behind our cabin, I dump the blanket and doll and run to the lakeshore where I throw myself down on my belly. Brian and Tony watch me wash out my mouth repeatedly and drink water to rid the burning in my throat. I sit up. Still breathing hard, I nod to Brian's questions fired at me, "Did you chew snuff?" His tousled, brown hair is falling over his big, curious eyes. "Did you get it from Bobby?"

Again, I nod. Now my stomach is trying to push its way up to my throat. I swallow repeatedly, silently moaning, "Oh, Mama, help!"

I stand up. Wave after wave of nausea washes over me. I stagger toward the cabin holding my belly. "Oh, Mama, help me!" I don't make it. When I reach the corner of the cabin, my neck lurches forward and my whole insides pour out of my mouth and nose, splashing my shoes and the front of my skirt. Retching and moaning, I stand bent forward with my hands on my shaking knees. When I am all empty, I lift my head and wipe my face with my sleeves.

There stands Mom, looking at me. "Go lay down on the bedding you put on the woodpile," she says before turning away.

Still trembling and dizzy, I make my way to the woodpile behind the cabin. I pick up my doll and the blanket and climb up to the comfortable bed I'd made this morning on top of the five-foot high woodpile. I pull the blanket over me and roll into a ball.

I must have dozed off. Mom had just turned away from me, stepping off a block of wood onto the ground to return to the cabin. I watch her. She's a tall woman, very solid and big, weighing about a couple of hundred pounds. When she emerges from the shadow of the cabin into the evening sunlight, her hair lights up like a halo in a fine spray of light brown. I can't believe I've slept that long. I can still feel the shrivelled skin inside my bottom lip. My head feels good, though, and I'm hungry and thirsty. Mom brings me a cup and a bowl. Her cotton print dress clings to her thick, stockinged legs. Her head appears over the woodpile. Her brown eyes look down her thin sharp nose, studying me critically for a few seconds, before she holds out the aspirins, tea and a bowl of stew.

"Did you eat anything this afternoon?" she asks.

Chewing snuff is not eating, so I shake my head.

I down the aspirins with tea. My mouth waters at the smell of the stew and I begin to eat. Mom has gone back to the cabin.

I hope my cousin, Joe, doesn't come looking for me. I can hear the door banging over there. He's a couple of years older than I am, about eleven or twelve. He's small and skinny and mean; he shoots stones with his slingshot at the girls' legs and ankles. He hangs around me a lot. He got me so mad once, I beat him up and made him cry. After that, he never bothered me much.

Joe lives next door, across the clearing in front of our cabin. Both cabins are beside the lake. There's a small island right across from our cabin, where the birds' nesting area is. There are lots and lots of blackbirds there, too. It's quite noisy there all summer, just like our cabin is most of the time.

There are seven of us in the family, four girls and three boys. My oldest brother got married and went away a long time ago. My other brother, Wess, spends most of his time at the cabin on our old trapline. The rest of us girls are all here. We live in a one-room cabin our father built before he died. Mom got someone to make a small addition at the back a couple of years ago. That's where she sleeps with our little brother, Brian. Brian was just a little baby when my father died and he's about six years old now. The rest of us sleep in the main room on two double beds and a bunk bed.

Three other kids live with us. Mom looks after them because their parents left their home. I guess three more doesn't make much difference aside from the fact that the food and clothes have to stretch a little further. The father came to see them once. I heard Mom say that she has never gotten a penny for their keep. Their mother has never come. Actually, I am closer to them than to my own sisters, since mine are gone all winter. Maggie and Jane have become my regular sisters and Vera and Annie are my special sisters when they are home in the summer. Maggie and Jane's little brother, Tony is just like Brian — the pests!

Twack! My bowl suddenly shoots straight up about a foot; the spoon twirls through the air and clangs on the ground. Here comes my cousin,

Joe, with his slingshot and a sneer on his face. Chuckling, he scrambles up the woodpile and picks up the tin bowl. It has a big dent on the side, the size of a large marble. He sees I'm angry so he suddenly decides to go shoot some birds off the Catholic church steeple behind his cabin. I'll never be able to shoot like him with my slingshot. He shuffles off, whistling, and I climb down the woodpile with a sigh. Feet dragging and head down, I walk toward the cabin.

Mom comes around the corner. "What did he want now?" she asks. I hand over the battered bowl and dirt-covered spoon. "Humph," she turns the bowl over in her hand and goes inside the cabin. I can hear the bowl spin and clatter across the table. I sit down on the porch steps.

Smoke curls over the roof of Joe's cabin. He stays there with his grandparents. Joe calls his grandmother Grandma, but I call her Aunty, because she is more like a big sister than someone's grandmother. There goes Joe's grandpa down to the lake. He's Uncle Bill to me. He always walks with his head down.

One day, walking home from school, I noticed a big crack on the front of my shoe. So I'd kick at the grass on the side of the path once in a while just to see how much grass my shoe's new mouth could hold. With my head down, I walked along, quite pleased at how much grass my shoe had taken in, when suddenly-oofff! My head bounced off Uncle Bill's chest. He just did a sidestep and continued on his way, hands still clasped together behind him. Oh, I like him. He didn't even get mad.

I remember another time when his oldest son came home for a visit and brought a bottle of wine for him. That evening he was left alone. We saw him come out of his cabin, headed for the outhouse. It was not unusual to see him go to and from his outhouse in his long underwear. But it was about a minute before cousin Joe figured out what was wrong with his appearance. He had his long johns on upside down. The short tight "legs" barely covered his knees and he had long, long, baggy "sleeves". And between his legs flopped an obvious hole where his neck was supposed to be.

I sit there grinning at the memory, until I hear Mom yelling about something in the other room. Then Brian and Tony come running out of the cabin with Mom on their heels, demanding, "Where is it? Where's that box of snuff that was on the table beside my bed? Come on, speak up!"

Tony kicks at the sand and mutters, "I didn't take it."

Brian sticks his hand in his shirt pocket and holds out a quarter. "He said to get him some snuff and he paid me for it. I was going to ask you. But you weren't around." Brian keeps glancing at me.

Then slowly, the light dawns in my head and I begin to feel sick again. Mom's eyes come to rest on me as she asks, "And who is 'he', I'd like to know."

Brian answers, "Bobby."

I remember Bobby had come down the path from where the boys were playing. Mom glares at me before asking, "I guess it was the snuff that made you sick?"

I nod. She turns and goes back in. I can hear her saying, "It seems The Owl tried to chew snuff and got sick." This is followed by a burst of laughter from inside. They call me The Owl.

Here comes Aunty now. She always comes to visit in the evenings. She's a short, plump woman with squint lines around her dark eyes. When she sees me, her round face breaks into a smile. Her glossy black hair hangs down in two braids on each side. A red sweater, buttoned only at the top, covers her sloping shoulders. At her chest, her shirt is lined by many safety pins between the buttons. They sway and tinkle when she sits down beside me. She wears the same kind of cotton print skirt that all the women have. My chest fills with love for this woman who is smiling down at me. Mom comes out of the cabin and sits down beside Aunty, and they begin to talk.

I'm still hungry so I go inside and search for something more to eat. One by one, the girls go out to sit on the porch. There are bursts of laughter among the drone of voices now outside the cabin.

The floor has already been swept clean. On one side of the door to the adjoining room stands the bunk bed where my sisters, Annie and Vera, sleep. On the other side, in the corner, is the double bed where my oldest sister, Barbara, and her baby sleep. Barbara's husband is away working somewhere, so she's staying with us, too. I sleep in the double bed by the front window with the three foster kids, Jane, Maggie and Tony. Our mattress is a big canvas sack filled with straw from across the lake. I remember the day we went to cut the long dry grass; we must have filled the canoe twice. Our blankets are all quilts sewn from discarded clothes.

The table and the bench are between the double beds. The dishes have been washed and neatly stacked on the shelves above the table and the cups hang from hooks underneath. I rummage around in the large, green, wooden food box beside the table. Finally, I come up with a chunk of bannock and a jar of jam.

We got our mugs from the gift boxes of oats, which have pictures of all kinds of funny looking dogs. Our hand towels come from the laundry detergent gift boxes. We try to guess what colours the towels are going to be from the pictures on the back of the boxes. Our plates, bowls and cups are assorted tin, stoneware and baked enamel, most of which are chipped.

I remember once, when Wess was home, Maggie and I were washing dishes after supper and everyone else was outside. I didn't want to miss the fun so I hurriedly put the cups in a row along the length of our six-foot table. We both stopped, wide-eyed as, one by one, the cups stirred and moved by themselves, glided along the table, smooth and easy, right off the edge. One by one, they crashed, chipped, bounced, or rolled away to the middle of the floor. The door flew open and Wess glanced at me, the cups, Maggie and back to the cups.

"What on earth is going on?" he demanded. "What's the matter with you two? You crazy or something?" He clamped his hand down on the last self-destructing cup. Our mouths hung open. He gave us this long explanation about soapy cups on the vinyl-covered, slightly-tilted table. It was a long speech for Wess.

I'll be in grade four this year. I am ten years old, I think. We don't celebrate birthdays. I know my birthday because it is on the day before Christmas. So I'll be eleven years old this Christmas. I don't know when the others have their birthdays. Maggie's older but we will be in the same row in school. The grades in our one-room Indian Day School are divided by the rows of desks, one row for each grade. The kindergarten kids sit by the window. I remember many days when I would daydream, looking out the window. Well, I still look out the window, I'm just a little further away, that's all.

The path to the store runs right by the school window, so whenever I see Mom coming with a toboggan in the winter, I know that Wess is home with a load of beaver pelts to trade at the store. At those times, it's all I could do to sit still until school was over. Sometimes I'd see Mom going back home with her toboggan full of grocery boxes. At other times, I'd catch her still at the store when the school doors finally flew open.

Each time Wess came back he seemed to be a little taller and I'd be shy until we had our punch and wrestle sessions and things would be back to normal again. Oh, I miss Wess.

My older sisters, Vera and Annie, go to a boarding school in the wintertime. Annie is a couple of years older than I am and Vera is about three years older than Annie. There are only four kids in the community who leave home to go to school. Mostly, the older kids avoid getting into the last row of desks. Otherwise, they get sent off to school far away. Annie left home early because there wasn't a school here yet. It's nice to have them home for the summer.

Our puppy, Jumbo, pokes his head in the doorway, licking his chops with a flick of his tongue. A fly must have told him that someone is eating again. After piling on the jam, I throw a piece of bannock at him. He's got such a sweet tooth that one.

Once our sugar bowl just disappeared. We questioned each other and searched everywhere, but it was gone. About five days later, Mom found it in the far corner under her bed, completely empty and very clean. Not a grain of sugar was spilled anywhere. Jumbo got the blame for that one. Mom always leaves the door open in the early mornings when she gets the campfire going outside. Jumbo probably came in while everyone was asleep, reached on top of the table, picked up the full bowl of sugar upright, and carried it under the bed where he ate every grain.

My skirt smells pukey. The gang is coming back in again with loads of blankets and quilts, including those I piled on top of the woodpile. I smile at one of Vera's usual jokes, which sets everyone off on another peal of laughter. Blankets and quilts fly everywhere with everyone getting the beds ready for the night. I slip out the door and lean against the porch post, facing the lake.

It has gone very calm and peaceful. I hear a loon out there somewhere. The village seems so noisy in the evenings, dogs barking, kids laughing and squealing over by the store. I can hear someone chopping wood over at the point. A mosquito has just landed on my arm. He walks around on his long skinny legs, poking at my skin with his needle, turns around and pokes again. Hey, he's pushing it in now. I don't feel anything. His belly is getting full. I squeeze the end of his full belly. He pulls out his needle. Whoops, I busted his belly! Yuck, blood, and my arm is itching now. I'd better go in.

Everyone is already in bed. My oldest sister, Barbara, locks the door behind me. After pulling off my skirt, I elbow my way between Jane and Tony when the nightly Bible reading starts. On a little table beside Barbara's bed among the clutter of Bibles and things, sits the blackened coal oil lamp that Mom reads by every night. The page-marked Bibles are always there. There's a thick, red Cree Bible which no one understands but it's read anyway. The other is a thin, black prayer book in Ojibway that she's reading now. Then, there's the thin, black one that holds the hymns which Mom sings, more often than we kids care to listen to.

A fly buzzes around the lamp, just barely missing Mom's nose a couple of times. At last, the reading's over. Mom goes into her bedroom, gets into bed and then yells, "Okay," for Barbara to blow the light out.

Now the jokes and stories start. Sometimes, we tell old Indian legends with some hilarious mistakes. When we know them well enough, Mom tells us another and we keep repeating it again till we can tell it correctly. I like the story time.

2

BLUEBERRY DAYS

Summer 1962

I stretch out with a big yawn and wriggle my toes. Tony shoves an elbow in my face. Jane throws a leg over me and I lay still while I unclasp a safety pin off my sweater. Slowly, I press the pin against Jane's skin above her knee until she pulls her leg away and turns over. Maggie's snoring softly on the other side of Tony.

I lift my head. We're laying like driftwood on a colorful rocky shore, our blankets having been long since kicked off. I smell wood smoke and fresh air comes through the open door. Dogs are barking somewhere and flies are buzzing around inside the house. Everyone's still asleep. I shall be the first one up again this morning. Mom is very happy in the mornings when everything is quiet. I like it best when there are just the two of us by the fire. Sometimes, Mom leaves in the canoe to check our fishnet and comes back before anyone is up. She likes to sneak off by herself in the early morning.

I'm hungry. I can't smell what's sizzling out there but it sure sounds good. Slowly, I climb over Jane and onto the floor. From the half dozen pairs of socks on the floor I pull on a pair and slip into a pair of running shoes. I run out the door; three steps and off the open porch, barely making it over the dog's head, and off to the outhouse. The outhouse stands about fifty yards in the bushes behind the cabin. The path forks into a Y, the other going toward the sand beach on the bay behind our cabin. What's that noise? Scratching. I peer around the corner of the outhouse. There's a dog digging behind the toilet. I grab a stick and throw it at him. "Get out of here. Go away!" I watch him slink off into the bushes.

Coming out at a run, I pause to listen to a bird chirping in the bushes beside me, "Cee-oh-dee, cee-oh-dee."

I ask, "C. O. D.? What did you order in the catalogue, silly bird?" I run back behind the cabin, past Mom who kneels beside the cooking fire. I grab a towel and soap from the block of wood and skip over the stepping stones to my special rock to wash my face by the lake. My rock shifts to one side but I know it well. Maggie tried to get to my rock one morning. She went off balance when it moved and then, splash, into the water. I laughed for days.

I breathe in the fresh air and hold my face to the warm sun. Oh, it smells so good. The water glistens and sparkles in the sunlight. Today is going to be a nice day again. I hop back onto the grass and drop the towel and soap back on the wood for the next person. I flop down beside Mom. She breaks off a piece of hot soft bannock, puts in a couple of pieces of salt pork she has fried, and hands it to me. Then she hands me another piece of bannock with butter and jam on it.

The flies are driving Mom crazy. She swats them and covers up the food. She also keeps a long stick beside her to keep the dogs away. They wiggle and crawl close to her, hoping for a taste of the morning meal. Jumbo, the black pup, had a long, long tail, until we decided he'd go crazy in the head if it were left that long. So we chopped off about six inches. It's stubby at the end now, but decent in length. The beige female by the door is very gentle. She used to be my father's favourite lead sled dog. She's Jumbo's mother. Her name is Rosiak. They're loose because the flies would get at them if we left them tied up and they're also a lot cleaner now. They can roll in the grass and swim and splash in the water with us. Like us, they get a dose of mosquito repellent around their ears.

Raised voices break out in the house. Mom sighs. Annie and Vera are up and at it again. I wonder if they fight like that when they're not home? Seems like a long time ago since we got out of school for the summer. I miss school. I miss the smell of crayons, paper, plasticine. Mom pokes me, "Gee, you're always daydreaming! Go get the pan of water I asked you to get."

In the cabin I watch Annie while I grab the pan from under the water pail shelf by the door. I fill it up from the lake and put it over the dying fire. It will be warm by the time everyone's finished eating. By now, the others are coming out of the house, racing for the outhouse. I smile. I won't be waiting in line this morning.

I sit again with my back comfortably against the tree, knees up. Jumbo comes over and licks my face. Eesh. His tail practically throws his whole back end from side to side. He's going to lose another couple of inches if he's not careful. "Hey Mom, I heard a bird this morning saying, 'C.O.D., C.O.D.' He thinks he ordered a C.O.D. from the catalogue." I giggle.

Mom says, "Well, I hope he realizes he has to pay for it before he can take it home."

I laugh again. Annie comes running from the outhouse and asks, "What are you laughing at?"

Mom answers, "Oh, about a bird that ordered a C.O.D."

Annie gives me a look that says I'm strange, shakes her head as she picks up the towel and soap.

Mom and Barbara are cleaning up inside the cabin and the quilts and blankets are already hung on the hanging pole behind the cabin for airing. I jump up and run inside. Mom is packing our lunch in a cardboard box while Barbara fills another box with cups, mugs and cans. We're going to the portage about three miles away to go blueberry picking. I carry things to the lake where Barbara and Vera have already turned the canoe over and lowered it into the water. Boy, that canoe looks great. A fresh coat of green paint. Mom worked on that last week. I wish I could ride in that canoe, but I usually walk on the railway tracks with the others everytime we go to the big portage.

Finally, everyone's ready. The door's locked and I watch them get in the canoe. Barbara gets in, then Cora, Brian, Tony and Annie. Vera smiles at me, "All right, get in. I'll walk this time."

I glance at Mom. She nods. I step into the canoe and sit down beside Annie. She is absorbed in folding her soft, delicate turquoise scarf on her knee. I reach over and touch the material before she tucks the scarf into her pocket. This is my first canoe ride this summer.

Mom gets in and pushes the canoe away. We wave to the others on shore. I know exactly what Mom will say next because she always says the same thing: don't run on the railway tracks and watch out for the trains. Then we paddle away. The water is sparkling and dancing in the sun.

With me paddling in the middle, Mom at the front and Barbara at the back, we glide across the water pretty fast. I love the feel of water against my paddle and get into the rhythm of pushing in the whirlpools created by Mom's paddle. I daydream while I paddle. The pains in my arms come and go in waves but I know if I slack off, I would get a poke from behind. Seagulls circle gracefully above; they screech occasionally. It is so quiet on the lake that we can still hear noises from the village we're leaving behind.

Cora, who's about three years old, sleeps at Barbara's feet behind me. Brian sits in front of Annie and drags a triangular-shaped board for a boat in the water. Tony sits behind Mom. Mom has that thick scarf over her head again. I don't know how she can stand the heat with that thing on. Once in a while Mom remarks on the beaver-chewed poplar sticks that drift along the shoreline or points out a dry tree that would be good firewood in the fall.

We have left the third island behind us now so we should be there soon. There's the point now. A breeze is coming up too. I hope the waves aren't too high by the time we come back. Well, I'll be walking home with Jane and Maggie anyway.

Finally, we slow down at the channel going into the portage. We're going to check our fishnet first. I rest my arms while they maneuver the canoe for Mom to fish the net cord up with her paddle. Mom pulls us along the net, lifting it to view the width. There's a good sized pike, some suckers and two pickerel. Mom is good at taking the fish out of the tangled net. She drops the end of the net back into the water and I watch it sink down in a straight line.

We start paddling again, softly this time, into the marshy bay where the portage is. The water lilies are so beautiful. As we pass by, the yellow and white flowers among the lily pads bob in the slight waves. I can smell perfume.

Silently, we check out each hidden bay and dark shadow. This is a moose-feeding area and there are always lots of moose tracks here.

Finally, we come to the end of the long bay to the portage and there's Jumbo, in a whirl of tail and excitement, prancing about.

Vera and Jane emerge from the bush to pull our canoe in. I step out of the canoe and hold it for Annie to step out. We run up the pathway to join Maggie in the shade on the soft moss. Mom calls us for tea and to hand out our containers for the blueberries.

After much shoving and pushing and squeals of laughter, we amble toward the railway tracks where the berries hang in thick clumps. The heat shimmers off the steel tracks. It is very hot here. I can feel the sweat on my neck already.

I step carefully around the bushes and rocks. On blueberry picking days at least two snakes will get their heads bashed in. The paddle for that job is brought up with the bucket for the berries. Sure enough, a yell and commotion on the other side of the tracks, "There. There it goes!" Maggie is yelling as everyone runs to help. Barbara has the paddle. I sink behind a bush, hoping no one will notice I'm not around. I don't understand why the sight of a snake could be such a bad omen that it has to be killed immediately to ward off the bad luck. I continue picking. Last summer, I'd made the mistake of saying that I had almost stepped on a snake at the corner of the cabin. Everyone stared at me, then dashed out the door. Later, I heard them yell. I felt awful. I saw them carry the dead snake at the end of a stick and throw it into the camp fire. Afterwards, every time I went near the fire, I kept thinking that I might see the bones of the snake or, perhaps, the head with eyes if it didn't burn. I shudder. It's not that I love snakes but killing them like that because they're messengers of the devil is scary.

It's so hot and that sun just beats down on my head. I've been day-dreaming again and my cup is only half full. The other girls are already dumping theirs into the large bucket that Mom and Barbara keep in the shade. Vera drops a handful of berries into my cup as she passes. I like Vera. Her shiny, curly, brown hair is so beautiful in the sun. I didn't comb my long, straight, black hair this morning.

I kick at an anthill to see how fast the ants will scatter. I remember the day Barbara, Vera and Annie came home laughing after they had gone blueberry picking along the tracks. Railroad section men in a motor car had stopped to chat and Annie stepped on an anthill while they were talking. Next thing she knew, she had ants up her pants, "What's the matter?" one of the men asked. Then, trying to be helpful, he advised "Take your pants off and give it a shake!" Yeah, right.

I'm hungry. It seems like hours and my neck is stiff. I've filled my cup so many times, I've lost count. Mom is very pleased and Barbara hasn't even said anything. I can see smoke and hear pots banging. They're making lunch by the lake on the other side of the railway tracks. That's the camping end of the portage. It's too swampy on this side. I hope we can swim before we eat. I see the others drift towards the fire I'm done.

Mom smiles at me when I empty my cup and head for the lake. I'm thirsty more than anything else. A train's coming, the third one since we've been here. The men in the caboose always wave at us when they go by. Must be nice to ride in a train all day.

The girls are jumping off the boulder to my left. I drop my cup, kick off my runners and flop into the water. Clothes and all, of course. We never bother taking off our clothes when we go swimming on blueberry-picking days. We take off our underthings and wash them and the clothes on us at the same time, while we're in the water. Also, we scrub our hair. That, I don't like. When my long hair gets wet, I have a big clump of pulled-out hair by the time Mom combs out the tangles. In a little while, the clothes we're not wearing are hung up to dry. The rest dries on us keeping us cool until the sun has us dry and hot again.

The girls are still in the water, swimming with bloated tops on the back of their necks. Jane looks like a humpbacked muskrat. I'm always afraid a bloodsucker might get into my blouse. Barbara comes down to the lake, yelling, "Tony, Brian, come out now!" The boys scramble up the sloping rock. Their pants are piled on a rock with their shoes and shirts. They're not allowed to get their jeans wet, they take too long to dry. I pull myself out of the water. Lunch is ready and we all troop to the fire, dripping wet and splashing each other.

Hot bannock, fried slices of bologna and a cup of tea. And, of course, blueberry jam for bannock dunking. After a while we are smiling with blue teeth, black mouths and sparkling eyes, laughing at each other. We head back up the trail with our containers. We have already wandered half a mile to get the best berries. Jumbo follows me. He moves from shade to shade at each place I stop, but then he wanders off. I've been here for quite a while. I'll look for a different spot. It's quite rocky here so I think I'll go across the tracks to where Mom is. More shade there.

As I come around a clump of bush, Jane looks up with a smile. "You going across?" she asks.

"Yep," I answer and hop onto the rock where she had her foot. Her other foot is on a small boulder a couple of feet away. She squats with her dress tucked under each knee, picking the berries with one hand and holding her cup with the other. Does she even notice the huge mound of an anthill directly behind her? Each time she rocks back on her heels to look up at me, her behind gets closer to it. I point to the anthill. "You're trying not to step on that?"

She glances behind and says, "That's an anthill. Some ants are black and some are small. Some can be quite big too."

I nod, not quite sure about the conversation, and jump onto another rock, going around her.

Jumbo's tail sticks out wagging from behind a rock. Sure enough, a chipmunk chatters and scampers onto the rock above Jane. It turns to give Jumbo a parting shot before it plunges into the thick weeds and grass in front of Jane.

Well, nothing could have saved that girl! Jumbo comes sailing over that rock with large, flopping ears, looking like a giant, black, ugly bird. He pounces on the ground in front of Jane. Jane gasps, waves her arms to get her balance. She looks like she's trying to fly. Then she grabs a branch and thinks she's safe. Jumbo's back end whips around and smacks her across the face with what's left of his tail. Almost in slow motion, Jane sinks down right in the middle of the anthill. Then she comes to life! She shoots out of that anthill. Some of the ants probably land on the nearby trees, as she flails away at her dress. Bounding and panting, Jumbo passes me and heads down the hill. I can't remember if Jane has made any noise the whole time. I disappear behind a boulder and stumble to the tracks with my chest and throat bursting. There, I finally clamp my mouth with both my hands and let my laughter out of my chest like a deflating balloon.

I had learned how to keep from laughing when I had been caught in situations where I couldn't laugh. Like the time our storekeeper served each customer with a smile, despite the fact that one eye was almost swollen shut from a mosquito bite. For me, that was torture. Mom's expression never changed. Or there was the time our minister gave a sermon from his open Bible, held upside down for quite a long time before he noticed it. Again, for me, that was murder. Mom's expression never changed. Then there was the time at church and that John, one of the older men, was a little tipsy and he toppled over backwards, chair and all, and went down with a mighty crash. All we could see were his feet sticking up. Oh, I would have died then, if I hadn't noticed that Mom was silently shaking with laughter, too.

I'm getting tired. I seem to be by myself, too. I don't see anyone anywhere. I don't like to be alone…I start thinking about bears. I've filled my cup. I'd better go. I see a snake and jump so fast I stagger and slip down the slope. My feet finally come to rest on the gravel beside the railway tracks. My cup tumbles down the slope. I almost cry when I see the empty cup at my feet. Mom is standing on top of the ridge about ten yards from where I was.

"What's the matter? Are you okay?" she asks.

I nod my head. She has been there all this time. I stand there blinking away my tears.

"Once," she says, looking at me, "Wess could fill his cup every two minutes, 'til one day, he tripped in front of me and out rolled a wad of moss he had been using to stuff his cup over halfway full."

I start to laugh, and she turns away to continue with her picking.

The rest of the afternoon goes quickly. Toward evening, we drift back to the fire. Supper smells delicious — fried fish with onions, mashed potatoes, canned corn and, of course, the hot bannock and blueberry jam washed down with camp-fire tea. We talk and laugh with our backs against the trees. Mom is telling a story again. The horseflies bite and drive us crazy because they fly around and around and around our heads. Too bad they don't get dizzy and crash into trees and things. I smile at the thought and then see Barbara glaring at me. Whatever Mom had been saying wasn't supposed to be funny. I put my head down and concentrate on finishing my supper.

After supper, Vera and I wash the dishes by the lake, while Jane and Maggie dry them. It's nice to be with Vera. She is always laughing. We begin carrying our things back to the other side of the tracks, down the portage path to the canoe. Rosiak has just emerged from the shade beside the canoe, yawning and stretching, licking her chops. The bay is absolutely calm. With the birds twirping and flies buzzing, it is so peaceful. "Get out of the way, will you?" Barbara marches by me with her arms stretched down by buckets full of berries.

I'm so tired after my full meal, I hate the thought of walking the three miles back home. But at least my arms won't feel like they're falling off; only my legs will.

Finally, we push the canoe away from the shore. Jane, Maggie and I, with Jumbo and Rosiak, straggle back up the path. Then, Jane pipes up, "Hey, let's see if we can get there before they do! It's not so hot now."

So, we walk and run for the first mile through two rock cuts. One more to go. Then just around the bend, we'll be at the edge of the village.

It seems like ages that we've been walking. Another train's coming. The dogs don't waste any time getting off the tracks. I hope it's not a cattle train...they stink. We wait by the shade of a large pine tree. A small path runs through here. This is called the "little portage" but it's a miserable looking place at each end.

The train whistle is loud. We turn our faces to the wind as the train rattles by. Again, we wave to the man in the caboose.

After the last half mile, we take the path that leads to our cabin by the lake. The dogs are already gone, probably fast asleep beside the doorstep by now. We run all the way to the cabin. There, the dogs are lying in the shade of the tree. Jumbo is cleaning his paws; good idea, he's got tar on them. He'll get clobbered for sure if he puts one dirty paw on our wood floor.

There's the canoe, with paddles flashing in the evening sun. The lake is very still and smooth, like a huge mirror. We splash water on our faces while we sit by the lake. I lean back onto the cool grass to catch my breath.

We'll all have a good sleep tonight. Tomorrow, we'll be going to the general store to trade in our berries. I hope Mom buys bananas and tomorrow is Wednesday, the day the way-freight comes to unload groceries for the general store. I lay on the grass with my eyes closed, smelling the earth and wild flowers beside me.

3

ORDINARY DAYS

Summer 1962

Cousin Joe lifts his head. He's chewing the last piece of bannock. He attaches a small ball of it to his fish hook and he says, "Run home and get some more bannock."

"Well, stop eating it! I just went and got a piece. Go get it from your place this time!" Very slowly, I edge my hook with its little ball close to the mouth of a four-inch pike. It fans the water with its fins to keep pace, backing up at the advancing bannock.

Joe grumbles, "Your bannock rolls better. Mine is too dry. It washes to pieces in the water." A school of pesky little fish attack his hook. The hard ones to catch are the small pickerel and pike. They're the ones we're after. "Come on, hurry up!" Cousin Joe sits down on a rock with a stick and empty hook dangling across his knees. "Why don't you go home to eat, if you're hungry? The bannock's supposed to be for the hooks and you keep eating it." I snap at him. He shrugs. "So? It's not my fault if it tastes so good." The little pike has just picked the small, white ball off my hook. The ball disappears in its mouth, and it swims away. I throw my stick on the rock beside Cousin Joe, turn and jump off the rock onto a boulder. I run along the rocky shoreline. The rocks are hot on my bare feet. Crouching under low-hanging branches. I duck beneath a mass of dry twigs. I lose a few strands of hair there. Passing Aunty's boat landing, I continue over the rocks till I come to the bush at the edge of the water. I dart onto the well-worn path around the bushes and back on the rocks again. I jump on my special rock, then hop onto the high rock. I leap to the ground and walk toward our cabin, my feet numbed by the rough, hot rocks.

Excited voices reach me as I near the cabin. Inside, everyone is dressed up. Mom has a bright dress on. Her brown hair is combed in flat waves on each side of her head with flashing crystal eyes on the pins at each temple. The rest of her hair hangs in long shiny ringlets over her shoulders and around her back. She looks beautiful. Barbara's dark eyes gaze beneath long curved eyelashes, framed by dark eyebrows. She wears a beautiful dress with ruffles cascading over her hips. She smells good, too. Annie's light brown hair is combed back and pinned on each side of her head with shiny colourful pins. They're going to the store. I notice the rows of baskets of blueberries on the table.

"I want to go! I want to go, too! Let me go!" I burst out.

Barbara scowls at me before she turns away. Pointing at me, Annie starts to laugh. My feet are white and water wrinkled, with mud and weeds wedged between my toes. My legs are scratched. My dress is wet and torn, and a piece of twig falls from my hair.

Vera pulls me into the back room where she promptly pulls off my sweater and yanks the dress off over my head. After a few swipes at my face with the wet hem of my dress, she seems satisfied. Quickly rummaging around in our clothes box, she comes up with a clean dress which I put on while she goes in search of a brush.

I grit my teeth while she attacks my hair. Finally satisfied, she twists it into two braids. My scalp tingles as I watch her pull out a wad of hair from the brush and roll it into a ball. They're ready to go, so I scramble in search of my old runners.

Off we go, Mom, Barbara, Annie and I, past Aunty's cabin, down the path by the Catholic church and then through the thick tall stand of pine trees. The path is very wide here. The ground beneath the trees is covered with heavy, dense foliage. It's always cool here. You can only see little patches of sky here and there. It's like going through a long, wide tunnel with life and light beckoning at each end.

We emerge into the sunlight, in front of the school. The path runs between the school and the store. The storekeeper's wife waves to us from their backyard where she's hanging her wash. She has a nice garden back there, too. On the right corner of the store stands a storage shed. It sits about three feet off the ground on huge wooden posts. In its shade sprawl the mongrels of the community, their tongues lolling. Some look nice and well-fed while others are so fly-bitten and covered with sores that they're obviously the homeless dogs. Sometimes, in the spring, a policeman comes to shoot all the loose dogs. That's when we have to tie up our dogs so they don't get shot.

People sit on the steps and platform of the storage shed and wait for the way-freight. A couple of dogs lie at each side of the door in front of the store, their owners likely inside.

Mom pushes the door open and a bell jingles above. The smells envelope us like a cloud: the tangy smell of tobacco, the sweet fragrance from the orange and apple bins, the new smell of rubbers and shoes, and, of course, the candy display rack.

Mom deposits the blueberry baskets on the counter. The store is packed with people; everyone is talking and laughing. Smoke hangs blue in the air above the huge beams running across the ceiling. In the middle of the beam sits a stuffed black squirrel. I look at that everytime I come in. I've never seen a squirrel like it. Above the door hangs a large picture of a huge black moose with the whites stark and clear in his terror-filled eyes. Advancing on him are vicious-looking wolves; deadly long white fangs bared for the final kill. Somehow I don't believe a moose like him would be caught like that. He looks too big, and healthy to me.

Amid the noise of shuffling feet and laughter, I hear the rumble of the approaching train. The store quickly empties out. We stay inside where it's cool and watch the way-freight come in through the large front window.

People are sitting on the grass by the station. Others are sitting under the shade of the poplar trees. The whole community must be out there.

The ladies in the shade show off their bright clothing set against the green grass and foliage. Their laughter spurs the men on to hoist boxes and bags of groceries from the boxcar of the train. Soon the boxcar is empty and the train pulls out.

The men carry the boxes and bags toward the store like ants, all in a row. I run to hold the door open for the first man who comes through the door. In the bustle and traffic, the storekeeper is darting here and there, checking, arranging and organizing. My mouth waters when a big, open box of bananas goes by on the shoulder of a small thin man. Bread, fruit, vegetables and meat are being dumped on the floor at the back. The huge pile by the station has now been rearranged into a couple of large piles inside the store.

The people file in for the fresh fruit. Mom is already at the counter with two boxes full of stuff. While the last group of people enter, I follow Mom out, squeezing by an old man. Once outside, she breathes deeply and waits for Annie and Barbara.

I hop up and crane my neck to see what Mom has in the box. After I see that the bananas are there, I skip ahead on the path home.

There are big, white, puffy clouds in the sky. The small island is just ringing with the high-pitched squawking from the hundreds of different birds nesting there. In the spring, I saw a bird fly off with a wad of Mom's hair. She had rolled it from the comb after untangling her fuzzy hair by the rock in front of our house. So there's a nest out there with Mom's hair in it. Jumbo runs up and jumps on us when we get home. You'd think he hadn't seen us in days.

As the boxes are emptied, I grab a bologna sandwich and a banana and go back outside. Cousin Joe comes up the path from the lake, kicking a rock in front of him. I'd completely forgotten about him. I duck back inside and break off a chunk of bannock from the food box. As I turn to dart back out again, a hand clamps down on my collar.

"You've been flying in and out of here with chunks of bannock all morning," Mom says, releasing me.

It's more like a statement, I guess, just to let me know that she had seen what I was up to when I thought I was sneaking the bannock out. We've been through this before with me wasting food. But, like Cousin Joe said, it's the best thing for bait.

I sit down on the steps and eat the bologna sandwich and then take my time with each bite of the banana. Joe walks up. "Where did you get that?" he asks.

"We went to the store. I forgot about the bannock. Where's my fish hook?"

"Oh, I left them over there on the rock where we were. I just finished my lunch. Come on, let's go." he says.

Mom comes to the door and hands Cousin Joe a big red shiny apple. His mouth watering, he studies it, then takes a big bite.

We decide to take the path through the bush, past their garbage dump, over a pile of cleared brush and down into the cool clump of bushes by the water. The path runs along close to the edge of the water. The small poplar trees and thick bush form deep cool caves where the girls often play house with their dolls. We hop onto the flat rock where we were before.

With the bannock still clutched in my hand, I search the clear water for little fish. They'll come soon enough. Just one of them has to see the bait and the rest will show up. I put the balls of bait on our hooks while Cousin Joe finishes his apple. The hooks are made of small silver safety pins pulled straight. The head is pinched together to form a closed loop where we tie the string. The sharp end is bent back to form the hook.

I break the bannock crust into tiny crumbs and throw them into the water. Now we're ready. And, here they come. They fight over the larger pieces while the smaller pieces just get sucked into their greedy little mouths. While these ones are fighting, we look beyond them. Hovering in the background is a four-inch pike. Cousin Joe has decided to go for that one. There's a small pickerel over there. They're a little easier to catch. Slowly, I advance the tiny, white ball and stop it about an inch from its nose. He hasn't moved. I move it a little closer. He fans the water then, suddenly, he darts away. Just then, my hook is swarmed over with the pesky, little ones. I caught one of the rascals. I jerk it out of the water. After yanking it off the hook, I throw it on the ground behind us. He'll make a snack for Joe's cat.

Suddenly, Joe's arm lashes out as he gives a triumphant yell. I hear the stick swish over my head, his arm crashes across my back and I splash knee deep into the water. I stand there dripping wet. Joe doesn't even glance at me. He's on the ground examining his prize. We have a can there for the little pike and pickerel that we catch.

"Hey! Come and see what it looks like. It's a big one!" Cousin Joe yells. He looks at me and says, "You should have taken your shoes off. Your Mom is going to get mad at you, going in the water like that!"

I blurt out, "You knocked me over! Why don't you watch what you're doing? And look! You stepped on my fishing rod and it's broken! Go get me another stick." I scramble back on the rock and wring out my socks and pour the water out of my running shoes. I can hear him rustling around in the bush. The water splashed clear up the back of my dress. After hanging up my shoes over a broken branch and my socks over a twig, I start wringing out the hem of my dress, a handful at a time.

Cousin Joe is back with a long slender branch. He takes his pocket knife out and he cuts off the leaves and rounds the ends clean. One of my shoes keeps falling off the branch. "Here," he says, handing me the stick. I like my nice new fishing rod.

"Give me your shoe. I'll fix it."

I hand over my shoe while I stand there admiring the stick. I glance at him in time to see him shove the blade of his knife through the tongue of my shoe. He makes a large slit through which he pokes his finger. Pleased with himself, he raises his hand with my shoe dangling from his finger and says, "There, now you can hang it up."

My mouth opens and closes before I reach for it. Wondering what I'm going to say to Mom, I hang the shoe on the branch through its hole. Maybe I can sew it at Aunty's. I tie the hook line on the new stick.

After a while, my back hurts and my arm is tired. We have five big ones swimming around in our now-crowded can. Three are Cousin Joe's and two are mine. The little pickerel have stripes on their bodies and the fins of their backs are pretty sharp. On the ground are four drying little fish. Joe says, "It's going to rain pretty soon. Look at those clouds."

I hadn't noticed. So stick in hand, I walk ahead up the path. Joe, behind me, keeps poking the back of my head with his stick. He's carrying the four dead fish, neatly skewered together in a row on a small branch.

As we come around the corner of his cabin, we spy the black cat sitting by the door, licking his paws. Joe grabs the cat and settles him on the step between us. He puts one little fish in front of the cat. The cat sniffs it and immediately turns away. Joe seems offended. "Hey, eat the fish! We caught four of them for you. See?" The cat again sniffs but isn't the least bit interested. So Joe clamps his hand on the cat's head, forcing its mouth open with thumb and finger.

The cat's sharp tongue flicks at the finger, as Joe shoves one of the little fish in the cat's mouth as far as it can go. He lets go and the cat pounces onto the ground. Gagging and swinging its head, it finally spits out the fish. Oh, he's mad. Hairs bristling, he stares at Joe for a second before shooting in a streak for the tree and up into its thick branches.

Laughing, Cousin Joe dumps the little fish in the cat's bowl beside the door. A few drops of rain pelt the roof when we enter the cabin. It's pretty dark in here with only two windows, one at the front and one at the back. Aunty sits on her bed by the back window, playing solitaire. I sit beside her. She smiles and asks, "What's your Mom doing today?"

I shrug, "I don't know. We were fishing. We caught some little fish. Would you give me a needle and thread? I have to sew up my shoe. See?"

She reaches for her sewing box from the table beside her bed. Methodically, as she does everything, she takes out a needle with a long thread dangling at the end and hands it to me. "That looks like it's been cut," she says.

"Yep. It's been cut all right," I answer. Pulling my shoe off, I begin sewing the hole together.

Cousin Joe turns from the food box. He stands there chewing and smiling before he explains, "It wouldn't stay hung. So I put a hole in it to hang it up."

The old man starts coughing. He lies propped up on the single bed by the front window. I know we shouldn't make him laugh. Aunty lifts her head from the row of cards and hesitates a moment before she asks, "But why did you want to hang it?"

Joe takes another bite of his sandwich. With his mouth full, he says between chews, "That's the only way to dry it is to hang it up."

Aunty sweeps up the cards with one hand to shuffle them again. "Your shoes were wet then." She glances at me and asks, "Did you step in the water?"

Joe's face stretches into a wide smile and he says, "It was a big one. I tried and tried a long time to get it. Then it grabbed my hook and we were both on the same rock and.... Oh boy! I pulled that little fish out so fast, straight overhead and it landed in the bush behind us!"

While Joe caught his breath, I added, "And I landed in the water."

The old man is coughing quite a bit now. A look of concern crosses Aunty's face as the old man continues to cough from a low rumble deep in his chest.

I bite the end of the thread against my shoe and hand the needle back. "I'm going to run home now," I say to Joe. I dash across the clearing. The rain is really coming down hard. I pounce on our porch with a flying leap. The door is held open by a block of wood. Mom is sitting on the bed sewing. "What's Aunty doing?" she asks.

I shrug and answer, "Nothing. Uncle is coughing really bad." Mom sighs and shakes her head.

I rummage around in the food box for an apple. The rain has stopped suddenly. I look around inside the cabin. "Where's everybody?" I ask.

"Cora is asleep in the next room," she says and spits out a stream of brown snuff into the spittoon beside her. "Barbara, Vera and Jane took Tony and Brian for a walk to the sandpit to see if there are any blueberries left. I hope they didn't get too drenched…." she trails off as she leans back looking at the sky through the window.

"Where's Annie and Maggie?" I say after another big bite of the apple.

"Oh they're playing around somewhere. Where have you been?" she asks.

"By the shore. Joe and I were fishing for little pickerel. Joe tried to force the cat to eat the little fish, but it wouldn't eat any."

Mom smiles as she says, "That might be because I took a lot of fish ends for the cat when I went over to give Aunty some fish. That cat must have a pound of fish in its tummy right now."

I kick off my shoes, crawl to the corner of the bed and curl up to watch Mom. I can hear a slow drip, drip, drip outside at the corner of the cabin. I yawn and take the last bite of the apple and put the core on the window sill.

"Take your socks off; they look wet," Mom says. She doesn't notice my shoes. I lift each leg and pull the socks off and fling them to the floor.

I stretch out on the bed, breathing in the smells of fresh rain and wet earth drifting through the open door.

4

ROCKY

Summer 1962

We're hiding.

We've been here on the small island all day. The baby birds have already flown away. We found hundreds of nests everywhere. Mom and Barbara have hidden the canoe at the back of the island. They had to make two trips to get us all here. We can't play at the front of the island because the drunks might see us.

The men that were away working have just returned this morning. They got off the train drunk and they had lots of liquor with them. We can hear them yelling, fighting and screaming from here. Every now and then a shotgun goes off somewhere. Dogs bark and children scream and cry. It's noisy and it's really scary.

We didn't have much time to get ready when we left the house. Mom said that rounding us all up took most of the time because usually we just scatter after breakfast. I was up in the tree with my slingshot shooting birds with Ben. He lives across the tracks. I went home with him once to get his jacket and his folks started teasing him for playing with a girl. I didn't like them much. I won't go there anymore. Anyway, we were up in the branches beside the Catholic church when Vera found me. Barbara found the rest of the girls playing on the beach behind the house and Mom found the boys with a jar full of frogs beside Aunty's canoe.

We've just had lunch and Mom says we have enough food left in the paper box for supper but we can't make a fire for tea. Barbara and Vera sit on blankets and sew. Mom works on a fishnet. Annie is lying on a blanket beside her, reading comic books. The rest of us play hide-and-seek. Sometimes we forget to be quiet and Mom has to get after us. Tony fell off the lower branch of a tree. He completely disappeared in the spongy moss and bushes. We kill ourselves laughing. He smells like rotten eggs.

Thick cedar trees grow all around the edge of the island. Boulders sit all along the shoreline. The interior is mostly dotted with small poplars and a few birch trees. Thick, soft, spongy moss covers most of the island. There's a large, flat, sloping rock at the front of the island and a smaller area of flat rock at the rear. I'm running along under the cedar branches, when I come upon the remains of a dog. Mom is waving at us to be quiet. I can hear a loud, cracking noise and my heart starts to pound. We creep to the edge of the island and peer out from the bushes. A strange man is staggering around on our porch, yelling. He's kicking our door and banging on it with his fist. He turns and sits on the step with his head in his hands. He's probably just noticed the lock on the door. We used to put the lock on the door, crawl in through the window and hide in the house. But then one man threatened to burn the house down. Mom didn't think it was such a great idea after that.

I'm glad Mom thought to bring Rocky. Lask week my big brother came and left his dog with us for awhile. He'll be back tomorrow to get his dog and leave on the evening train.

Rocky is a beautiful, big intelligent, black and white dog. He decided to rescue Jane when we tried to swim with him. He swam directly toward the first kid, grabbed Jane at the back by her shirt and dragged her back to shore. Then he watched us sheepishly by the shore when he realized we weren't drowning. We keep him tied up behind the house by the lake.

Mom remembered to bring him in the canoe because she figured he'd bark and howl for us all day. He's stretched out fast asleep beside Mom right now. He's got his chain on because Mom didn't want him running around; the drunks would see him.

Our other two dogs, Jumbo and Rosiak, know enough to make themselves scarce when we're not home.

"Has he gone yet?" Mom asks softly.

I look through the bushes again and reply, "He's gone, Mom. I can't see him around anywhere."

The shadows are getting longer inside the tent we've made with a couple of blankets. Cora, Tony and Brian are asleep. Jane, Annie and I were going to go swimming at the back of the island but Mom thought we'd make too much noise splashing. So we washed our clothes instead.

I yawn. I'm getting bored. I've gone over every foot of the island already. Mom has just put aside the fish net she is making and lays back on the moss to rest. She's already made her new net quite long since this morning. I sit down beside her and pick up the net. The rectangular wood and the spindle of twine are quite large in my hands, but my fingers are long enough to hold the knots as I pull in each loop. It seems to take forever to do one row of squares. After finishing the third row, I decide I've had enough.

Time to eat. We each have a bologna sandwich and there's enough bannock left over for jam and butter sandwiches later. All we have to drink is a package of Kool-Aid someone thought to throw in the box, but we don't have much sugar left. Anyway, it's better than warm water.

The sun is now just above the treetops. If anything, the noise of the drunks seems to be getting louder in the evening calm. The small kids are getting tired and miserable despite their afternoon nap.

Mom starts packing the things. We're going to go home now. First Barbara, Mom, Annie and Jane are going across with our things. Rocky is to go in the first canoe trip, too. Mom lets the dog run around for awhile to stretch his legs before she calls him into the canoe. Vera, Maggie and I, with the three little ones, stay out of sight till Barbara comes back for us.

It's almost dark when Barbara returns. Quietly, we paddle back. Rocky is tied up again by the shore. I can see him wagging his tail as we get close to shore. The canoe is pulled up and turned over quickly. The blankets and quilts are all inside the cabin already. Mom tells us to get ready for bed. Inside, we grope around in semi-darkness because we can't put the lamp on. Finally, we're all in bed.

We tense in a hushed silence when we hear the raised voices of men, arguing and wrestling each other, coming down the path. They get closer. With a sigh of relief, we hear the voices go by our cabin and fade away. Then the loud voice of the town bully echoes in the silence and a door crashes at the cabin behind us. The sound of his shouting is coming towards our cabin. Again, we hold our breaths when he reaches our turnoff from the main path. But he doesn't go by. Swearing and ranting, he stomps across the length of our porch, kicking the door with a force that rattles the cups and plates in the cupboard. Every nerve in my body is jarred by each kick and punch at the barred door. Finally, leaving splinters chipped off the door frame, he stomps away cursing loudly about blasting the door down and shooting us all.

When the footsteps fade, Mom and Barbara debate in hurried whispers whether we should get out and make a run for it or stay and hope he doesn't come back. The vote is to run till we realize that the little ones have slept through all the noise. Well, now it's too late; we hear footsteps coming at a run. He's ranting and raving at the top of his lungs! He kicks at the door with all his weight. Mom orders us all under the beds. Quick! The door is falling through, I'm sure. In five seconds, we're all crammed under the bed.

A shotgun blast shakes the cabin. Then a heartrending wail pierces our ears. It takes a few seconds for each of us to identify the horrible sound. We hit the door in the next second, clumsy, childish hands, struggling and fumbling, as we rip the door bars down. We throw the door open and see that Rocky is crawling away in a trail of blood. He's about eight yards from the corner of the cabin. Red, frothy bubbles form from a big hole in his back. I couldn't look at the bloody mass under him.

I hold his head and lay my face against him as he whimpers his last breath. I am crying so hard. I don't care who hears me. I scream as hard as I can. My cries mingle with Annie's sobbing as she runs her hand down the dog's bloody back.

Someone pulls me up and we are all ushered back into the cabin. Annie starts to get very hysterical inside the cabin which calms me down. My grief is replaced by anger and hate like I never felt before.

I sit at the edge of the bed totally still, breathing deeply. I'm thinking of all the times we've had to run out of the cabin, in the middle of the night — spring, summer, fall or winter, dodging this drunk and others like him.

Annie is still cursing and swearing between each sob, but I sit in silence while the anger and hate settle like a ton of cold cement deep inside me.

We are so vulnerable, this cabin full of children. No father or brother protects us; no police to come to our aid. We're at the mercy of all the evil out there. Very calmly I get back into bed. It's very dark in here now. For the first time, I lay down without fear. The man can come again and kill us all; I don't care. I'm not afraid.

Through a series of nightmares, I hear low voices. I open my eyes. It's early morning. Barbara and Mom are washing their hands; their eyes are red and puffy. Then I remember. I slowly climb out of bed and go outside. It was no dream. They've poured water over the thick trail of blood, leaving brown blotches and little rivers flowing from the grass onto the sand beside the door. The dog is gone.

I walk down to the lake and splash cold water on my face. I notice how large my hand looks when I hold it under the water. I plunge both my arms into the water. I feel an irresistible urge to plunge my whole body in. Lowering myself to my belly, flat on the rock, I push my arms into the water almost to my shoulders past my rolled-up sleeves. My chest aches. I submerge my face in the cold water. The dull cold ache and pressure from the water feels good on my arms. Raising my face, I let warm tears flow over my cold cheeks before I plunge my face in the cold water again.

I lift my face again. This time, I feel clean on the outside but empty inside. Very empty. When I open my eyes, Jumbo is on a rock beside me, wagging his tail and turning his head sideways, looking at me, almost like he's asking, "What are you doing?" I sit up and he leans over to lick my face then splashes me with his wagging tail.

It's quiet inside the cabin this morning — no fights, no arguments and no laughter. We pick at our breakfast and sit around. Each of us knows we're all waiting for the train that will bring our brother to pick up his dog.

The community is totally quiet this morning. Those who've caused so much suffering are now peacefully sleeping it off or they've crawled away sick somewhere to recover. I hate them. I hate them all. I go and sit outside on the rock beside the tree. Mom calls me to do something. Everyone is busy dashing around in a flurry of activity — doing nothing.

Finally, we hear the train coming. We all stay home listening to the train stopping and pulling out again. We look down the path where he'll pass the bush by the church. A few minutes later, sure enough, here he comes.

A surge of love flows through me like a healing balm when I see my brother come down the road. He seems to glide gracefully on the balls of his feet. He's very tall and weighs about two hundred pounds. His belly is flat and the huge hams of his arms and shoulders swing slightly at each step. A curl of brown hair bounces over his right eyebrow. My chest tightens with a squeeze as his white teeth flash in a smile when Mom moves to the open door.

He stops, framed against the doorway, surveying us all. His smile slowly disappears before he asks, "What's happened? What's the matter?"

Mom quickly answers, "We're all fine. It's your dog. Everyone was drunk yesterday and John Bull decided to come and shoot us all. I guess your dog must have figured we were threatened and came to help. We had tied him up good but he snapped the buckle on his collar. He must have just come around the corner of the cabin and John Bull just shot him. John must have left pretty fast because there wasn't anyone out there when we all rushed out to the dog, the children first... ." Mom's voice trails off. My brother moves across the room and stands looking out the window for a long time.

Most of us wander down to the lake where we sit talking about this and that, but our minds are still on our brother inside. Lowering our voices, we try to guess what he might do. We've never seen him angry; we don't even remember him ever raising his voice. He gets attention wherever he goes. Maybe it's his smile. I imagine it would be hard trying to argue with someone that's smiling at you. Well, he isn't smiling now. Maybe he's never realized how much we have to live with here. All his visits have always been happy family gatherings. We never tell him anything.

Some time later we drift back into the cabin, one by one. Brother Dave still sits by the table. Mom and Barbara attempt to lighten the air with smiles and everyday conversation. Making the most of everyone's attention, Brian and Tony provide a bit of amusement.

Just before lunch, Jane busts through the door, "I heard John Bull yelling at someone outside his house!"

Silence settles over the room as Dave scrapes back the bench. He slowly stands up, turns and goes out the door. He stops at the edge of the porch and cups his hands over his mouth and yells, "Hey you, John Bull! You bloody coward! Come over here!"

Well, at least half the community hears that yell. What else can John Bull do? He comes down the path, very cocky and insolent and saunters over to our cabin. The big man approaches looking like a battle-scarred, back-alley dog and stops a couple of yards from Dave.

Dave does not move, but his eyes blaze while he says quietly, "Does it make you feel big and strong when you go around scaring women and small children and shooting down dogs?"

Then Annie, who is standing beside me looking out the window, suddenly screams out, against my ear, "Kill him! Kill him, David! Kill him!" I don't hear any more of the conversation outside because Mom has just come to grab Annie and push her into the back room where she is trying to calm her down. Barbara stands by the open door blocking it. John Bull turns and goes back home. Dave comes back inside. Whatever was said, that particular man didn't bother us again for quite awhile.

Feeling a bit let down, I sigh and make myself a cup of tea.

David has to go back on the evening train so we try to make the rest of his visit as pleasant as possible. Barbara and Vera have gone to check the fishnet and Aunty has come over to see Dave. Dave likes to tease her to make her laugh. They enjoy each other's company. Soon Barbara and Vera are back with some fish. David lounges around under the shade of the tree while Mom and Barbara clean the fish by the camp fire.

Oh, no, here comes the Town Joker. He strolls over with loosejointed legs toward Vera and Barbara and starts his usual joking and bantering. He is slightly deaf so everyone has to talk a little louder to him. He grabs Barbara and tries to tickle her. Barbara slips around quickly and throws him right into the large piece of cardboard covered with piles of fish guts and scales. The poor guy slithers around in the slimy fish guts before he can sit up. A string of grey stuff still sticks behind his right ear as he makes another lunge at Barbara. She makes a dash for the cabin and slams the door behind her. We see her laughing at him through the window. The Joker is by the water now washing his jacket as best he can.

David laughs so hard he has to wipe his eyes by the time the Joker leaves. Swinging his wet jacket at us and showering Mom with a spray of water, he walks by with a sheepish grin. Barbara comes out when he is gone. If someone is keeping tabs, this is one on him.

After a meal of fried fish, potatoes and canned peas, David's ready to go. The train will be here soon so we all walk him to the station. The usual number of people are here to see who gets off or on the train.

Some are still drunk but they're the harmless ones: the old man doing a two-step with one of the giggling, young ladies at the corner of the store, the old lady who's always singing at the top of her voice, staggering around in complete circles with arms swinging around her, the old man sleeping under the storage shed with the dogs, his knees tucked against his chest .

The train is gone now. I look at the steeple of the Catholic church but no birds are there now. The sun's gone down. A calm, peaceful evening settles over us, the same kind of evening as yesterday, yet nothing is the same. Nature is friendly and true while our own kind tears us and leaves us bleeding inside, all in the same space of time.

A warm, gentle hand settles on my shoulder when we reach our cabin. Unconsciously, I move away from Mom. I cannot handle any comfort at this moment. I'm afraid I might cry again. We go about the usual routine of getting ready for bed. When someone mentions the recent exploits of the Town Joker, a reluctant smile comes to my face.

A shadow crosses the front window and footsteps sound on the porch. The door, not yet bolted, opens and the boyish face of Wess appears. "Hey, how come it's so dark in here? I was beginning to think you weren't home when I didn't see a light at the window!"

With a cry of joy, Mom springs up from the bench and plants a loud kiss on his cheek. I snicker and giggle because I know he hates to be kissed or shown even a bit of affection. Come to think of it, I don't usually see Mom kissing anyone.

Our world explodes with laughter as the lights go on. The shoulder bag that Wess carries is dropped on the bench. Something wriggles inside. Mom pulls the flap back and a little brown head pops out. A puppy scrambles out and shakes its little body before being swept up in Brian's arms and covered with hands from every direction, reaching out to pet it.

Both coal oil lamps are shining their brightest. Even the stove digests the week's accumulation of paper, dust and woodchips long enough to make a pot of tea and warm a late supper of fish for Wess and the pup.

Long after the lights have gone out, the girls are still whispering and giggling. Wess makes a comment here and there that sets the girls off laughing again. Vera has given up her bottom bunk for Wess. She now sleeps with Barbara on her double bed with Cora cuddled between them.

I lay on my back, staring into the blackness of the room. Everything is alright again. Everything is the way it should be. Smiling, I imagine being a blackbird. The warm air gently lifts my breast, filling me, through me, and I become one with the night, only to emerge again as Me, to honour the sun, in the early morning light.

5

WESS AT HOME

Summer 1962

I wake up to a voice saying, "If you want to sleep inside my house, there are a few things you'll have to learn!" I lift my head from my pillow. Mom is kneeling on the floor talking to the puppy. "You see this here? Do you know what that is?" The puppy is sitting on its haunches, head turning left and right.

The pup gives a yelp when his nose is rubbed on the floor. Then Mom's voice comes again, "Now that you know what that puddle is, little dog, here is where you go next time!" Mom pulls the puppy by the scruff of the neck and out the door.

I hear Wess chuckling from his bunk. Everyone is still asleep. Mom comes back in again with pail and scrubbing brush. I lay there listening to her scrubbing the floor boards.

Wess says from his bunk, "I guess this is the first time he's ever been inside a house. I got him from an old man at the portage on my way in. His dog had five puppies."

Mom has gone out with the pail. I can hear her laughing outside. When she comes back in, she says, "That puppy has found a new mother. He pounced on Rosiak and he's plaguing her to death right now. Rosiak hasn't had puppies in a long time. She doesn't want anything to do with that puppy out there!" We hear a yelp of pain and the pup comes in, standing uncertainly by the door. Then he runs joyfully nudging and licking at Wess's hand dangling from the bunk.

I jump down from the bed and kneel on the floor beside the bunk to pet the puppy. It's dark in here; there is no sunshine today. Wess's face is very dark with his summer tan. I watch his eyes shine above his cheeks. His teeth look very white as he returns my stare with a big grin. I giggle and say, "Toby, all I can see are your eyes and teeth!"

Wess gets up on his elbows. He has a T-shirt on and now he looks like he has long brown gloves on. His skin is very pale where the sun hasn't touched it. "Toby yourself! You're at least two shades darker than the last time I saw you!" he says. Toby must be the darkest Indian anyone has ever seen. He's up north somewhere. So when we tease, it's Toby this or Toby that.

Mom comes in with an armful of wood and starts the fire in the wood stove. "It's going to rain soon, again." she says.

After tucking the puppy inside Wess's warm blanket at his chest, I pull my runners on and dash out the door for the outhouse. It must have rained hard early this morning. The air is cool and damp. The leaves hang dark and heavy on the branches. Wet leaves and grass whip my legs as I run to the outhouse. My steps echo within the walls of the outhouse as I step in. Pulling the heavy door shut, I slip the long wooden latch in. It's very dark in here, even with that opening above the door. There's a box of old rags on the floor beside the door. I smile, remembering the time I lost my rag doll. I searched everywhere and couldn't find it. Then one day, I pulled out a piece of rag from the box and out came my doll. That Wess.

I dash out again and something smashes against me and crashes into the bushes. I swing around to keep my balance. When Tony gets up from the bushes, he sniffles and whimpers. He wipes raindrops from his clothes. I start to giggle and when he smiles, I let go into a rolling laugh. Holding my sides, I continue down the path to the cabin. Poor little guy, I didn't even hear him coming.

I grab a facecloth from the sink beside the door and run down to the lake. The rocks are slippery wet, so I carefully hop onto my rock. I dip the cloth in the cool water. Lifting it by the ends, I slowly lay it over my face. Then, jerking my head down, it falls off my face back into the water. I retrieve it once more, laying it over my face, till I notice the water is dripping on my chest. I wring it out and vigorously dry my face and hands. A light wind causes little ripples of water to touch and disappear against the rocks along the shore. The millions of wavelets of water, one behind the other, march closer and closer, disappearing and emerging, drawing near to touch the rocks and then vanish. A few birds twitter and chirp from the bushes to the right. The wind whistles through the needles of the pine tree above me on my way back up to the cabin. The stovepipe belches out smoke which quickly disappears over the rooftop. Getting closer, I smell the wood smoke. I hear the door open and close over at Aunty's cabin. It's the old man slowly making his way around the cabin to the outhouse. There is no smoke at their cabin yet.

Our door flies open and Maggie and Annie giggle and race around the cabin to the outhouse. Mom comes out and hands me the water pail and I throw the facecloth at her. Back down to the lake I run, skipping over a puddle beside the rock. The rain is starting now. I fill up the pail of water and turn to go. The raindrops plunge in and merge with the water on the lake and fall steadily faster while I hurry back to the cabin with the pail sloshing and splashing at my side.

Barbara is jamming the door open with a block of wood when I approach. Without a word, she takes the pail from me and puts it on the shelf behind her. With a sigh of relief, I brush by her. The shelf is a bit too high for me to lift the heavy pail. I usually spill or splash water because the bottom of the pail always bumps the shelf.

Mmmm! Mom is frying bacon on the wood stove. Her frying pan is wedged in the opening by the stove, lid tucked in the back. There's a pan of bannock rising and browning in the bubbling lard at the corner beside the stovepipe. On the other side of the pipe, the pot of coffee is brewing.

The cabin is full of noise: people talking, laughing, feet shuffling over the wooden floor, along with clanging utensils, cups and plates, and sizzling and sputtering grease from the frying pan. The stove is roaring and crackling, giving off warmth and drying off the side of my dress where the pail of water splashed.

The sound of rain pelting on the ground drifts in from the open door. Jumbo and Rosiak lay on the porch kept dry by the overhanging roof. I notice the puppy making a dash for the door. I edge around behind the stove to see what he's up to. There he is, falling all over Rosiak. His little behind is wagging so fast he loses his balance once in a while and he's frantically licking Rosiak's face, biting and pulling on her lip. Rosiak looks very annoyed and disgusted. Wess comes to stand beside me at the door to watch the puppy.

"What are you going to call him?" I ask.

"Oh, Little Dog, I guess," he says.

"But how about when he gets big?" I said.

"Oh, then I'll just call him Big Dog," he answers, poking me in the ribs.

"Come and eat now," Mom says, and everyone takes their turn at the table, helping themselves to bannock and bacon and finding a place to sit down on the edge of the beds. Eleven of us are in the room. Mom, Wess and Brian sit on the bench at the table. Maggie, Jane, Tony and I sit eating on the edge of our bed and, across the room on Barbara's bed, are Barbara, Cora, Vera and Annie.

Mom is telling a story about the time we lived at our trapper's cabin. I get up and pour myself a cup of coffee from the stove. I reach across the table for milk for my coffee. Next I look for the sugar when Wess hands me a spoonful. I smile gratefully and dump the contents into my cup, stir it and stroll to the open door. I smile at the puppy curled up inside the hollow of Jumbo's body lying asleep on the porch.

The cup is warm on my hands. I trace the figure of the polka-dotted dog on the side of the cup before I lift it to my lips. About the time the coffee covers my tongue, Wess breaks up, sputtering and giggling from the table. I spit out the salted coffee onto the ground, along with the contents of the cup, before I march back to refill my cup. Mom pays no attention to us and continues on with her story without even a pause. The sugar bowl has magically reappeared.

After breakfast, the dishes are done; garbage pail dumped; floor swept and puppy dragged out by the scruff of the neck. The rain has stopped now, but it's still cloudy. Mom has gone over to visit Aunty. I don't know where everyone else has gone.

Joe and I sit by the table fixing our slingshots. Wess is in the back-room. He takes out his guitar from under Mom's bed where she had it hidden while he was gone. He tunes it and begins singing songs. He sounds like a guy on the radio. We love to listen to Wess sing.

Our slingshots are now in good working order, but we hang around by the door to the little room listening to Wess sing. The puppy is pouncing and hopping around trying to catch Wess's tapping foot on the floor. After a couple of songs, Wess enjoys his audience and starts another song.

I glance down at his tapping foot and notice a splash, splash, each time his foot comes down in the puddle deposited by his puppy. I start giggling and whisper to Cousin Joe. He laughs too, after looking down at Wess's foot. When the song is over, Wess looks down to see what was so funny. By this time, the pup has already gone out the door.

I am left to scrub the puddle on the floor while Joe and Wess go to try out Joe's slingshot. He found a piece of rubber from the store garbage dump this morning. Just when I'm finally done, the girls come back in, laughing. They had gone to see the old lady across the tracks and found the Town Joker there, cutting wood for the old lady.

I find Wess and Joe behind the house by the lake. Wess has decided to replace the rubber of his slingshot with the one that Joe found. I am sent back to the cabin for string and a pair of scissors. Grabbing them off the table, I hurry back to Joe and Wess. After cutting off a strip, Joe shoves the remainder in his back pocket. Wess cuts the knots at each end off his slingshot with his pocket knife and pulls the old rubber off.

Someone's calling Joe, so he runs off to his cabin. I sit down beside Wess on a rock, watching him. "Here, put your finger on this," he says after he has tied a knot.

I put my thumb on the knot and Wess makes another knot on top. Wess pulls the string hard. It breaks and his fist hits me in the chest, knocking the breath out of me. I go flying backwards into the bush. I roll over on my tummy, trying to catch my breath. My chest hurts. I lay there moaning, trying not to cry. The pain eases when I sit up. Wess sits there, laughing. "Are you okay?" he asks.

So I smile and say that I'm fine and it didn't hurt too much.

The puppy has found us. He's running around, biting and pulling my hair and pulling at my shoelaces.

Slingshot done, Wess picks up the pup. He hops up onto a rock by the lake, scratching the pup behind the ears. Then he swings him back and forth and throws him into the water about four yards away. The pup's head immediately pops up and he starts thumping and splashing in the water, going in the wrong direction. Wess whistles and the pup turns, frantically swimming towards us.

"Dogs instinctively know how to swim," Wess says, pulling the pup out and petting him. After a brief rest, he throws the pup back in. Halfway back, the pup ceases to splash and swims quietly. Another rest, he throws it back in. This time, the pup swims quickly and quietly. Then Wess puts him back on the ground. The pup shakes himself and dashes back toward the cabin. Grinning, Wess wrings his shirt dry at the front where he held the pup.

I remove my slingshot from around my neck and pull and pull on the rubber, snapping it, while we walk along toward the cabin. Wess gets ahead of me while I insert a pinecone on the leather piece. I let go. Whack! It hits Wess right on the seat of his pants. Well, I know I'm in trouble now. I take off as fast as I can around the cabin among the trees and past the clothesline pole. Laughing and panting, I dart back around the cabin with Wess close at my heels. Right behind the cabin I feel a hand close on my shoulder. He pulls me around and throws me on the ground. Laughing, he pins my arms to my side with his knees and sits on me. He sits there laughing down at me... and then I notice he has one clothespin in each hand.

Slowly, he attaches a clothespin on my left earlobe. Pain registers. I struggle and shake my head. He says, "Oops! I've got it on crooked."

So he removes it. My ear burns, and he quickly attaches it again. Strangely, it doesn't hurt as much the second time. Then he attaches the other on my right ear. I yell. I wriggle and blink away the tears that spring to my eyes. I'm not going to cry. He has never made me cry yet and I'm not about to now. With the clothespins on both ears, it hurts to move my head. Laughing, he jumps off me. I grab the pins off my ears and jump up. He takes off around the cabin and I run after him. He disappears into the cabin

Just then, Maggie comes around the corner from the outhouse. I wait for Maggie and she goes in ahead of me. As soon as she crosses the open door, a pillow-wrapped fist shoots out and catches her on the side of the head. Her head jerks to the side and her knees just about buckle beneath her, as she sets up howling and crying in pain.

Mom quickly emerges from her room, asking, "What's going on?" Seeing Wess with the pillow, she asks, "What did you do that to her for?"

Maggie staggers to the bed. I quietly snicker. I love it. Caught red-handed, Wess returns the pillow to the bed with a bashful, guilty look on his face.

There's a pot of partridge stew with dumplings on the stove, so Wess and I help ourselves. Some have eaten already and the others will eat when they get home. Wess brought the partridge when he came home last night. I watch every move he makes. He has a trick of moving the bench just as I sit down. We eye each other, smiling and giggling as we eat. We pull a partridge wishbone apart; my side breaks. Wess wants bannock and there's none so he nudges me. "Make some. See if it's any better this time."

After throwing a couple of logs in the stove, I mix up a batch of dough, knead it and put it into the pan. I turn it when it's brown on one side. I also make another pot of tea.

Mom sits on our bed by the window doing some beadwork. When the bannock is done, Wess pulls out a knife and cuts off a piece. I guess I've passed the test because he doesn't say anything and helps himself to a second piece. Then Cousin Joe comes in. After a while, they decide to go for a walk down the railroad tracks.

I sit down beside Mom and string some beads for her. Aunty comes in and sits down on the bed, too. I give them some tea, while they sit talking.

I get restless, so I decide to go and find something to do. No one's around so I walk toward the store to see if I can find Annie anywhere. Just before the tall stand of trees, I hear Ben calling me. He lives across the tracks. I see him now coming up the trail from the big dock. He's holding a small, black kitten in his arms.

"Where did you get that?" I ask.

"I saw the old man over there throw a bag in the water with a rock tied to it. I took a stick and fished her out. See? She's fine now." He proudly holds up the kitten. I take it and stroke its small body. It starts to purr and settles against my arm. Ben stands there smiling, his face covered with white blotches, scars from sores left by the summer flies.

I hear Wess calling me from the path by the Catholic church. I give the kitten to Ben and run to Wess. He asks, "What's he doing with the kitten?"

When I tell him, he shakes his head and says, "I suppose he'll save all its kittens, too, when that cat has babies. Then they'll all starve to death."

I shrug. As we near our cabin, I take his slingshot, but it is so wide I can't pull it. Smiling, he says, "Hit a partridge on the head with a stone from this, and you can have a good meal."

By the time we get home, it starts to rain again. Pretty soon, everyone is home, drying off around the stove. The rain continues. Mud is tracked in and the pup periodically gets dragged out the door.

The sound of laughter and voices, and the smell of wood smoke and wet clothes drying fill the cabin. Brian and Tony are sound asleep on Mom's bed. Raisins are scattered on the blanket between them.

Finally, the rain stops and out comes the sun. It's evening now and its rays cast an orange tint on everything. Over to the east is a rainbow, its end dipping somewhere beyond the island. We start running and fooling around again.

I notice Uncle Daniel's cap tucked in a comer on the ceiling beam inside the cabin. He left it here when he was a bit tipsy last week. He doesn't visit us very often but I'll return it to him the next time I see him. I had washed and ironed it for him. Uncle Daniel always asks me the same question everytime I see him: "How are you, Indian Maid?" and always, I'd smile and answer: "Fine." Sometimes when I'm sad I often wish I could tell him that I'm not fine and tell him all my troubles but I always give him the answer he expects.

He calls me "Indian Maid" because I'm the darkest one in the family. He always teases me, saying there goes Mom with brown-headed kids in tow behind her, and right behind them comes one dark one, black head and all. Proudly, I pull the cap on my head and run out to show it to Wess. I can see a gleam in his eye and he lunges for me. I run. No, not the cap. He catches me behind the house. By the largest puddle, he picks me up, turns me upside down and dunks my head, cap and all, into the mud puddle. I almost cry. Wess lets me go, laughing at me while I stand there, mud dripping down my long hair and streaking down the length of my dress. I wipe the mud off my face. I'm not smiling. Wess stops laughing and disappears around the corner of the cabin. I go inside and wash the cap first before I wash my hair and change my dress. Mom watches me from the bed but doesn't say anything. The others are too busy going about their own business to ask how I've gotten so muddy.

I sit down on the bed and look around the room. From the constant scraping sound of feet on the floor, I get the impression that something important is happening. But when I look closely, the people in the room aren't doing anything special. Vera is washing her socks in the sink and hanging them on the line behind the stove. Annie is looking in the mirror by the door, putting cream on her face. Barbara is at the table making cocoa for Cora. Maggie is scraping mud off her shoes into the garbage pail. Jane is bringing in an armfull of wood. The two boys, Brian and Tony, are laying small stones in a circle on Wess' bunk. And Wess... a guitar strums softly from the next room.

6

CAMPING

Summer 1962

Mom coughs outside the tent before her footsteps fade away again. It's a very quiet morning. I hear the lonesome cry of a loon, somewhere out on the lake. A few seconds later it's answered by another much closer to the tent. Mom would never make it as a loon. I hear her footsteps coming and the crash of wood on the ground. She pokes her head in the tent flap, rummaging around in the paper box in the corner for the matches.

I prop up onto my elbows and smile at her. She whispers, "Don't get up yet till I get the fire going. There are a lot of mosquitos out here." She ducks back out again.

I lay back down and pull up my knees, snuggling into the warm blankets. I sleep at the edge and my face is about a foot from the tent wall. I can smell the pine branches that we're sleeping on. The bottom of the tent wall is tucked and weighed down with rocks around inside the tent. A mosquito bounces along the tent wall and settles on the rock in front of my face. I put my hand out and squash it.

The fire crackles now and soon the smell of birch bark and wood smoke drift into the tent. Something small is scratching, scratching, then bounces off the tent wall in front of me. The canvas wall is a little loose between the rocks and I can see the imprint of the frog each time he bounces against the wall. I hold my hand against the canvas, my middle finger tight against my thumb, waiting for his next jump. Here he is. I let my finger go as hard as I can. Snap, the frog is gone. After a pause, he is back again. I look down the length of the tent wall and see one of my old runners. I nudge it up with my foot till I can reach it. The frog is still bouncing off the wall. I hold my shoe, flat side against the wall, waiting till he lands on the tent again. Whack. I got him good. The tent vibrates clear across the top centre beam. Maggie pops her head up behind me. "Wha… what's that?"

Giggling I pull my shoe on and rummage around the pile of shoes for my other one. I step out into the fresh, clear morning air, then around the tent and into the bushes. After a battle with the mosquitos, I hurry back to the clearing.

Mom sits on fresh, broken pine boughs, making breakfast by the fire. She leans back, squinting her eyes each time the smoke sweeps around towards her. “The smoke just can’t decide which way to go,” she grumbles.

I pick up the soap and towel from the top of an old tree stump and head down to the lake. I slowly wash my face and hands. A mist hangs over the bay where the little portage is. We came here yesterday. Mom and Barbara came by canoe with the tent, groceries and camping stuff with Cora, Brian and Tony perched on top of the boxes and sacks full of blankets. Wess, Vera, Annie, Jane, Maggie and I walked the mile on the tracks to get here. We helped carry all the things across the portage and Wess and Mom carried the canoe over. Then Mom and Barbara made several trips with the canoe to get us all here to this island on the lake. Boy, our canoe was packed full.

The island is only about fifty feet from the main shoreline which is mostly swamp. There are some rocky slopes on the other side of the lake; some are quite steep. Here comes a train. I can see the tracks from here. Funny, I never even heard the trains that must have gone by during the night.

“You got the soap and towel?” Maggie comes walking down the rocky slope towards me. Rubbing her eyes and yawning, she squats down beside me by the lake. Slowly, she dunks both hands in the water and wipes her wet hands over her face. I hand her the wet soap. As she takes it, it squirts out of her hand and into the water. The soap sinks and slides along the rock, deeper and deeper. Maggie plunges her hand in quickly, trying to reach it. She loses her balance and falls over, her chest and shoulders sliding into the water. With a gasp, she scampers back onto the rock, dripping wet, but holding up the soap.

I start giggling and finally break out laughing. Oh, she looked so funny. Her wet hair is plastered to her head. After throwing the soap on top of the towel, she dashes back to the tent to change her shirt.

Mmmm… I smell bacon and I rush up to the campfire. Mom has made raisin bannock, bacon and a big pot of boiled eggs. My mouth waters as Mom hands me my share of the breakfast. I find the nearest rock and settle down, enjoying every bite.

After breakfast, we wash the dishes and pans. The blankets are hung on a rope stretched between the trees. Then the camp settles down to some quiet, peaceful hours. Annie and Maggie are reading Annie’s endless supply of comic books inside the tent. With Barbara’s help, Mom is stringing up her newly-finished fishnet. Beside the tent, Cora, Brian and Tony are building a miniature log cabin with twigs and dry sticks.

Mom sends Wess with the axe, and Vera, Jane and I to gather a pailful of pinecones. She wants to use them to dye her new fishnet. After an hour of tripping over brush, swatting flies and throwing pinecones at each other, we emerge from the bush with Vera carrying the pailful of cones. Our hands are black and sticky, the resin gluing our fingers together. Wess rubbed some of that sticky stuff over my left eye. Now my eyelid sticks everytime I blink.

Giggling and pushing, we file past the fire where Mom has a tub filled with boiling water. Her fishnet is ready. She dumps the cones into the boiling water. She gives us each a dab of mosquito repellent to strip the resin off our hands. After washing our hands clean by the lake, we decide to have some tea.

I sit leaning against the tree with my tea cup, watching Mom stirring her pinecone brew with a long stick. Small puffs of clouds are slowly moving across the sky, sometimes covering the sun. Flies continually buzz around the campfire. Mom's satin-white fishnet lays folded in layers on a white sheet to protect it from the moss and twigs on the ground.

Wess and Vera are in the canoe calling us. I drop the cup by the tea pot and skip over the rocks to the lake.

"We'll pretend we're the train. Get in." says Wess.

"Where to?" he asks, after Annie gets in.

"Sioux Lookout!" she says.

"Where to?"

"Armstrong!" says Jane, settling down beside Annie.

"Where to?" Wess shouts again.

"Savant Lake!" says Maggie.

"Where to?"

"Fort William!" I step in, quite proud of remembering the name of that place.

"Sorry. You'll have to get off. We don't go there on this train." Wess shouts.

My mind scrambles for another town. "Okay, I'm going to Long Lac then!" I say and sit down beside Maggie.

"All aboard!" Wess shouts in his conductor's voice.

Mom yells at us from the campfire to be careful. Wess chuckles as the canoe is pushed away from the shore. Having gone only about the length of the canoe, he steers the canoe to shore. "Armstrong." he yells and points to the boulder by the shore.

"Aw-w-w, already?" says Jane, getting off.

Wess chuckles, "Well, Armstrong's not far, you know."

Off we go again, this time, he steers the canoe straight across the lake. Thoroughly enjoying the ride, I don't realize we are approaching a small, flat rock about two feet across, far from the main shoreline. I smile at Wess, who chuckles again and brings the canoe to a stop. He yells, "Long Lac!"

Well, what can I do? I have to get off. I step off onto the rock which is only a couple of inches above the water.

The canoe turns and heads back to the island. I stand there, and glance at the bush behind me once in awhile. I can see them paddling around to the side of the island where they let Maggie off. Then I see the canoe disappear around the other side of the island. I stand there listening to all the little noises from the bush behind me.

Feeling dizzy from all the shimmering water around me, I try squatting on the rock. Soon my calves start to ache. Oh, I wish they'd come back. I try sitting down with my legs crossed in front of me, but the hem of my dress falls into the water on each side of me. The rock hurts my ankles and I almost lose my balance. Still no sign of the canoe.

Time passes. The mosquitos and horseflies from the bush have found me. I'm getting desperate. The wind has picked up and little waves are starting to lap at the rock in front of me, splashing my feet. I need to go to the bathroom.

Should I disgrace myself by yelling for help? Should I yell? I'll wait a little longer. More time passes by. I try standing up and stomping my feet but I almost lose my balance. I try sitting very still but my foot starts to fall asleep. More time passes. I can't wait any longer. I fill my lungs to yell. Then I see them picking up Jane. Slowly, the canoe approaches me. "Oh, thank you, thank you." I whisper, as they come closer. Vera with her bright smile and curly head at the front of the canoe, is a welcome sight.

"What took you so long?" I ask meekly.

"Well, Long Lac is pretty far you know, so we had to stop for lunch first!" Wess answers with a chuckle.

Around the side of the island, Maggie comes out of the shade, stretching and yawning after a nice rest on a comfortable moss-padded clearing. We go around to the other side of the island. When we come upon Annie stretched out on top a large boulder with a comic book over her face. Then we slowly drift towards the campsite. I am the first one out and head straight for the makeshift bathroom back in the bush.

When I return, Mom hands me a bowlful of macaroni in tomato sauce with a piece of bannock. I notice the new rust-coloured fishnet gently swaying in the breeze while it hangs in long sweeps over a rope strung between the trees. It looks silky soft.

Mom, in the shade under a tree, pounds a pile of lead sinkers apart to hold the bottom rope of the net. Beside her is a tub of multi-coloured floats Barbara has finished stringing. They will be attached to the top rope on the new fishnet.

After lunch, I run down to the lake and wash my bowl and spoon. Soon Maggie and Annie come to wash their bowls, too. We watch a big flat bloodsucker approaching in a steady wavy motion. "It probably smelled the food washed from our bowls," says Annie.

"How would it smell? I don't see a nose on it," I say.
"Maybe it just sees the pieces floating around," suggests Maggie.
"Well, he must have eyes for sure, because he seems to know exactly where he's going," says Annie.
I say, "You know, he looks like Crazy Bill's bottom lip." We all run up to the tent, laughing.
Mom has decided to put rabbit snares in the marshy area across the bay. Wess is going with her to hunt for partridge. He's taking the small .22 rifle. Barbara will take them across in the canoe and come back to pick up Vera, Jane, Maggie and the little kids. They're going to the tracks to pick some late blueberries.
Annie has decided to stay in the tent to read her comics. Mom calls me over to her sewing bag and indicates the left over spools of twine from her fishnet. "Look how much was leftover," she says to me.
"Would that be enough for a little net?" I ask excitedly.
"Oh, it could be about two feet wide and about seven feet long," she says.
"Oh Boy! I'll start it right away!" I run my fingers over the satiny-smooth surface of the nylon twine.
I'll need a little rectangular piece of wood and a small spindle. Mom hands me a piece of cedar wood. I decide to get busy right away. Mom warns me to be careful with the knife before she heads down to the lake with Wess.
I love to carve things and I'm the knife and axe sharpener, when Wess isn't home. But I still manage to cut myself a lot. I must have over a dozen scars on my hands.
"Hey! I'm asking you if you're coming!" Barbara yells at me from the canoe.
"No. No, I'm staying here," I answer and make myself comfortable on the rock. I already see in my mind the small spindle that I am going to make.
I've got a sore neck. The rectangular crossbar I've made is about an inch and a half wide; that's how wide the squares are going to be. I've sanded it smooth so that the twine doesn't catch. The spindle I've made is about five inches long and about an inch wide, with a long pointed tongue in the middle. I've sanded and smoothed the inside, all along the tongue around the sharp curved tip and down to the nicked flat bottom. The red stains along one side are from the small cut on my middle finger.
The girls came back awhile ago with a pot of blueberries. The branches of the pine-trees above me interlock together and part again, gently swaying in the breeze. I hear a long whistle from the shore. That's Wess's signal that they're ready to come back. Barbara heads down to the lake and into the canoe to pick them up.

I sit up again and start winding the twine on the spindle. Starting from the bottom, I bring it up; loop around the tongue; down the bottom and around. Faster and faster I go. The spindle gets fatter and the twine climbs higher and higher up the tongue. There, it's full!

I'm done and here comes Mom, twigs clinging to her hair which has escaped from around her scarf. A pleased look crosses her face when I place my new crossbar and full spindle beside the shiny white nylon spools on her sewing bag.

"Oh, you've finished them." she says smiling.

"Yep!" I answer, grinning, quite pleased with myself.

Wess snags my hair with the protruding sights of the .22 gun, when he passes behind me. "Oops!" he chuckles.

Mom and Barbara go to check the fishnet. Inside the tent, I lay down with Annie who just woke up from a long nap. I look at one of the "Archie" comics. Maggie lays sprawled on the other side, giggling and turning the pages of a "Sad Sack" comic. With Wess in there, our comic reading quickly turns into a pillow fight. My ears burn from a whack on both sides of my head. I dodge out of the tent. Mom is starting to fry fish in the two frying pans. The sun has already gone down behind the trees.

Vera and Jane are getting the bedding down from the line and into the tent. Cora is grouchy and tired. Brian and Tony are almost leaning on each other while they sit waiting for their supper.

I sit down under a tree, watching them and listening. Barbara has just put down her sewing—a baby bonnet? Gee, it looks pretty small. My heart fills with love as I watch my mother, there by the fire, swatting flies away from the food. Her hair is very tangled now and blowing in a fine fuzz all around her head. She's asking Jane for a long piece of wood by the fire. As Jane pulls it, the end flips up and knocks the teapot over. Barbara is mad. She had just made the pot of tea. I study Barbara for a moment and decide her belly must be getting fat.

At last, supper is ready and we're all having our fill of fish, potatoes and bannock. The wind is completely gone now. I sit there thinking we should all chew at the same time, so there'd be some silence. I turn around and face the lake. It's calm and peaceful now. Almost as part of the nature all around us, the voices grow quiet, turning into a low drone mixed with twitters of laughter.

I sit there daydreaming, having long since returned my plate to the pile by the fire. Maggie and Annie are washing the dishes by the fire. The little ones have gone to bed now. Mom sets the last log in the campfire for the night. I linger by the fire watching the flames greedily devour the dry wood until it is almost burnt out.

I stand up and brush the twigs off my dress. After a big stretch and a yawn, I shuffle along to the tent. Everyone's already jostled to a comfortable spot when I poke my head in. Mom sleeps by the door so I look along the row of bodies until I spot a space at the end, beside Jane. I start gingerly at first, until I hear the first, "Ouch!" Quickly removing my foot, I get another, "Ow!" Then in rapid succession, it is "Ouch! Awoo! Hey! Watch it!" Stepping and slipping on feet and toes, I finally make it to the end, where I drop down quickly before someone throws a shoe at me. Jane giggles beside me, as I take off my shoes. I pull the covers over me and stretch out on my back.

Mom, grunting and sighing, settles down on her bedding beside the tent door. Quiet settles over the group as she digs in her bag. She clears her throat and reads from her worn Cree prayer book and a chapter from the red Bible, a nightly ritual. Small lights flicker across the tent front from the dying campfire outside. The reading is done and the nightly jokes and stories start. Mom tells a legend of two sisters who went on a journey. They had looked longingly at the brightest star and that star came and took them up to where they found an old woman fishing from a hole in the sky. They asked her to let them back down to earth with her fish line. My eyelids grow heavy as Mom's voice drones on and on....

I'm awakened by Jane poking at my back and saying, "Come with me. I have to go to the bathroom."

Grumbling, I follow her feet as we crawl to the door. It's pitch black inside and everyone's sleeping. Jane is already outside waiting, as I quietly stand up and step over Mom. Then I realize, I've left my shoes back there. Well, I grope along the edge of the tent flap until I find Mom's shoes. I slip them on and duck out of the tent. Jane is hopping around now, telling me to hurry up. Still grumbling, I follow her into the bush, occasionally scraping her heels with my large shoes.

The moonlight floods our camp area when we return from the bush. The clouds have parted a little but they quickly cover the moon again. We scramble to take advantage of the brief light. The mosquitos are bad. Somewhere back there on my last step, we were enveloped in darkness again and I heard a "squish" and a definite "pop" under my foot. With a sickening feeling, I lift my foot up. "Jane." I whisper, "I've stepped on a frog!" Touching only the heel of my yucky foot on the ground, I limp along behind Jane. I quickly kick the messy shoe off my foot and we duck back into the tent.

As I settle down to sleep again, I wonder what Mom will find plastered to her shoe when she goes to put it on in the morning. We'll be going home tomorrow. I miss our dogs, Jumbo and Rosiak. Joe insisted on looking after Wess's pup. With a drowsy smile, I picture Jumbo wagging his tail. I snuggle deeper into the blankets.

7

GATHERING FIREWOOD

Fall 1962

Black blobs drift across the sky. I try to make the black blobs catch up to that seagull up there. So white, its belly flashes in the sun. So graceful, it glides across the clear blue sky. But if it flies across that sun again, I'll have so many blobs in my eyes that I'll... Ouch! Mom taps me on the side of the head with her paddle. "How many times do I have to talk to you before you hear me?"

Water drips off my hair and into my ear. "Now hand me my bag there in the box beside you!" Mom says in her high, angry voice.

The canoe rocks to the side when I lean over and yank the bag out, and turn around to hand it to her. "Watch her now, she'll have us all in the water yet!" she says, glaring at me.

Sinking my head lower between my shoulders, I settle back on my seat at the bottom of the canoe. In front of me, Annie's back is shaking with laughter. I feel embarrassed and humiliated. The blobs are still drifting across my eyes, too. Impatiently blinking away the blobs, I look up at the sky but the seagull is gone now.

I study my broken dirty thumbnails, thinking how I've been trying to be so grown-up and nice. My older sisters, Annie and Vera will be going far away to a city to go to school pretty soon. They'll be gone all winter. Maybe they'll come back during Christmas holidays. They sometimes do. I swallow a lump in my throat.

I glance back at Mom who's putting her snuff box back in the bag. Her voice gentle now, she says "Here, put it back in the box." With exaggerated care, I slowly lean over and shove the bag back in the box.

Mom is quickly pulling in her trolling line. She's caught a fish. Finally, she pulls it out in a spray of water and drops it inside the canoe. Brian and Tony scramble to get out of the way. After moments of frenzied thrashings, the fish lies still long enough for Mom to yank the hook out of its mouth. It's a jackfish. It lays there at Mom's feet, its red gills opening and closing. Curiosity brings the little boys closer. Suddenly, the fish flips up and slaps Tony right across the face. Tony howls in pain and surprise and frantically wipes the fishy slime off his face with his sleeve. Brian is killing himself laughing, pointing at Tony's face, which only sets Tony into full gear with his sniffles. Mom says, "That'll teach you to try to smell a live fish."

Wess chuckles from the front of the canoe. Annie hasn't looked up at all from her comic book which she grabs each time the paddling stops.

I study Mom before I see, beneath the straight face and calm voice, that her eyes are filling with swallowed laughter. Mom is wiping Tony's face with a wet cloth. There's still slime on his eyelashes. Giggling, I turn away.

Barbara's new grey canvas canoe has reached us now. Flashing us a smile, Vera, at the front, grabs the front of our canoe. "What's he crying about?" asks Barbara.

Mom answers, "The jackfish slapped him on the face for smelling him." That did it for Mom. I felt it from the canoe first, as her big body quivered and shook before she let out peals of high-pitched laughter. That got us all laughing. It's not very often we hear Mom laugh like that. Even Tony manages a sick smile, blinking aside the drying slime off his eyelashes.

Behind Vera, sits Jane, choking and gasping in that weird laugh of hers. Maggie sits smiling in the middle of their canoe, her paddle across her lap. All around her are the handsaws, axes, grocery boxes and pots. Barbara sits at the back end. Cora is sleeping at her feet. Barbara's husband, Allan, comes home to visit a couple of times each month. The last time he came, he brought the canoe with him. It was great watching them take it off the train boxcar, so shiny and new.

Mom has finished baiting her fishhook again. The tea pot has been passed around and now we're on our way again. It's my turn to paddle now. Annie and I are taking turns paddling. We're one paddle short in our canoe, which suits me fine.

We're going to the end of the lake to cut some firewood for the winter. Mom says we'll have an early lunch there first before we start. There's lots of dry wood there. We do this every fall. Sometimes we sleep overnight in the tent. But we're not going overnight this time. After we get the wood cut and piled by the shore, we leave it there. Then Mom and Wess or Barbara and Vera make trips once in a while, hauling back the wood in the canoes, till they get it all home. I'm glad our cabin is by the lake. It would be even harder getting the wood from the bush to the lake and then carrying it inland to the cabin like the others do.

The breeze feels so good on my face when I tilt my head back. It's getting hot now, though. There's not a cloud in the sky. I yawn. We were up pretty early this morning.

Along the shoreline, the water reflects the many shades of yellow, orange and brown leaves. The birch and poplar trees are now so beautiful among the evergreens. It must look like flowers of gold, orange and yellow, blooming in a field of green grass to that seagull up in the sky. It's back again. My arms are hurting. They feel like they're falling off. But I clench my teeth and force my arms to keep moving back and forth, back and forth. Soon, the ache recedes and my mind wanders again.

The water glistens and dances in the sun. I imagine invisible giant wings, gently fanning the water from the west, sometimes from the south, causing the water to continually gurgle at the front of our canoe. Mmmm, I smell peppermint. Annie is chewing away, lounging with her comics with a pile of jackets under her head. Wess is popping his gum and Brian has just popped his bubblegum over his nose. I turn around to Mom and ask, "Hey! Where's mine?"

She pauses to dig in her sweater pocket, saying, "I offered you one but you didn't answer. I'm telling you, girl, your daydreaming will get you into trouble one of these days!" I accept the gum with a bashful smile. Fancy me missing an offer of gum.

I hear a train whistle. That must be the morning passenger train. Everyone pauses to look back. We can see the train like a small, black garter snake with a white stripe, inching along the tracks that run along the bay. The village itself is now hidden by the islands we've passed. Mom says, "Well, I wonder who it's stopping for this morning." The train never stops unless someone is getting off or on.

Annie has settled down for a nap with a jacket thrown over her shoulders to protect her arms from the sun.

My gaze drifts along the shoreline. A dead, black tree is leaning into the water, its branches somewhere beneath the muddy bottom. Another tree with its gnarled, dead branches, rakes the surface of the water. It's leaning at such an angle, I wonder what's holding it up? It's tempting to get up there, jump up and down and make it fall.

It looks so cool and dark, deep in those bushes by the shoreline. If I were tiny, I'd walk in there and lay down on top of that leaf and watch us go by. I can smell the decaying leaves of fall already. The rich earth and pine scent... I breathe in deeply.

My arms are aching again. I can feel the burning sensation starting from my wrist, up along my arm and into my shoulders. I spit out my gum. It even hurts to chew. It's getting awfully hot, too. I glance back at Mom. She has put on her thick scarf. How she can wear that thing in this heat, I'll never understand.

I hear laughter from the canoe behind us. Barbara and Vera are always talking and laughing about something. Oops! My paddle has slipped from my hand and hit the water at such an angle, it looks like a pail of water descending on Annie, fast asleep in front of me. "Ahhhh!" Annie jolts up, gasping and wiping her face frantically with her hands. She spins around, blinking water out of her eyes and fixes a stare on me that tells me what she'd like to do with my scrawny neck. I lamely try to explain how my paddle slipped because my hands are sweating. She turns with a "humph!" and sits there with her back stiff and she proceeds to wring out her shirt. I feel just terrible. Is the canoe shaking again? I glance back at Mom. She's looking across the lake, biting her lower lip. Brian and Tony are playing finger loops with a string. I'm glad they put the fish into a box in Barbara's canoe, but Tony still smells fishy.

I continue paddling. I'm getting hungry. We're almost there. Mom has told us to stop paddling. As she waits for Barbara's canoe, she pulls in her trolling line, . Barbara says, "There at the point, how does that look to you, Mom?" Up ahead is the point, fronted with flat rocks that slope down to the water, framed with short spruce and birch trees.

Mom nods and agrees, "Good spot. It's shady. We'll have our meals there."

Smiling happily, I let my paddle drop across my lap. Mom and Wess paddle slowly, guiding the canoe in between submerged rocks, toward a grassy spot to the side of the rocky area. One by one, we get out of the canoe. Mom steps out last and we pull the canoe onto the soft earth.

Maggie and Vera are already lugging the boxes to our lunch spot. I run around exploring the area. From where I stand, there's a swamp behind and a little stream on the right. A thick bush and a muddy bank are at the left side. With the canoes now empty, Annie, Jane and I help Maggie gather wood and twigs for the fire.

Cora is awake now and playing with a bag of sugar from the box closest to her. An axe rings out in the bush behind us. That will be Wess cutting two logs to hold the firewood. Annie scoops up Cora and we shake the sugar off her blanket. Mom is cleaning the fish by the lake. Boy, am I hungry. Finally, the fire is going and the groceries and pots are arranged nearby.

The camp smoke drifts almost straight up. The wind seems to have completely disappeared. I splash water on my face at the lake and give Maggie a splash, too, when she comes to see what I'm looking at in the water. I smile at Annie, as she emerges from the bush where she has hung her shirt on a branch. She has her sweater on now and she just walks right by me.

Mom and Barbara are almost finished cooking and it sure smells good. Tony's climbing in and out of the canoes which brings a sharp order to stop from Mom. Cora is stuffing her face with jam from the box behind Barbara. Wait till she sees her. I smile when Brian trips and goes tumbling into the bush. Maggie is frantically searching the boxes for some paper. Barbara has finally noticed the sticky strawberry jam all over Cora's hands and beaming face. She looks funny. I make my way over to a small birch tree where I flop down and lean back in the shade. Vera and Annie are sitting side by side, laughing and talking like old friends. Vera is so beautiful. Her brown hair, always curly and shiny. Annie is a few inches shorter than I am. She has light brown hair which she sometimes curls and she looks so creamy and delicate. My eyes drift down to my runners, holes in both toes. My white socks keep falling down. My long, boney legs are covered with a pair of old stretchy, brown pants pinned with a big safety pin to the front of my sweater to keep them up. I've a blue sweater on, with a long string of tiny safety pins pinned to the front. I think they look nice. And I have great big holes at my elbows. Heaven knows what my long black hair looks like. I can't remember if I combed it this morning. I sit picking at the imbedded dirt under my thumbnail. Before we left I peeled some dried mud off a ball I found.

Annie kicks my feet. Between each chew of her mouthful, she says, "Better hurry and get some lunch or you won't get any!"

"Oh!" I'm off to the fire where I stuff myself with bannock, bologna, a piece of fish and a cup of tea.

After lunch, everyone is resting and talking and laughing again. I'm washing the dishes while Jane puts things away. Mom and Barbara decide we'll tackle the bush to our left first for the firewood. So off we go, into the canoes and across to the other shore. Mom has piled our lunch boxes and pans by the dying fire. Scrambling out of the canoe, we dash into the bushes. It's so beautiful. The leaves haven't started to fall yet. The colours are just brilliant in the sunshine. I'm standing around under a poplar tree, looking up at the colourful leaves almost transparent in the sun, glowing like a stained glass window.

Barbara, Vera, Mom and Wess are carrying the two axes and hand-saws. Annie has Cora by the hand. I'm running around in circles with Maggie and the little boys. Jane comes up the trail last with the teapot and cups. Maggie and I glance at each other guiltily and I ask, "Anything else down there?"

Jane shakes her head smiling, "No, your mother has the medicine bag."

I go skipping along again, telling Tony and Brian not to run too far. After watching everyone drop the things in a clearing, Maggie and I are off, crawling over logs and branches. We already see some dry trees for firewood. Mom and Barbara have set to work with the axe and hand-saw while Wess takes the other axe to cut down trees. Mom and Barbara saw off the downed trees to short lengths and get them ready for carrying to the lake.

Logs are lying there ready to be carried down to the lake. All afternoon squirrels scold us, scampering around, while the woods ring with axes, saws and laughter and tears. Cora has scratched her exposed tummy on a branch. She got sawdust in her shirt top which made her itch. Tony and Brian are kept busy running back and forth for tea, bandages and occasionally, mosquito repellent.

It's getting very hot working in the sunshine with not a breeze going through the bushes. I take a towel to the lake and get it wet so it'll be here for someone to wipe the dust and sweat off their faces. It's so nice at the lake, I can take a deep breath and splash some cool water on my face. My mind is ahead of my body again. To get to the lake, I have to carry something down there. So, throwing the towel over my shoulder, I pick up a log of drywood from the pile. It's not too heavy but it is very sharp. Almost like handling a cactus. Making my way down to the lake, I carelessly throw it on top of the growing pile. As I kneel by the water, I notice something under the overhanging bush by the shore. It's about a foot and half long, about six inches wide, tapered at the end and painted green, round and smooth. I grab a long pole and nudge it out from under the branches to where I can reach it. Throwing aside the stick, I jump on a rock and stretch out my arm till I reach the front of it. It is very heavy and soaked through. It's a canoe, carved beautifully-smooth right around the flat bottom. The back end is all rotted through and worn off from the constant rub on the rocks but I could put a new back-end on it. It will be like new. Mom might even let me use some of the leftover green paint. It'll be so beautiful. I pull out some rotted leaves and brown scum from the bow of the canoe and rub it dry on my clothes.

I'll show it to Wess, maybe he can help me fix it. Cradling my precious find, I dash off through the bushes. I can hear Wess's axe and I run and brush past the branches, crashing through the bushes towards the sound of the axe. There he is. I suddenly come to a complete stop. His face is furious and he's shouting at me, "Get out of here! Go to where the others are! Hurry up! Go!"

I turn and run. Why is he so mad at me? I run on, blinded by tears and sobs that choke me. My feet stumble over brush and twigs, till I finally stop. A tree crashes in the bushes behind me. My legs start trembling. I sit down on an old stump. I had forgotten he was chopping a tree down.

He's chopping the tree in half, severing the branches now. Soon I hear his footsteps. With the long upper half of the tree over his shoulders, he walks by me, then turns. He regards me for a few seconds before saying quietly, "Don't ever do that again."

I jump to my feet and say, "No, I won't do that again." Remembering that I still clutched the canoe, I hold it out, "I was so excited, see? I found it by the shore. We can fix it and it'll look just like new!" Lovingly, I run my hand over the smooth, wet bottom of the canoe.

He smiles and turns. "Maybe," he says and continues toward the lake. I scamper along behind him, jumping over roots and twigs.

Suddenly, he stops. I just happen to put my head up when I brake to a stop and stare at the jagged end of his log about a foot from my face. He chuckles and continues on his way. That was close. I'm ready the next time he stops, I hold on to the end of the log and he has to do a quick double step back when he starts to go again.

When we get to the lake, I notice the towel on the rock where I had dropped it. I push the toy canoe into the narrow bow of our canoe. Wess has gone back up the path again for the other end of the log. I wash my face and carry the dripping towel toward the clearing. With a sigh of appreciation, Barbara holds it to her flushed face.

After many more trips, I flop down beside Maggie at the clearing. The shadows have lengthened; it's late afternoon. All of us have gathered at the clearing. Mom and Barbara are laughing behind the bushes. Finally, they come out bearing the last log, a six-footer, which they put down in the middle of the clearing. They stand there wiping the sweat off their faces. Gee, Barbara's tummy is sure getting big!

Mom says, "Is everyone here? Then, let's go."

We each get busy grabbing something, not wanting to be the one to carry the heavy log.

Then Mom says, "Tony, pick up that log and carry it to the lake!"

Everyone stops, turns and stares at Mom, then at Tony.

Tony, who is already down the path, slowly returns, taking one step at a time, his eyes never leaving Mom's face. He finally blurts out, "I can't! It's too heavy!"

Mom, in a very commanding voice now, says, "Pick it up! And take it down to the lake!"

We stand transfixed, while Tony, lips trembling now, stands looking down at the six-foot log at his feet. He looks like he'll bawl at any moment. Then with one more look at Mom, he bends down and puts his slender arms around the rough bark. Suddenly, he jerks the log up so fast he just about throws it over his shoulder. He staggers before he regains his balance. A look of utter disbelief and astonishment crosses his face and everyone cracks up. Those of us who weren't in on the joke, rush over to investigate the log. We find that it was like dry straw all packed in tight, surrounded by a thin layer of brittle dry bark that is still intact. The sawdust had plugged in the porous core so that it looked solid at the ends where Mom and Barbara had sawed it. Maggie calls it a giant cigar.

Tony smiles sheepishly, as Mom ruffles his hair, and says, "Do as you're told right away, Tony. I wouldn't expect you to do something I know you couldn't do."

Laughing and skipping, we make our way down to the canoe. Proud of our day's work, we stand back and look at the two huge piles of dry wood by the shore. I'm glad we're having supper here because I'm starving. We paddle back across the calm water to our boxes of groceries.

Mom makes a quick supper of corned beef and macaroni. With bannock and tea already made, we have supper in no time. Soon, the dishes are washed and put away again and slowly we drift down to the canoes. It is so nice here that everyone is reluctant to go home. Mom says, "We should have brought our tent and blankets."

I'm paddling again. Annie says she's too tired. I can hear Cora crying behind us in the other canoe. Brian and Tony are laying down behind me. Tony is still talking about the log. This time, Mom has her bag of necessities beside her, in which she keeps her snuff box. I can hear her spitting into the water behind me. I wonder how she can make her spit shoot out so far. I tried to spit like that once but it fell on my foot.

The lake is so smooth, it looks like a giant mirror. And there's that seagull again and another one. I wonder when they'll leave to go south. It seems that one or two seagulls hang around after the rest have gone. I don't blame them. It's so beautiful here, I wouldn't want to leave either.

We've passed the two islands now. I hear a dog barking from the village already. There's the point up ahead where we once had a shore lunch. We'd been playing by the canoes and our cup floated away. So I climbed to the end of the canoe, which lifted the front off the ground where it was pulled up. When the cup was close, I grabbed it and turned to scurry back. There I was with no paddle and the shore about two yards away. It's a good thing Wess came by then; he pulled me in with a long stick that he grabbed from the bush. Boy, did I get a tongue-lashing from Mom.

Jane is singing behind us from the other canoe. I wish she'd shut up. She sounds horrible, like a strangled cat.

The Catholic church is set in a clearing by the lake. You can see the white steeple from far away. The village is so noisy. I can hear the dogs barking, kids screaming and laughing, someone chopping wood, and the generator running at the general store. They only use it for light and they shut it off at bedtime. That's how the kids know in the village when it's bedtime. I can hear the old lady at the point giving somebody heck. She's always mad at kids, that one.

Rosiak our dog, has seen us already and she's wagging her tail by the boat landing. Jumbo and the pup are lying fast asleep by the doorstep. It's nice to be home.

8

THE NEW TEACHER

Fall 1962

Mom is cooking breakfast outside, but what is Wess up to? I heard him sneaking out and later he came in and tiptoed back to his bunk. He's gone back to bed.

I push the blanket off me. Everyone's still asleep. Wess is curled up under his blanket facing the wall. I slip my shoes on and go out the door. I jump off the porch and head for the outhouse at a run. Shucks. I've got sand in my shoe. I stop and pull off my shoe to shake the sand out. I kneel down to pull my shoe back on and... look at that! There, a couple of feet in front of me, is a string strung across the path. It's about ten inches high off the ground and tight. Oh Wess! He must have noticed that I'm always the first one out of bed and he decided to lay a trap for me. I giggle as I deliberately step over the string and continue on my way to the outhouse.

Just as I am taking the latch off the door to come out, I hear someone running. Oh no! I fling the door open to yell a warning. Too late. Jane crashes into the bushes head first. Oh my gosh. I run forward, heart pounding. I reach her just as she sits up. Oh, she's hurt. She sits there gasping, holding her knee. She has skinned her knee real bad. Blood runs down her leg. There's a large scratch across her cheek. "I'll help you back to the house," I offer.

"No, I have to go to the bathroom first," she moans.

I help her to her feet. Limping, she slowly makes her way to the outhouse. Oh my. She's also has a gouge on her right palm and it's bleeding, too. I wait for her till she comes out again. The blood is starting to dry on her leg. Slowly, we return to the house. As we pass the broken string, she asks, "Who put that string across there?"

Feeling quite guilty, I hesitantly answer, "Wess, I guess. He was ' trying to trip me but I saw it. I was going to pull it out on my way back. I didn't know anyone was going to come behind me...". My voice trails off.

We head towards Mom at the campfire. "What happened to you?" she asks, after casting a sweeping glance at Jane. I get a cloth off the line and Jane washes her wounds off by the lake. Mom sends me for her medicine bag.

As I enter the cabin, Wess looks at me and I say, "Nice try, but you got Jane instead!"

He chuckles and swings his legs off the bunk. I deliver Mom's medicine bag. She's examining Jane's hand. Pulling out band-aids and ointments, she sets to work patching up Jane.

After breakfast, Wess and I decide to go shooting birds with our slingshots. Or rather, he shoots the birds while I follow, stones filling my pockets, so that my sweater is weighed down and stretched almost down to my knees. The stones rattle and grate from my swinging pockets that bounce off my knees with each step, while I hurry to catch up to Wess.

We're following the narrow footpath along the shoreline. It is very quiet here deep in the shade. The bush is very tall and dense. As we come around a curve on the narrow path, I almost bump into Wess, who suddenly turns around, saying, "Turn around; we have to go back."

"Why?" I ask and crane my neck to see that, beyond him up the path, someone's lying acoss the road. "Who's that?" I whisper.

Wess smiles and whispers, "It's that old lady, Sally, passed out drunk!"

We hastily retreat back up the path. Taking a detour up to the tracks, my pockets are quickly getting lighter while Wess shoots off stones at every moving twitter in the bushes. After refilling my pockets again by the railroad tracks, we make our way home through the bushes.

Hot, tired and panting, I stumble out of the bushes behind the outhouse. Wess is nowhere in sight. As I near the cabin, I can hear someone talking inside. I see Wess take one look through the open door and head towards Aunty's place. I step inside and stop at the door. A stink fills the cabin. Mom is sitting on our bed, doing her beadwork, nodding at her visitor, Ben's mother. She's drunk and filthy. She's sitting on the bench by the table. She must have fallen in a mud puddle by the looks of her dress. Her messy hair is all over her face which she occasionally brushes back with blood-crusted hands. She has scratches all over her hands. Mom gets up and gives her a cup of tea and offers her some snuff. The woman takes a large pinchful and shoves it under her bottom lip. Then I notice her face when she turns her head to send a splatter of spit on the floor. The whole half of her face is swollen black and blue. Blood is caked on the corner of her swollen lip. I can't understand what she's saying. In slurred sentences, she's telling Mom a story, only pausing to spit on the floor again.

I slip back out and wait around by the lake, until I see her come out and make her way down the path towards the store. I enter the cabin again. In a flurry of activity Barbara has emerged from Mom's room, mumbling and grumbling. She wipes the spit off the floor with an old rag which she throws into the fire. Then she viciously attacks the floor with a pan of water and scrubbing brush. Amused by all this, Mom continues with her sewing as Barbara thoroughly wipes off the bench.

Mom sends me out to bring in the towels and dishcloths from the clothesline. Taking my time, I lower the pole that holds the line high until I can reach the pegs. I walk along the line, releasing the towels from the pegs. Finally, arms overflowing, I make my way back into the cabin. I sweep past the stove and bump into something and the stove lid comes down shut with a clang.

Barbara sets up a screech and I dump my load on the bed. She is frantically scrambling around behind the stove, before pulling out a long stick. I can hear something sizzling in the stove. The fire grows into a louder roar. Barbara is still babbling at Mom, "Did you see what she did?" And to me, she screeches, "Gee whiz! Do you know what you did?"

I slip by her to reach the door. "Get out of here before I hit you with this stick." She flips the stove lid up to reveal the frying pan handle sticking up. The smoke now belches up the smell of burning meat. I must have bumped into the frying-pan handle causing the frying-pan to slip off the stove lid that it was resting on and fall inside the stove along with the contents of whatever Barbara had been frying.

Mom just claps her hands over her mouth. Shoulders shaking, she sits there laughing. One quick look at Barbara, and I dash outside. Boy, she's really mad.

I see Maggie coming up the path. "Hey, did you hear? The new teacher got off the train yesterday!" she says.

"Oh yeah? What's he look like?" I ask.

"I don't know. I didn't see him yet, but Rita says he's tall and slim, has dark hair and he's not old at all."

"Come on! Let's go see Rita!" I say and grab her arm. We run along the path to the big dock, past the store's garbage dump and up to Rita's cabin. Poking our heads in through the open door, we find her sitting by the table, eating lunch.

Rita's mother glances at us. She's filling a bowl from a big pot on the stove. "You kids had lunch yet?" she asks.

"No," we shake our heads.

"Here, sit down. It's just duck-dumpling soup," she says. We plunk ourselves down beside Rita and set to work on the bowls placed in front of us. Rita's mother is back playing solitaire on the bed by the window.

We quickly devour our lunch, laughing and talking about the new teacher. Rita is the same age as I am and will be in the same row with us this year. After our lunch, we decide to play with Rita's dolls. We pack a box of dolls, a blanket and some other things to play with and head toward the rock slope by the lake. A gentle breeze blows across the water while we stand in the rock clearing, facing the bay. A little stream empties into the bay but we don't go there often; it's too mucky.

We spread the blanket and get out the dolls. We find some empty, old cans and we mix some mud pies. Then, somewhere along the way, I end up being Rita's baby and Maggie's the daddy. I lie on my back on the blanket, pretending to cry. Rita rocks me and slips a round rock, about the size of a robin's egg, into my mouth. I suck on that, pretending it's candy. Rita continues to rock my head on her knee. Suddenly, the rock slips pass my tongue. I frantically try to sit up, but Rita pulls me back down and continues rocking my head back and forth. Choking and gagging, I swallow the rock. When I catch my breath, I push Rita back and, horrified, I wail, "I swallowed it! I swallowed the rock! You pushed me back down! Oh, I'm going to die now!"

Terrified that I am going to die for sure, I feel my heart thumping very hard against my ribs. "Oh, what am I going to do?" I lay back down, checking for pain that will lead to my death. I'm breathing okay. I'm not hurting anywhere. I don't feel any different. Somewhat relieved, I sit up again, "I guess I'm all right. I don't feel anything…" Rita and Maggie are sitting on each side, watching me, intently, "… unless, I die a slow, painful death. Maybe the rock will block something inside me or maybe get stuck inside somewhere. Then I'm going to get sick and die!" My heart is thumping against my ribs again.

Finally, Rita suggests, "Let's put our toys back and we'll go and tell my mother."

I slowly get to my feet and follow behind them to Rita's cabin. But there is no one home when we get there. Rita says, "Well, let's go to the store. Maybe she went that way."

I'm still not feeling any symptoms of sickness, so I relax a little and slowly walk behind Rita and Maggie. As we come around the corner of the store, I catch a glimpse of Ben taking off as fast as he can towards the sand pit down the road by the tracks. "I wonder what's up with Ben?" I say.

Then, we hear the commotion by the store's storage shed. Ben's father's beating up Ben's mother. My heart is thumping very hard now as I watch the man crash his fist into the woman's face, sending her flying to the ground, blood splatters on the front of her dress. My knees are trembling and I'm starting to feel really sick to my stomach. The woman is screaming and crying and the man draws his foot back and starts kicking her. I look for a way to escape. I feel like I'm going to throw up. I shudder.

"There's Mom, over there," says Rita, pointing toward the station.

The rock in my stomach is quite forgotten now. "Hey, there's my mother, too!" Five ladies are sitting in the clearing by the station, Mom among them, being entertained by the Town Joker. Mom has a grocery box beside her. I take a peek inside just tea, lard, canned milk, baking powder, matches and some packages of Kool-Aid.

I glance back at the fight, but there's no one there now. No one here even mentions it. They totally ignore the couple. Soon, I forget about them, too. It's getting on evening and I'm getting hungry for supper. I notice Ben by the railroad tool shed.

I take off at a run towards him. He turns when he sees me coming, and heads towards the sand pit again. I finally catch up with him. He gets some stones from his pocket. "Give me your slingshot!" he says, holding out his hand.

Hesitantly, I pull out my slingshot from my waist band where I had it tucked in. He looks nasty. I hand over my slingshot. I watch him fire stones as hard as he can all over the place. He's really pulling hard on the rubber. "Hey don't break it!" I say. He glances at me with a smirk on his lips. "Give it back to me!" I say. He swears at me and tucks my slingshot into the back pocket of his pants and turns to walk away.

I lunge forward a step and yank it out of his pocket. Eyes blazing, he swings around and comes at me with both fists clenched. I freeze and stand there. I face him, feeling the anger rising in my chest. He stops and stares at me. I take a step towards him very slowly and we are still staring at each other. I hiss at him, "Don't you dare hit me! You understand? Nobody, is ever going to hit me!"

I turn and run back to the station, feeling the strength leave me with each step. Mom is ready to go home when I get there. So we say goodnight to Rita and her mother and Maggie and I follow behind Mom.

Mom decides to take a shortcut through the bush path to our cabin. As we pass the school washrooms, I decide to make a stop there. Maggie and Mom go on ahead. After glancing warily at the teacher's house and assuring myself that he isn't anywhere about, I slip into the "girls" side.

My footsteps echo loudly when I step in. I like the echo so I try out a "La, la, la..." Then getting a little carried away, I let go with a loud, "Go tell it on the mountain, over the hills and everywhere..." My voice carries loud and clear.

Finished, I slip back the door latch and skip out the door. I dash around the corner of the outhouse and come to a complete stop. There in front of me, coming out of the boys' side, with a wash-pail in one hand and a cleaner in the other, stands the new teacher. He's got a big smile on his face. Dark, curly hair and the bluest eyes I've ever seen. "Hi. What's your name?" he asks, with laughter in his voice.

Then it dawns on me... . He was on the other side while I was in there, separated only by the thin wall and the screen at the top. I look down at my feet, my face burning. If the earth opened up at my feet and swallowed me, I would be so grateful.

He takes a step towards me, and softly this time, he asks again, "What's your name?"

I lift my head and my face breaks into a grin as I look into his merry, twinkling eyes. I say my name but it comes out like a squeak. Then I turn and take off as fast as I can down the path through the bush. Halfway home, I let go, laughing long and hard.

When I get home, everyone is bustling around, and it looks like everyone's here. I'm hungry! Then like a flash, with a sick feeling in the pit of my stomach, I remember the rock I swallowed. Getting scared again, I start thinking, "What if I die tonight, they won't know what happened to me!"

I finally corner Mom in her bedroom. "Mom, I swallowed a rock about this size," I say, bringing my thumb and forefinger together to form a circle. Waiting to hear my death sentence, I hold my breath.

She looks at me, and asks, "Why would you want to swallow a rock for?"

So I tell her the whole story. She looks at me again and says, "It'll probably pass through you." She turns away, muttering, "You do such stupid things sometimes!"

A flood of relief flows through me along with a mixed dose of shame. Stupid? Yes, I guess it was — but I had no intention of swallowing it in the first place.

Supper is ready — spareribs with potatoes and carrots. Everyone's sitting on the porch eating supper. I carry my plate outside, too. With tails wagging, the dogs lie on the grass in front of us, gnawing on the rib bones.

Oh no. Here comes the Town Joker. "What's that you're eating?" he asks Mom. Barbara comes out with a plate for him. He sits down on the porch and eats with us. Amid bursts of laughter, he continues with a story between each mouthful. Mom refills his plate again and gives him a piece of bannock and tea.

Dishes done and house cleaned up, we join in the fun outside. Wess has found a heavy, brown ball. Everyone is standing around in a circle while the ball is thrown from person to person, faster and faster around the circle. The laughter and squeals get louder until finally someone drops the ball. Even Aunty has come to join us.

A couple pass by on the path and they stop and join us. The circle grows. Oh, here comes Cousin Joe with another ball. They start that ball going the other way. Oh, the laughter is really loud now. The two balls meet at Aunty's hands and we just about kill ourselves laughing. She gets mixed up and doesn't know which ball is going where. The balls are in play again, and they're going faster and faster, until the Town Joker gets hit on the side of his head. He was busy teasing Vera next to him.

Mom, holding her sides from laughing, goes and sits on the porch. Then the rest of the adults also go and watch from the porch as the Town Joker begins chasing the girls around.

It's getting dark. The couple and Aunty leave and the girls finally chase the Town Joker away. Barbara takes the blankets inside. Wess and I play ball a bit more. Wess throws the ball over the cabin roof and I catch it on the other side. I really have to run to catch it because I've no idea where it is going to come over. Then Wess hits the stove pipe. Barbara sets up a howl inside the house. I run around the cabin to see. The pipe is sticking out crooked. Chuckling, Wess climbs up on the roof to straighten it up again. That is the end of our ball game. I run inside the cabin for a cup of tea. I am very tired.

9

SALTED PORRIDGE

Fall 1962

I awake to hear Mom and Barbara talking in hushed tones. Mom is making a fire in the stove. The lamp is on. Why are they up in the middle of the night? I'm so hot. I hope Mom doesn't get the stove too hot. I listen to them, vaguely wondering who they're talking about. "Her fever is very high," says Mom.

Barbara, from her bed says, "She didn't get up for supper. Come to think of it, I didn't even see her eat any lunch."

"No, she's been in bed all day," Mom says. "I really think we should get her to the hospital. She's been moaning in her sleep and her fever is higher than it was earlier when I checked her."

I hear Barbara moving in her bed, "Maybe Vera should take her."

I must have dozed off because now Mom is standing over me. Vera is at the foot of my bed, all dressed and drinking coffee. Mom is talking to me slowly as if I were deaf, "Sit up. I have to change your clothes."

I pull the blanket back over my shoulders again. My mouth feels very clumsy as I murmur, "That's okay. I'll change my clothes in the morning."

Mom pulls the blanket off again and says, "No. Vera is going to take you to the hospital. Now sit up."

I struggle to sit up. My head is very heavy and I hear a constant buzz in my ears. "Why is it so hot in here?" I ask. My tongue isn't working properly. Mom yanks my slip off over my head, then, pulls a clean slip and dress over my head again. "Why is this dress so hot?" I ask.

Mom answers in an annoyed voice, " I warmed it by the stove first. Now put your coat on."

My arms slide into the armholes and I gratefully lie down again. I'm so tired. I can feel Mom pulling on my socks and feel her slipping on my shoes and tightening the shoelaces. Too tight. Mom is shaking me again. The light is turned down very low. The stove air vent has been closed. Mom has her coat on and Vera is standing beside her, ready to go. "Come, it's time to go. You're too heavy to carry, so you'll have to walk between us. Now, come on," says Mom.

I sit up again. Oh, I want to take my coat off. It's too hot. My legs feel shaky, when I stand up between Mom and Vera. I walk towards the open door. I step outside and the cold air makes me gasp. It's very dark. I smell rotting leaves and wet ground. We pass Aunty's cabin. Mom's flashlight sways with each step. It's making me very dizzy. A heavy mist off the bay hangs frosty white in the ray of Mom's flashlight. My teeth are chattering. Now I'm very cold. I realize I have a blanket over my head when Mom ties the ends tighter around my middle. When we enter the path through the tall pine trees, the mist disappears.

I'm too tired to catch my breath to say anything, but I notice a pair of shining eyes at the end of the tunnel . And I'm afraid. My legs are really shaking now. Each time Mom's flashlight flicks down the road, the eyes flash back. I keep my head down till I get dizzy again with the ground travelling so fast beneath me. When we come out in the open, Mom's flashlight passes over a dog sitting on the path watching us. I realize it was the dog's eyes I saw.

My fear has made me hot again. Mom and Vera turn at the store's storage shed to wait for the train. Mom sits down and I gratefully lie on the platform, my head on Mom's lap. She pulls the blanket tighter around me. I see tiny lights moving around by the station; cigarette tips glowing, people waiting for the train. I no sooner settle down when we hear the rumble of the approaching train.

Groaning, I slide off the step and back on my feet again. I just want to lie down. Off across the open field to the station, I shuffle my feet one in front of the other between Mom and Vera. The train engine passes the station when we reach it. I can see the conductor's flashlight flashing down the length of the train, coming closer till he's in front of us.

With a hiss, the train screeches to a halt and the conductor jumps down with a little step stool. I feel the blanket slide off my shoulders as I go up the steps. I stop at the top to wait for Vera. With the blanket draped over her arm, Mom waves to us and the conductor runs up the steps and opens the door to the coach. The door bangs shut behind us and the train lurches forward.

The smell of upholstery and cigarette smoke hits my nose. Lurching from side to side, we hang onto the back of the seats and slowly make our way down the aisle to the first empty seats. Everyone is asleep in the dim light; some snoring loudly over the clickety-clack of the train. The seat opposite me is occupied by a lady sleeping. I can just see the back of her head, all white; the rest of her is covered with a shawl.

The conductor returns with a small white pillow which he puts on the window side of my seat. I lie down gratefully. Vera settles into a seat across the aisle from me. The train is deafeningly loud. Bang, bang, clickety-clack.... I stare at the sleeping body in front of me jerk, shiver and bounce with each movement of the train. Soon my burning eyes close.

When I awaken, it's still. The train has stopped somewhere. The old lady is gone. Vera is sitting across from me, smiling. There is a low murmur of voices at the door from the people getting on. Then the train lurches forward again, the wheels squealing and screeching. The monotonous clickety-clack starts again and I close my eyes.

Vera is shaking me. We're here. With my heart pounding, I follow Vera down the aisle. The train is slowing to a stop now. Most of the people seem to have come to life for the aisle is suddenly packed and we're lined up behind each other. The train pulls into a flood of lights.

Soon we're on the platform of the station. People are hurrying everywhere. We walk into the waiting room where Vera speaks with one of the men behind a glass partition. Soon a man comes in and we follow him outside to a car. I feel very sick. I'm just barely able to follow Vera. I haven't the energy to look around. The seats are very soft inside the car. I think this is my first car ride. I just can't remember right now if and when I'd been in a car before.

With Vera beside me, I feel a little better. The car moves slowly at first, then it goes fast. I see lights go by, one after another, in a blur. It makes me very dizzy. It feels like we're gliding or flying low over the road; it's so smooth. Soon we come to a stop in front of a low house. I'm feeling very sick. I feel the man's arm come around me.

Cigarette smoke escapes from the man's coat as he carries me up to the house. When I'm on a soft bed, a woman's voice whispers for me to go to sleep. I hear them talking in low voices in the dimly lit room. I fall asleep. I wake up once. Someone has taken off my shoes and coat. Vera is sleeping in the next bed. In the faint light, I see a row of beds, all filled with sleeping bodies and in two rows on each side of a long narrow room. We're in one corner. So I turn my back to them and concentrate on Vera's relaxed, sleeping face and soon drift off to sleep again.

When I wake up again, I poke Vera and whisper, "I have to go to the bathroom!" She rubs her eyes and pulls on her shirt and skirt over her slip and helps me off the bed. My legs are shaking and my head still feels strange. I follow her into a little room. She turns on two shiny knobs and out comes warm water from a spout. She washes my face and hands after I'm done. I jump when all of a sudden behind me, comes a loud gushing of water in the toilet when Vera pushes a little lever on the side. I'm getting very tired again. She leads me back to bed where I promptly fall asleep again.

Vera is shaking me awake. All the bodies on the beds are gone. There, in a room off to the side are voices. Vera leads me into a room with two long tables filled with people already eating breakfast. My mouth waters at the bowl of porridge that is placed in front of me. Vera passes me the milk and sugar. I put in a tablespoon of sugar and pour the milk in my porridge. I stir it up and promptly pop a spoonful into my mouth. I stop. My throat closes and my stomach gets ready to chuck it out if I dare to swallow it. Grabbing my glass of orange juice, I wash it all down before I can breathe again. I poke Vera and whisper, "Somebody put salt in my porridge."

She smiles and says, "Some people make porridge with a bit of salt in it."

I sit there feeling cheated out of a good breakfast. I nudge her again and say, "Mom never puts salt in our porridge!"

She looks at me and says, "I know. Just eat."

I look at my bowl again. There has got to be nothing more awful then the taste of salt and sugar mixed in a bowl! I poke Vera again. "How can people be expected to put sugar in it, if it's already got salt in it?"

Vera is getting annoyed with me. I can tell when she starts to breathe deeply like that. I sit there looking at my bowl. What a nasty joke to play on a hungry person. A woman comes to ask if I'd like to go back to bed since I'm obviously too sick to eat. I nod my head, get up and head straight for my bed and lie down. I listen to the clanging of pots and tinkling of spoons and bowls, accompanied by the murmur of voices. I realize I can't understand some of them. What language are they speaking? I go to sleep again. I wake up later to the sound of shuffling feet on the old, worn linoleum floor. About a third of the people have left with the car driver. Lunch is ready. It's a delicious soup and I feel much better. The soup is so good that I forgive the woman and give her a smile when she asks if I am feeling better. Then she refills my bowl.

Just as I'm finishing my second helping, the car driver comes again. After calling off a list of names from the paper in his hands, he's followed by half of the people who go out to the car with him. We're left to wait some more.

I feel fine now and I begin to take an interest in the people around me. One of the men in the room has a huge white cement shoe on his foot. I nudge Vera and ask, "How come he's got that on his foot?"

She answers patiently, "It's a cast. He must have broken a bone in his foot." An old lady on one of the beds is coughing very badly. The room is very stuffy, dark and dingy. The old linoleum on the floor is worn down to its black tar bottom in many places. The painted walls are peeling and globs of brown stains spread over the surface.

I go and sit on a chair by a window. Kids are playing by the road. They're very dirty and they have scabs on their legs. They're kicking cans and throwing stones at the cans. They look mean. I don't like this place. I wish we would go soon.

A long time passes while I sit there by the window. Vera is lying on the bed reading a book. A car comes down the road and stops in front of the house. It's a green car but rusty at the bottom and it's very dirty. Some of the people who left this morning are getting out and coming back in. The car driver now names the rest of the people who are left, including us. So off to the car we go. Vera and I sit in the front. There's that exciting, gliding feeling again. We whiz by the houses. Cars of different colours, some shiny new, are on the road. I almost hold my breath when we turn a corner. All too soon we come to a stop in front of a long building with many windows—the hospital. I recognize it now. I've been here before when my nose was bleeding and they couldn't stop it at home or on the train. I didn't even remember getting to the hospital, I just woke up in there.

The driver directs us to a room where we take seats on the chairs lined up against the wall. Vera leaves the room with one of the nurses who has a handful of papers. When Vera returns, she says we have to wait until they call me. We sit for a long time when finally a nurse comes and puts a thermometer in my mouth.

I sit there with the long stick of glass under my tongue until my mouth fills with saliva. I'm afraid to swallow in case I accidently bite the glass off. Vera turns and studies me as if something has just occurred to her. She pulls the thermometer out of my mouth and looks at it. Thankfully, I swallow. Then she glares at me. "There's nothing the matter with you." she says, as she looks at the numbers again. "The doctor is going to get mad at me for bringing you here for nothing." She shoves the glass back in my mouth and says, "Hold your breath. Maybe it will make it go up a little."

I look at her and hold my breath till my chest starts to ache. I think my face must be turning blue before I gulp in some air at the side of my mouth, still holding the glass tube with my tongue. I sit there panting while Vera checks the thermometer again.

Desperately, she says, "Do it harder. It hasn't even moved yet!" She pushes it back in my mouth again. I'm getting pretty tired but I hold my breath again. I'm not anywhere near desperate for air yet when the nurse comes back. She plucks it out of my mouth and writes something on the paper she holds. Then she asks me to follow her into a room off to the side. She tells me to sit on a padded table and there I sit, perched at the edge while the nurse leaves the room again. Later, I hear the doctor talking to Vera outside in the waiting room. Then he comes in and checks me over. I realize that I didn't understand some of the things he said. My English isn't that good.

I wouldn't dare talk English in school. I'd be embarrassed and teased to death if I dared to talk English in front of the whole classroom. So the most we ever say is to answer shyly, "Yes" or "No" to the teacher's questions. Any English I know is only from what I read in my school books and by listening to the teacher talk. I would never dare try to talk to him. If only I saw him by myself, maybe I would try. I sometimes wish I could talk to the teacher easily like I talk Ojibway to Mom. But I wouldn't dare, I'd be too embarrassed.

"Feel this here?" the doctor is talking to me, guiding my fingers to my left collar bone; there's a sharp bump there. "Now, feel this here." He traces my fingers along my right collar bone; it's flat. "When did you get hurt there?" the doctor asks in the same tone.

My mind scrambles to remember. I shake my head and shrug my shoulders. Inhale, exhale; he's listening to my chest with that thing that looks like a slingshot, stuck in his ears. He runs his fingers along my ribs. Again he picks up my hand and traces my right ribs downward. "Do you feel this bump here? And feel that space?" I nod. He continues, "That's a broken rib. Do you remember what happened there?"

I remember that one. I smile and nod, "It was a low stump on the ground."

"A low stump?" he repeats after me.

Again I nod. "I fell on it from the tree."

"From a tree?" he repeats after me again.

I nod. "I fell off."

"Oh, you fell off a tree. What were you doing up there?" he asks.

Hesitantly now, I answer, "I was shooting birds."

"Shooting birds?" he repeats after me again.

Slowly I nod, "Yeah, with my slingshot."

A smile tugs at his lips as he says, "Oh, you were shooting birds with your slingshot up in the tree and you fell down right on the stump. Right?"

This conversation is boring. I nod. I give a big sigh of relief when he finally turns to the counter behind him.

"Do you like to fish, too?" he asks enthusiastically.

"Oh yes, I like fishing." I reply, thinking about the little minnows and baby pike and… .

"And, I suppose you dig up your own worms?" he asks, turning from the counter with a smile.

Thoroughly puzzled, I ask, "Worms?"

"Oh you know, worms for bait." he says, holding a tube upside down on something in his hands.

I answer, "I use bannock for bait!"

Then my eyes fall on the needle in his hand, while he dabs some wet stuff on my arm with the other. I don't know what else he said to me for I've closed my eyes and forced my mind on something else when I feel the sting and ache on my arm. Suddenly, it's over. He turns back to the counter again and picks up his papers to leave. He turns and looks at me. "All finished. Are you okay?"

I nod and slip off the table to my feet. I take two steps, when suddenly the floor comes up to meet my face. I feel his hands grab me and lay me back down on the table.

There is still the twitch on his lips and he stands looking down at me. "Now, you stay here till you feel better, you understand?"

I nod and he leaves. I can hear him talking to Vera again outside the door. I lie there looking at the counter beside the door. My head still feels funny. On the counter is a long row of big and little jars filled with white fluffy cotton, flat sticks and round sticks with white fluff at the ends. There are two little sinks, side by side, with the long spouts where the water comes out.

My eyes travel back along the counter to the window with its faded curtains. Then I turn my head and my eyes fall on the dark bottom of a row of cupboards all along the wall above me. I begin to feel very uncomfortable, as if I were lying under a ton of bricks hanging about six feet above me. I'm getting out of here. I swing my feet down again and sit up. My head feels light but, otherwise, I'm fine. I get to my feet. I feel okay. I walk out into the waiting room where Vera is waiting.

Then the car driver comes in and we return to the house again. The people are already sitting down to supper. The woman meets us at the door and ushers us straight to the table. I sit fidgeting at the table; I need to go to the bathroom badly. I don't enjoy the supper much; I feel my tummy is as full as it can be. As soon as the people start to get up, I dash for the bathroom. When I come back the woman gives me a second heaping bowlful of the wiggly, jiggly, delicious stuff, which Vera says is Jello. I remember when I was really small I tasted this stuff once in the hospital. They did something to my throat and I couldn't eat for awhile. All I had was this delicious stuff.

It's dark now and I'm tired. Gratefully, I crawl into bed and go to sleep. Sometime in the early dawn, Vera shakes me awake. It's still dark. It's time to get up and I dress quickly. We have breakfast of boiled eggs, sausages and toast with four other people who are also getting on the morning train.

Soon, the car driver shows up at the door again. When we're ready to leave, the woman appears with a sandwich bag for each of us. I clutch mine tightly while we all pile into the car. Quickly we're whisked off to the train station. The driver disappears again. We sit for a few minutes in the busy station when the train pulls in amidst the hissing and squealing of its wheels. Then we follow the long line of people to the train. Some go left, some go right as the conductor asks, "Where to?" to each passenger who comes through. We're directed to the coach to the right and soon find two empty seats facing each other. We watch the scurrying activity down below on the ground. The sky is getting a little lighter when the train jerks forward. This time I sit up, bright, alert and taking it all in. The beautifully-coloured houses go by. Then come the lakes, marshes, and rock cliffs, each different from the other.

One after another, the endless telephone poles march across the windows: some high, some low. The wires are sometimes level with the train before plunging down or springing up to a pole on a hill top. I doze off.

I wake up and my glance falls on my lunch bag. I grab it and peer inside. I pull out a sandwich, an apple, and two cookies. Carefully, I open the plastic wrapping on the sandwich. Such soft white bread. I take a bite. "Mmm… hey, Vera, what's this thin meat in here?"

Glancing from the book she's reading, "That's ham," she says.

After taking another bite, I ask, "What's this orange stuff in here?"

Looking up again, she says, "Oh, that's cheese." She's getting annoyed.

After another mouthful, I ask, "What's this creamy, white stuff in the green leaves?"

"Oh, be quiet! Don't be so stupid." she continues with her reading. I shrug and slowly eat my sandwich, thoroughly enjoying each bite. Mmm… . After the sandwich, I promptly chomp through my apple. I save the cookies.

I poke Vera when I see two bears by the tracks, eating something. I watch the people get off and on at all the stops along the C.N. main line. The conductor is always coming by, teasing Vera each time he passes. He brings her another book. Soon we're home.

We get up and walk down the aisle to the door. We hang onto the backs of seats, as the train jerks and comes to a stop. The door is flung open and the conductor jumps off the step and sets a stool down with a flourish for Vera to step down beside him. She's giggling. I walk carefully down the steps and on to the ground. There's Mom waiting for us by the station. Smiling, she comes forward. Oh, it's great to be home.

10

JUST US

Fall 1962

Mom's hands dart in and out with her needle through the shiny, glittering beads. She sits in the middle of the bed by the window. A cool breeze comes through the door past the roaring wood stove.

The newly-patched door with its fresh white boards reminds me of last night's episode when the man from across the tracks kicked our door open again. We were already lined up in the dark behind the stove when the door crashed open, splinters flying, and the man strode in. We slipped out behind him. I heard something behind me when Mom hurried us out the door. We ran across to Aunty's and she opened her door before we even reached it.

"I heard your door being kicked open." she said. We trooped in and stood in the dark by the door. Mom peeked out from the small opening by the window to watch for the man to leave.

Mom whispered from the window, "I had to help him inside a bit. He stopped too close to the door, so I gave him a push. I heard him crash and roll around on the wood blocks I laid all over the floor by the door." She chuckled. We heard him walk across the porch and disappear down the path.

Then we returned home and crawled back into bed. Mom had to use all the knives to hold the door closed. Next time, we'll have to get a new door.

"I'm talking to you." Mom sighs.

"Huh? What?" I ask.

"Get me some water in this cup," she says. I jump up and pour water from the dipper in the water pail. When I hand her the cup, my last step kicks her spittoon over. She gasps at the sound of the spit-can, rolling and bouncing off the wall. The brown liquid spreads on the floor and I decide to get out of there, quick.

I slow to a walk on the path leading to the beach. The rotting leaves swish under my feet. I wish Wess was here. He's gone far away somewhere. Mom says he's got tuberculosis and he's in a sanitorium. He'll be gone a long time. Vera and Annie left on the train last week to go to school far away, too. I kick at an old root sticking out on the path. The yellow, rotting pieces of wood spread under my foot. Barbara and Cora are gone too. My brother-in-law, Allan, came and got them before Vera and Annie left.

No one is at the beach and I sit down on the grassy bank. I hear a rustle of dry leaves from the other end of the clearing. It's an old black dog. Huge blobs of yellow stuff are caked in the corners of its eyes. It just stands there, staring at me. It makes me nervous. I pick up a piece of driftwood and hurl it. "Get out of here!" I shout. Slowly, it turns and disappears behind the low cedar bushes.

Someone's blue shirt lays washed against the rotting logs of the small dock jutting out from the middle of the beach. It's too far to reach. Forget it. I'm not getting my feet in that cold water for someone else's shirt.

I sit back down again on the sand cliff. Picking at a piece of driftwood with a couple of knobs at one end, I hear shuffling feet coming down the path. It's Joe. I still get an attack of the giggles everytime he opens his mouth. He went back home to his parents for about a month and when he came back, he sounded so funny. The first time he talked to me, I thought he had a cold. He just glared at me and ran off. Then I heard Aunty talking about Joe's voice change. I didn't know about things like that. It's still pretty funny, the sound that comes out everytime he opens his mouth.

He jumps off the path to the beach a couple of yards from me. Then that weird, low voice comes out of his mouth. "What are you doing? And don't laugh!" he orders.

I look up at him for a second. "Oh, I'm just trying to see a figure of an animal's head or something in this,' I said.

He chuckles, "Looks like the thing between a man's legs to me."

I jump up, really mad now, "You get out of here!" And I throw the driftwood at him. He jumps back and, whistling, he disappears behind the bushes down the path.

I kick the sand. "Mean dog! Dirty old dog!" I mutter.

I take off at a run, up the path toward the tracks. Oh no, the dog. It darts from the side of the cabin and comes at me barking. "Aw shut up! Shut up! Get out of here!" The dog stops, looks at me, then turns around and lies down again in the shade by the cabin. I run until I reach the tracks. I take out my slingshot from my waistband. I'll do some target shooting. At my first shot, the rubber breaks and slaps the back of my hand so hard I almost cry. I hurl it into the bushes as hard as I can.

I run across the sandpit by the railroad tracks. With each step, my feet sink into the soft sand. I punish my legs still harder for slowing me down. Then I reach solid ground. Suddenly my foot hits a root. I crash and slide on the ground so hard, I lay stunned for a second, before I catch my breath. Then I lay my head down and cry. The tears come hot and fast from my eyes. I feel them drip, drip, drip off my nose. Then I notice the dusty sandballs of tears all in a row on the hard sand. I can make a heart design. I get up on my elbows. The first three tears take the first curve up the side, then more teardrops down the dip at the top, more tears coming around the other curve, then I run out of tears. I blink and squeeze my eyes shut — no tears. I still have one side to go down on the heart. I'll finish it with tiny spit drops. There, a perfect heart.

I sit up and examine my knees. Both palms are bleeding. My skirt has protected my left knee somewhat but my right one is bleeding. My baggy stocking is ripped through and blood is running down my right leg.

Slowly I get to my feet, wincing at the pain on my knees. Boy, you sure couldn't hide anywhere around here; all the leaves are gone. I can even see our cabin from here. The scene here looks exactly as if I were standing right in the middle of Vera's hair brush.

No one is around when I enter our clearing. I head for the lake to wash my hands when I hear Aunty talking inside. Passing by our open door, Tony and Brian are by the lake. What on earth are they doing? They have sticks and the flat rock is covered with... bloodsuckers! Tony is cutting some in half with a rock. I limp up to them and order, "Put those back in the water! Remember, Mom says you'll be crippled if you maim any creature! Now, put those back!"

Brian glances up at me and says, "We got lots of big ones from those fish guts in the water by Aunty's canoe! See?" He shoves a stick at me with a huge black bloodsucker writhing at the end.

"You stop that or I'll break your neck!" I yell at him.

After studying me for a minute, Tony asks, "What happened to you? You've got blood running down your leg." Bloodsuckers forgotten, they skip over the rocks, toward me, "Let's see? Oh, look at your hands!" They sit and watch me pull my long baggy stockings off and wash the blood off. Then they wince each time I pull the shredded skin off my knees where it was hanging loose. Behind them, I watch all their bloodsuckers wriggle to the end of the rock and plunge safely into the deep water.

They go off playing and I make my way toward the cabin. I glance at Jane who's by the stove stirring a stick in a tubful of clothes on the stove. I groan, "Oh no! Not dishtowel washing day again!" I hate the smell of Javex. It makes my eyes water and it gets in my nose. Even the food tastes like Javex to me. All I smell is Javex for a whole day afterwards. Aunty must have gone home already.

I throw the stockings in the laundry box and climb up to the top bunk where I sleep now. I try to look at some of my school papers, but my eyes are watering too much. I climb down and pull out the fishnet bag from under Mom's bed and tie a couple more rows on my fishnet. It is very grey with dirt, especially the knots. They're almost black. Remembering how white and satiny Mom's net was when she finished it, I feel kind of disappointed with my net. It doesn't look new at all. I only have a little more to go and it will be all done. Maybe it won't look so bad after I dye it. Quickly losing interest, I shove it back in the bag. Sighing, I settle myself at the edge of the bed. Mom sleeps here on Barbara's bed now. We filled Mom's room with stuff we don't need. Only six of us are left here now. I glance out the window. "Hey Mom! Here comes John Bull! He's drunk." I whisper quickly, just as his footsteps pound on the porch and the big ugly man walks in.

He strides over to Mom's bed, stands looking down on Mom's bent head, and finally asks, "Hey, Delia! What you doing?" His voice booms in the small room.

Mom glances up, continues sewing and says, "What's the matter John? Can't you see very well?"

Grinning, John Bull seems to relax and folds his big body to sit on the bench by the table. He looks around. Jane has promptly disappeared out the door.

"Where's your young boy, Delia? I thought he was home," he says.

Mom pauses while rethreading her needle. Slowly she answers, "Wess has T.B. He's in the sanitorium."

John Bull clucks his tongue and shakes his big head, "Bad thing, that T.B. but he'll be okay. He'll be home in no time. Hey! How about some tea, eh?"

Mom glances up again. "There should be some in the pot there. Help yourself." She continues stringing the colourful beads.

John Bull chuckles deep in his chest. "Help yourself, she says," he mutters filling the nearest cup with tea. He sits there looking around the table, so I guess he's looking around for a spoon.

I stand up and go around to his side. "Move your elbow," I say. He moves aside and from beneath the table I pull the spoon drawer open and put a spoon in front of him. I move the sugar and can of milk toward him.

John Bull stirs his cup with relish and says, "Hey, Delia, you have a good kid here! Hey, you go to school?" He directs the question at me. I nod. "You see anybody fighting my Tommy, you come and tell me, huh?" I think about the snotty-faced, loud-mouthed Tommy; I don't say anything.

Then John Bull exclaims, "What the heck is that evil-smelling stuff you've got on the stove? Pee-ew! What a stink! My eyes are starting to water. I'm getting out of here!" He throws his head back and downs the rest of his tea.

Mom smiles, "Yes, that Javex might steam some of the dirt off you if you stay any longer."

John Bull's laugh echoes over the ceiling beams. He stands over Mom again, points a finger at her and says, "You make me a nice pair of mitts sometime, eh?" Then he turns and strolls to the door.

With an amused look on her face, Mom answers, "You'll have to pay me good money, John, otherwise, you'll not be getting a pair from me."

John Bull chuckles, then points a finger at me, "Hey you! If anybody ever bothers you, you come tell me, eh? I'll fix 'em for you!"

I just sit and watch him turn and stomp out the door and across the porch. We can hear him yell and sing, going down the path.

A thought comes to me. It's like I've just discovered Mom's secret. A smile tugs at my lips and I look at Mom. I've just discovered her name. Delia! I just never thought about the fact that she had a name. She was always just, 'Mom' or 'your Mother'or 'my Mother'. Now, I was looking at Delia.

Mom looks at me and begins laughing. "I don't think there will ever come a day when you go running to John Bull for help!" It's a ridiculous idea and I, too, start to giggle.

Mom takes the tub of Javex-soaked dishtowels off the stove and sets the stew pot on. Somehow, I didn't mind the javex smell so much anymore. Jane returns with the two boys and Mom dishes out spareribs and dumplings from the pot. It seems awfully quiet now with just us at the supper table.

Halfway through the meal, Maggie busts through the door, "John Bull! I saw John Bull at Rita's. He must have got off the train this morning!"

We look at each other around the table and smile. Jane calmly says, "Yes, we know. He was here."

Maggie's jaw drops, "Here?"

We nod and continue eating. Maggie says no more and starts eating her supper.

Mom asks me, "Where's your blue shirt? I haven't seen it for two washings already."

I was ready to say that I didn't know where it could have gone to, when Maggie pipes up, "Oh, it's by the beach. It was floating in the water between the logs the last time I saw it."

My eyebrows shoot up and I glance at Mom and murmur, "I couldn't reach it. I'll get it right away after supper."

"And another thing," Mom continues, "you stop carrying a slingshot around. You're getting too big for that. They say that as far as a girl can stretch a slingshot, that's how long her tits will be!" There's a sudden explosion of choking and giggling all around the table.

"I don't have it anymore. I already threw it away..." my voice fades away.

The conversation turns to the coming school day; that's tomorrow, Monday. Brian exaggerates my accident and I'm in trouble again, "She had large, bloody holes in both knees of her stockings, blood running down her legs and big holes on her elbows."

Mom glares at me. "Your new stockings?"

I drop my eyes and put my head down. It's getting hard to swallow. I murmur, "No. They weren't my school stockings. I couldn't find them..." She continues to look at me, waiting for the rest. "I found a pair in the box over there. They were your stockings."

Mom takes a deep breath, then totally ignores me. "Maggie and Jane, you wash the dishes this evening." The conversation starts again with Mom pretending I'm not even there. I stand up and walk out. Kicking the old stump as I walk by, I head down the path toward the beach. When I get to the bay, the water is now washing over the shirt with each wave. I kick off my shoes. Deliberately, carelessly splashing down with each step, I march toward the shirt. The cold ache is travelling up my legs and I jerk the shirt off the log so fast—rrripp! It catches on a rusty, old nail. Now it has a big hole in the middle of the back. Sigh. I walk back to the sand and wring out the shirt. As I'm sitting there trying to shove my wet feet back into my shoes, I notice a big furry thing over by the rocks, beneath the overhanging branches. Each wave lifts and flows over the long, black ... fur. It's the black dog, I saw. It's dead in the water.

A shiver runs down my back and I jump up, grabbing my shirt. I spot Ben walking by. "Hey, Ben! You know that old man's black dog? It's dead. Right here in the water," I yell.

Ben stops. "Okay, I'll go and tell the old man." I see him turn and run up the path. I run home as fast as I can. I stop long enough to fling my shirt on the clothes line. But it goes right over. So I stop to grab it and — rrrippp! It catches on something on the ground and, oh, I can imagine how big the hole is now. I fling it on the line again and dash into the cabin. The lamp has been lit but no Mom.

The door opens and Mom comes in. "Hey Mom! Know the old man over there that owns that old, black dog? He's floating dead in the water at the beach!" I pant.

Mom looks at me and asks, "The old man or the old dog?"

Impatient and excited, I blurt out again, "The dog! I saw the dog floating in the water. I saw him today and I thought he was going to bite me, but I guess he was just dying."

The door opens and Ben enters. He is breathless from running. "Did you tell him? About his dog?" I ask, still panting.

He stands there looking at his feet. When he lifts his head, I see his lips twitch at the corners before he says, "Ever see that bearskin the old man always sits on outside?"

I nod, waiting. He takes a deep breath before continuing, "He said he took it down to the water today and weighed it down with a rock to make it clean. And his old black dog just about bit me when I came out of the cabin!" He grins at me then runs out.

I glance at Mom. She has her back to me. Do I see her shoulders shake? Presently, she turns around. "Get to bed. You have to get up early for school tomorrow."

I sigh and kick off my shoes and climb into the top bunk. I am very tired. I start muttering, "Stupid dog! Stupid bearskin! Stupid old man! Stupid Ben! Stupid old stockings! Stupid old slingshot and long tits…."

Snuggling deeper into the blankets, my mind conjures up an image of long tits on my chest, swinging and slapping together, when I run to school in my baggy holey stockings… with the old, black dog close at my heels in his borrowed bearskin….

11

COAL OIL, CRAYONS AND SCHOOL BOOKS

Fall 1962

The radio is on, playing country music and Mom hums over the noise of the splattering bacon grease on the stove. It's nice and warm inside in the soft lamp light. I smell the bacon and coffee. I stretch and yawn, kicking my blanket off.

Mom glances at me and says, "Go out first and I'll have your breakfast on the table when you come back."

I jump off the top bunk and slip my black rubber boots on and dash out the door. I slow to a walk when the cold damp air hits me in the face. I can't even see anything. No island, no Aunty's cabin, no outhouse. What a weird feeling. Like I'm the only person in the whole world; white mist all around me. It's like standing on a tiny island with just naked branches all around me and no noise, just my heart beating and the sound of my chattering teeth. I'm cold. I walk briskly toward the outhouse.

Coming back, I can smell the wood smoke from the stovepipe and the bacon. Once I reach the porch, I dash into the cabin. "Hey, Mom. I can't see a thing out there. Our cabin has floated off somewhere by itself into a big white cloud."

She smiles at me and says, "Sit down and be quiet. The others are still sleeping." I gulp down the bacon strips in thick, soft slices of bannock. Mom is shutting down the stove and turning down the lamps. She's putting on her boots and thick coat.

"Where you going? Can I come with you?" I ask between mouthfuls. She glances around at the sleeping bodies on the bed and smiles. "Sure. But finish eating first. We'll go and check the fishnet by the island." I quickly wash down my last mouthful with the sweet creamed coffee and rush to put my coat on.

Softly, Mom closes the door behind us and we go down to the shore. It's getting a lot brighter but the fog is still pretty thick over the water. The noises seem to amplify in the stillness as we turn the canoe over and into the water. I get in first, then Mom gets in, pushing the canoe off with her foot. In the stillness, the drip and swirl of the water over our paddles is very loud and clear. I breathe deeply, holding my paddle still for a moment. Mom also stops and the only sound is the gurgle of water at the front of the canoe. My coat swishes against my arm when I turn to give Mom a smile and then we paddle on again.

The morning train comes early in the morning now. We can hear the screech of the wheels and the *sh-sh-sh-sh*, when it stops. We're at the west end of the island. We drift a few feet before Mom lifts the lead rope with her paddle and starts pulling us alongside the net, lifting it out of the water at each arm's length.

The train pulls out, moving faster with each roar of its engine. It's click-clack sound grows fainter down the tracks.

There's one fish, a large trout. Then another, and another one! The fourth one is a slimy, old catfish. Mom throws him back in the water. She swishes the net in the water a few times, washing out the slime before we move forward again. There are no more fish. She drops the net back in the water.

I hear a door shut. "Look." I point. "Who's that?" The fog has partially lifted and I see someone coming out of our cabin! The figure walks down the road.

Puzzled, Mom says, "I don't know," Then she shrugs. "If he's someone who's just gotten off the train, he'll come back later."

We paddle toward home. I smell wood smoke. People have gotten up and started their fires. I like the morning smell. Mom looks pleased with the trout piled at her feet. We can see a shadow inside the cabin moving across the window. It must be Jane looking for her socks. I've got them on. Anyway, I have to put on my long stockings for school, so I'll just tell her I kept them warm for her.

The lake has gone down a bit. I can tell because a rock, which used to be underwater, sticks out by our boat landing. I hop onto it now and pull the canoe to the shore. I hold the canoe steady while Mom steps out on a rock. "Get a knife and pan for me," she says, reaching for the trout.

I run up and dash into the cabin. Everyone's awake and eating breakfast at the table. "Lazy bones and sleepy heads!" I say to them, whipping out the dish pan.

Grabbing the knife, I dash down the lake to Mom. She's already pulled the canoe up and turned it over. The early morning sun is slowly drying up the mist. Mom looks up at the sky. "It will be a cool, clear day, today. Go and get dressed for school now."

The old man next door comes out and heads for his outhouse. I know one of Mom's trout will be going to them. Reluctantly, I leave Mom cleaning the fish and walk back to the cabin, bursting now with the sound of sharp voices and clattering dishes.

Brian and Tony are arguing. I push the door open, just in time to see a wet shirt fly over the table and smack the side of Jane's head. Brian clamps a hand over his mouth before blurting out, "Sorry. I was trying to hit Tony. That's his shirt."

Jane picks up the shirt off the floor while Tony is bending over, laughing. Suddenly, Jane's foot shoots out and boots Tony squarely in his pants and flings the shirt at him. "Hang up your shirt, you!"

I glance at her, wondering what's eating her? Quickly pulling the socks off, I decide not to say anything about them. I've already changed my clothes when Mom comes in with the three fish, their dark shiny backs curved inside the pan.

"Where's the comb, Mom?" She reaches up high on the top dish shelf. "How is anyone going to find it when you hide it way up there?" I ask.

"If I didn't, I wouldn't know where to look for it when you ask, would I?" she answers.

Smiling, I sit down on the bench and tug at the tangles in my hair. The door opens and in comes a man with grey hair jutting out from the side of the dark green cap on his head. But it's the sparkling eyes and the smiling face that brings a thrill of excitement, love and respect; it's the Medicine Man.

He surveys the room with joy on his face. His eyes laugh into mine and my face stretches into a wide smile. Mom rushes by me and ushers our visitor to the table where she promptly makes breakfast for him. He is the one we saw walking away from the cabin after the train left. He lives far away in a town by the train tracks. He comes when someone calls him for medicine and he usually stays at our place. Now he says Rita's mother called him. Mom reminds him that our canoe is there when he needs it. He usually goes off to gather the plants he uses.

Oh, I hate to leave. Sometimes I don't understand some of the things they're talking about, but I could listen to him talk all day. How I wish I could follow him around, and find out what he does and see how he makes his medicinal brews.

"Are you finished? I need the comb." Maggie is poking me in the back. I hand the comb over my shoulder to her. He has a strange accent. He's not from around here, that's for sure.

Jane walks by and grumbles, "Where are my socks? I couldn't find those socks anywhere this morning."

Feeling a bit guilty, I point to the laundry box in the corner. "I saw them in there."

Mom announces, "It's almost time for school," and glances at the clock on the shelf.

I linger as long as I can as I put my coat on. Finally, I blurt out, "Are you going to be here when I come back for lunch?"

The Medicine Man chuckles and winks at me. "Yes, I'll make sure I get back in time to see you at lunch." I smile broadly and dash off.

The sun is shining on the sides of the cabins now, but the tall weeds and twigs are still very wet. I run as fast as I can through the bush path, my shortcut to school. I emerge behind the school house. The teacher is just coming out of the school with the bell. He usually hands the bell to one of the kids to ring it but there isn't anyone outside yet. He glances at his watch and smiles at me. "Good morning! Would you like to ring the bell this morning?"

I smile and shake my head, "No."

He glances at his watch again, then starts ringing the bell, ding-dong, ding-dong. Giggling, I step up to him and say, "Everyone's going to go to church."

Misunderstanding me, he asks, "Right now? Is the minister here?"

I giggle again, pointing at the bell. "You ring it like the church bell. Everyone's going to go to church instead." He throws back his dark, curly head and laughs. Encouraged, I continue, "You have to ring it faster to make it sounds like a school bell!" Smiling down at me, he shakes the bell, ting-a-ling-a-ling. I nod and smile, "Now it sounds like a school bell."

I stand around by myself for about a minute before the kids come scurrying in from all directions. The teacher stands on the wooden steps, as the kids jostle each other into two crooked lines. When Teacher finally satisfies himself that there are indeed two lines, he flings the door open and, one by one, we troop in.

The smell of coal-oil permeates the room, almost blanketing the smell of crayons and schoolbooks. We hang our jackets and coats on the tinkling hangers and kick off our boots and shoes. The one-room school now echoes with the sound of chattering voices, scraping chairs and shuffling feet.

Order and quiet follows the teacher's steps from the back of the room to the front. Roll call brings forth cries of, "present," "present," "present." I recall my kindergarten days when it took me awhile to figure out what "present" meant. All I knew was that it's what you had to say when your name was called. Suddenly, all is quiet. Then I notice all eyes are glued on me. Teacher repeats my name! Startled, I quickly answer, "Present!" Amidst the giggles and twitters, I bury my burning face into my book.

Like a sponge, I soak up the words from the teacher, but I get bored when it comes to writing it all down. I love the stories in our English lesson. I always leaf through the book far ahead, sometimes to the end when I'm supposed to be writing. Jed pokes me and points at Liza's back. A big louse is making its way down her back. What if it falls on my desk. Then I feel the teacher brush my arm as he walks by. My eyes widen when his hand hovers for a second on Liza's back. He bends to correct her on a word and moves away again. The bug is gone! Those of us who notice, watch him make his way to the stove while talking about the chapter we've just read. His hand stops for a second over the stove top before he continues, slowly circling the room talking and explaining. Jed and I glance at each other, smiling.

An awful smell keeps getting worse. Soon the kids are giggling again. It's Ben's stinky feet. Then Cousin Joe leans back and stretches; a fresh burst of laughter erupts. His big toe is sticking out of a hole in his sock. I giggle into my hand so hard, it makes a snorting noise. I'm about to burst.

Then quickly the laughter dies when Teacher stands up from his desk and stares at each of us with that look that says "No more." Heads down, we continue with our work. Finally, he says, "Books away! Fifteen minutes for recess outside."

With sighs of relief we leave, one row at a time, coats and boots on and out the door. Laughing and squealing, we chase each other around the school and the swings. I think Cousin Joe is mad at me for laughing at him. Teacher is coming out with the basketball. He plays with the boys all the time, so I head for the swings. Rita and I decide to sit together on one seat. Since I'm bigger, she sits on top of my lap with her legs on each side of me. Who will push us now? Oh no! Here comes Cousin Joe for his revenge. I can see his face.... Suddenly, Teacher calls, "Joe! Catch!"

The ball comes flying and Joe catches it and drops it to the ground. He kicks it, right smack in Tommy's face. That's John Bull's son. Tommy sets up howling. Blood gushes from his nose and runs down the front of his shirt. Quickly, the Teacher ushers Tommy into the school. Now, a thought has just occurred to me: I grin, thinking I could threaten to tell John Bull on Cousin Joe if he comes after me again. Teacher comes out and blows the whistle; it's time to go in.

Still giggling, Rita, Maggie and I stay at the end of the lineup for the cup of milk and large vitamin biscuit. Yuck. It's powdered milk mixed in warmish water and the biscuits taste like old socks. I tuck my biscuit under my waist band; Rosiak likes them. Jumbo won't eat it though; he makes that face and drops it on the ground. I watch Ben, Jed and some others, asking for more biscuits and I realize that it is probably their breakfast.

It's back to lessons; this time, with math on the chalkboard. I like writing on the board; if only the others didn't have to see it. I'm always afraid of making a mistake for all to see. Whenever someone makes a mistake, everyone starts laughing. I feel a hand tuck my hair back over my shoulder and I glance up to smile at Teacher. He looks at my sketch of Rosiak and Jumbo on the corner of my book. I quickly put my hand over it. He continues down the aisle. I smell crayons and plasticine from the little kids by the window. Brian and Tony are whispering quite loudly. It seems like such a short time before Teacher says, "Time to put your books away. It's lunch time."

Noise and activity fills the room again as we leave. I run as fast as I can through my shortcut home. The dry brown leaves crackle and swish under my feet. The air is crisp and cool. A flood of joy fills me as I dash into the clearing. Our cabin door is open; smoke is coming up in blue wisps and I hear voices and laughter.

I skip across the porch and stand at the open door as the Medicine Man turns from the stove, "Oh, there you are. So did you learn something new this morning?"

I nod, "Yep."

He stands by the stove, stirring a pot of strong-smelling stuff on the stove. He grins at me. "Don't worry, you won't have to eat this for lunch."

I giggle and sit down at the table where Mom dishes out boiled trout and potatoes. Oh, I'm hungry! Then Brian and Tony come running in, panting, with Maggie right behind them.

Jane seems to be in a better mood and she hovers over us to pick up the dirty dishes. She does not go to school; she's too old.

After lunch I ask the Medicine Man, "Would you give me some medicine, too?"

"Oh? And what's the matter?" he asks.

"I have a very sore arm. It hurts!" I gasp, holding my arm.

He takes my arm and turns it over examining it. "Did you fall down? How did you hurt it?" he asks.

"No, I didn't fall down. I've been writing and writing all morning and my arm is very sore now." I groan.

He chuckles and Mom sends me off to wash my face and hands. I sit and listen to him again, watching him take so much care of the pot on the stove. Finally, Mom says it's time for us to go back to school again. The Medicine Man is going back on the train this afternoon, so I won't see him again.

I pause at the door and say, "Goodbye."

He gives me a big smile, saying, "I'll tell my wife that the trout I'm taking home is from The Owl. I saw you checking the fishnet with your mother this morning."

I turn and run down the path, embarrassed that he called me by my family nickname. The Owl; what a silly name!

The boys are already there when I approach the school. Teacher comes out of his house and falls into step beside me. I'm embarrassed. I slow down, as I look at his shirt. He has mud on his sleeve from the ball. Hey, that's the shirt he had on his clothesline on Saturday. Aunty and I were coming around the corner of the store when she started giggling and pointing at the teacher's house. Then I noticed the most jolly and cheerful looking clothes I have ever seen on a clothesline. The shirt was bouncing and swinging in the breeze, hanging by its wrist cuffs. The collar was pinned straight across by half a dozen clothespins. One minute it would do chin-ups, the next, forward swings.

And his pants were hanging over the clothesline by the knees, swinging back and forth, doing occasional sit-ups. The socks were dancing and flipping on their own individual pins. And his shorts, oh, Aunty nearly died laughing. The shorts were hung, flat as you please, with about four pins straight across the waist... I can feel my face burning at the thought. Aunty had said, "No modesty at all!"

People usually use one pin on the back or side of the underpants, so they won't hang so obviously. And, right between his shorts, hung his dish towels. Aunty told it all to Mom when we got home and they all laughed so hard, I started to feel sorry for Teacher.

He stands facing me. "Huh?" I ask.

"Say 'pardon me'."

Oh, oh, I can feel a giggle swelling in my chest, I swallow it down.

He continues, thoughtfully, "I said, that you have a very expressive face when you're looking at me." His eyes twinkle with amusement. I look at him totally confused. I have no idea what he's talking about. He guides me ahead and rubs my head with his hand, saying, "Oh, never mind."

We resume walking towards the boys. And then it starts; I knew it from their faces. They tease me about the teacher. In our language, they chant, "Teacher likes her-er; Teacher likes her-er."

I ignore them and begin going out of my way to avoid the teacher. I no longer speak to him outside the school and I always wait till lots of kids are in front of the school so I can stand at the back of the line.

It is a very slow afternoon. After recess, I watch the same kids stock up on the vitamin biscuits and milk again. They probably won't have another meal till tomorrow's recess. Once back at our seats I hear Cousin Joe say loudly, "Hey, Ben! Why don't you go for a walk in the water with your socks on before the water freezes?"

Ben promptly answers, "Aw, shut up! We can see your toe but we wouldn't see any brains sticking out if I put a hole in your head!"

The whole class roars with laughter. Of course, we all speak our own language, so after surveying the class, Teacher raps a ruler on the desk and says, "Joe, Ben, save it till after school, eh?"

In quiet titters, we resume our work on the books. I hear the train coming. That's the one the Medicine Man is getting on. I imagine him boarding the train, the conductor getting back on behind him, the door clanging shut and some delay... maybe he dropped his fish and had to get down to pick it up again. Oh, there it goes; I can hear the roar of the engine as the train pulls out.

Finally, the time comes to go home. It's after school and, without looking back, I dash out of the door and straight through the bushes on my shortcut. The door is closed. As I near the cabin, I can see the padlock on the door. A grip of panic seizes me. I stop and listen—no sound. "Mom!" I yell. "Mom!"

Wandering toward the canoe, I smell something I've smelled before. It's tanning smoke. I can see the smoke drifting over the bay now. I dash down the path behind the cabin toward the lake. Behind a windscreen by the lake, Mom kneels in front of a long roll of moose hide, suspended over a pot of smoking sticks. I like the smell. With a big smile, I kneel down beside her and watch spirals of thick smoke escaping from the numerous stitches along the seams of the hide.

With a sigh of contentment and happiness, I turn to watch the lake, so dark and so cold. Mom squints against the smoke to peek through a hole and plug it up again. A few wisps of curly hair have escaped the cotton kerchief over her head.

We hear Brian, loudly yelling, "Mom! Mom!"

Grinning, I look at Mom and ask, "If I was that loud, how come you didn't answer me?"

She looks at me with a smile. "I figured I'd just see if that button nose of yours works!"

I laugh. "Oh, it works all right. I had to put up with the stinky smell of Ben's feet all day long!"

She hands me the keys and says, "Go open the door and make sure you leave the keys in the lock and put them away on the very top shelf, understand?"

I nod and grab the keys. Feeling quite important, I unlock the door and fling it wide for Brian and Tony. Maggie is just getting home. "Where's Jane?" I ask.

She shrugs and says, "How should I know? You got home first!" Then we both remember at the same time. Their father came yesterday and asked Jane to go with him to his trapline this winter. We both dash out the door, around the corner toward Mom.

"Hey Mom! Where's Jane? Is she going or not?" I ask.

Mom is putting her things away. She looks at Maggie and answers, "No, she's not going with your father. But right now, she's with your mother. Your mother got off the train this afternoon. Go and see her before I get supper ready."

Maggie sighs, "No, I don't want to see her. When's supper? I'm hungry."

"Is your stomach all you ever think about?" asks Jane, as she comes up behind us, smiling at Maggie.

Mom looks toward the house, as she shakes out and hangs the freshly smoked hide on the line. Who's kicking the door? Walking behind them towards the cabin, I feel a knot develop in my stomach.

There, at the door, stands Brian. All eyes now fall on the shiny padlock securely locking the door. Brian sheepishly looks at his feet when the kicks come again from the inside. "Tony's got the key," Brian murmurs.

Feeling sick, I refuse to look at Mom. I feel her eyes on me. Jane sits down on the steps to wait for someone to figure out something. My mind is scrambling but I can't think of a crack big enough to slip the key through. Mom has already sealed the windows and reinforced the boards all around the door.

I hear Maggie ask, "Is the stove cold?"

Mom nods, "I didn't add any more wood after lunch." She glances at the chimney pipe sticking out on the side of the roof. I'm missing something here. Nothing more is said as Mom gets a length of string from the woodpile and ties a small rock to the end. Maggie has scrambled up the log ends at the corner of the cabin and crawls along the edge of the roof to the stovepipe and Mom throws her the string. Mom calls through the door, "Tony? Look inside the stove. Maggie is letting down a string. Take the rock off and tie the key on."

We can hear the stove lid banging open. Maggie's laughter echoes down the stovepipe. Soon Maggie swings the key on the end of the string down to Mom.

Without a word or glance at me, Mom unlocks the door and they all go in. I sit down on the porch steps, wishing Little Dog was still alive; he got hit by the train before Wess left. Jumbo doesn't play anymore and Rosiak is always the proper dignified lady. There are no more birds on the island and everything is peaceful, quiet... and cold.

12

THE NEW DOOR

Winter 1962

Mom scolds from her bed, "You, Owl. Go to sleep. It's Saturday tomorrow, so you'll have all day to talk all you want. Now, go to sleep."

I stop in mid-sentence and let my laughter die in my throat. It is very dark inside. Only occasionally, light flickers from the dying embers in the stove. It's getting cold inside too. I touch my nose with my finger. Yep, it's cold in here.

Suddenly, I'm wide awake. There it is, the noise that woke me; snow squeaking under footsteps coming toward our cabin. I'm out of bed and slipping on my boots when the first kick on the door shatters the stillness. Everyone's out of bed and dressing now, while the door continues to rattle and bounce on its hinges. Shaking so badly from cold and fright, I can hardly button my coat as I stand in line behind Maggie and Tony against the wall behind the stove. Jane and Brain are behind me and Mom is standing beside us, waiting for the door to come crashing open.

Finally, with a tremendous crash, the door flies open, bouncing back against the far wall. At the same instant, a man bursts into the room and crashes into the stove. With a loud crack, the stovepipe breaks above our heads. We shoot out of there instantly, into the cold night air. My feet fly swiftly over the snow, ahead of Maggie and Tony toward Aunty's cabin. I hear Mom screaming and I swerve off the path toward Aunty's woodpile, where I stop. Maggie and Tony follow me. Then, Jane and Brian come running and stand beside us, panting.

"Mom! Where's Mom?" I demand and lunge, to run back to our cabin.

Jane clamps a hand on my shoulder. "No!" She hisses, pulling me back. Holding me, she whispers, "She'll be okay! He'll catch you, too, if you run in there!"

I start struggling violently. This is the first time anyone has ever been caught. He'll kill her! "Let me go! We have to help her! Come on!" I try to pull Jane forward, but she holds me back. I continue to struggle helplessly.

When at last we hear footsteps crossing our porch, I stop struggling. We poke our heads around the woodpile and see the drunk stumble off. I dash out with the others close behind me. The light comes through the gaping door as we approach it. I bound onto the porch and through the door. Mom's back is towards us, her shoulders heaving. She turns from the lamp, pushes back her tangled hair from her face, and begins to tidy up. Then her eyes seem to focus on us standing together by the door. She squares her shoulders and says in a low voice, "Come on, get back into bed before you freeze to death!"

We come to life and scramble into bed. I climb into the top bunk where I sleep. I watch Mom push the stove back into place and join the stovepipe together. My teeth are still chattering so hard my jaw is getting tired. Then I realize I'm not cold; I'm just so tense. In fact, I'm getting hot under my blankets with my coat still on.

Mom looks at the hopelessly broken door, hanging crooked, attached only by the top hinge. She tries to straighten it, then she starts muttering louder and louder. She curses in a quivering voice. My heart is pounding in my chest again. Suddenly, she grabs the flashlight from the shelf and runs out the door. I can hear her hurried footsteps to the outhouse. All is quiet. I hold my breath and then try to breathe quietly so I can hear better. The lamp sputters a few times. The others are breathing softly in sleep again. I'm not sure, but I thought I heard Mom. I'm just about to get up and check if Mom is all right when I hear her footsteps coming. I breathe a sigh of relief. Mom pours some water into the basin to wash.

Then she picks up the axe and sinks the blade into the frame to hold the door in place. At the sound of the axe, all four heads on the beds shoot up to see what the noise is. Quickly, Mom says, "It's only me. Go to sleep now."

I watch her shove all our knives around the door. Finally, she blows the light out and goes to bed. Darn, Maggie is snoring. Gradually, I stop shaking and warmth comes over my tired, tensed, aching muscles. Slowly, I relax into sleep.

I awake to country music drifting into my ears under my blanket. My foot taps to the music. The stove is crackling and roaring happily with its belly full of wood. The lamp shines softly from the table. Mom is chipping away at the ice on the bottom of the water pail. I look at the white frosted heads of the nails on the cardboard wallpaper in front of me. Mom is humming to the tune on the radio.

Everyone else seems to be still asleep. The room isn't warm yet; I can see the white steam of my breath. Yep, my nose is still cold, too. Mom is struggling with the door, trying to slide it open far enough for her to squeeze through. She's out and slowly she pulls the door back into place and heads toward the lake. The snow crunches under her feet.

I throw back my blanket. Brrr, it's cold! I jump down from my top bunk and stand shivering by the stove, holding out my hands to the heat. When I look at the door I feel like crying. I wish I were big, very big and strong; I'd squeeze that hateful man like a piece of cloth wrung out to dry, and then I'd... I can feel warm tears running down my cheeks. No, I won't cry. I pull back the curtain at the window. It is all white with frost. I put my hand on the glass and melt a big circle. Now I can see Mom chopping at the iced-over water hole, with the axe. After that, she chips away with the ice auger. It must have been very cold last night. I can see her kneeling now, pouring water from the dipper to the pail. The sky is red on the horizon behind the island.

Suddenly, with a slow squeak, the door falls over and crashes, hitting the floor as heads pop up again. I smile and go over and try to pick up the door to prop it back into place. Oh, here's Mom. She hands me the pail before she struggles with the door. Finally we have it standing and she sinks her axe into the door step with the handle holding the door up.

By now, everyone is awake. We change our clothes with Mom pointing to the warm water in the basin, saying, "Wash your faces well and comb your hair. There, now stand by the window. The sun is just about to come out. When the sun comes over the horizon, he will see you and be very pleased that you're all ready to greet him and he will bless you."

Sure enough, the orange ball emerges over the tree tops on the distant hill. Oh, it's always so beautiful. Then it gets smaller, lighter and brighter, making the snowflakes dance and sparkle in glorious rays on top of the snow. Every morning we stand here ready for the sun to come out. Mom puts a hand on my shoulder. "Mark where it's coming out on the hill. It will appear at a different spot down the hill each morning, until it comes up right at the tip of that branch on the island on Christmas day. See how far it has to go in a month?" she sighs.

I'm hungry. I hear the porridge bubbling in the pot on the stove behind me. The bannock and coffee smell absolutely delicious. "Can we eat now?" I ask.

Mom laughs. "Sit down," she says.

After breakfast, the dishes are done, the floor is swept and the bedding is folded on the beds. I glance through a clear spot at the front window, "Hey, Mom. Here comes the Town Joker. Hurry, pull that axe out and see what happens!"

Mom glances at me with a twinkle in her eye and carefully removes the axe just as the footsteps fall on the porch. One push on the broken door and it comes crashing down, throwing our unsuspecting visitor off balance. With a quick lunge, Mom saves him from falling on the stove. Shaking her head at me and sighing with relief, she says, "You'd think I'd know better than to listen to you."

I was laughing so hard my face hurt. His mouth had fallen open with such a look of surprise. He's leaning the door against the wall now and Mom is hanging a blanket over the door frame.

With a whistle, the Joker says, "What the heck happened to your door? Never mind, that's a stupid question. I can see what happened to it." The Joker clicks his tongue and shakes his head, "You should call the police from the next town, you know? Just so they can see this."

Mom smirks, "And have the door leaning against the wall for three days and the kids freezing in here in the middle of winter? Besides, I called them many times last year; they can't do anything, at least not by the time they get here three days later."

The Joker examines the door, "I can tell you for sure, you can't fix this door again."

Mom nods, "Yes, I know."

Grinning, the Joker asks, "Got any boards and nails?"

Mom smiles, "Yes, I knew I'd need a new door before the winter was over so I put some boards behind the woodpile."

The Joker turns to go out for them.

"Wait, did you have breakfast yet?" asks Mom.

The Joker chuckles. "No. Old Man across the tracks was cooking beaver," he says, "and beaver and I don't get along too well in the morning."

Mom laughs. "Well, do you get along okay with bacon and bannock?"

The Joker has a wide smile now. "Oh yes, we're very good friends, bacon, bannock and I!"

I laugh, saying, "You guys are crazy!"

The boys are dressing up warm to play outside. "Hey, Brian! Those are my wool socks! Give 'em to me. I'm going out, too, you know!" I shout.

Brian throws the socks at me, saying, "Why don't you stay home like all the other girls? Joe says you're bossy and try to be like everybody else and do things like them!"

I yell back, "Joe says! Joe says! Joe was just mad at me 'cause he was showing off in front of Teacher, trying to hit a can with his slingshot and he missed. Then I took his slingshot and hit the can. First shot!"

Brian's nose twitches, "Girls aren't suppose to use slingshots, anyway. Right, Mom?"

I throw a pillow at him, saying, "Aw, shut up!"

Brian and Tony whisper something to each other and dash outside. I take my time getting dressed. I can see them walking around outside; Tony still buttoning up his coat. Finally, they stop by the woodpile. Tony settles for a piece of cardboard and Brian has a large piece of plastic. Off they go, across to the small island. I chuckle. I brought the toboggan inside yesterday to change the rope. That's what they were looking for out there. I go into the back storage room and bring out the toboggan with its new rope. Mom and the Joker have already pulled out the nails from the broken doorframe. I squeeze by them with the toboggan under my arm. I jump off the porch and suddenly, I spin around and hit the snowbank with a thud. The Joker is killing himself laughing. I had the curved front of the toboggan around my arm and the Joker stepped on the rope of my toboggan. I grab a pile of snow and throw it at him. Mom's voice comes, "No, no, no! You're throwing snow inside!"

I laugh and walk away, pulling the toboggan behind me toward the island. The boys are already there, sliding down the slope. There's still not enough snow. We can see some bare spots all the way down the rocky slope. It's pretty hard landing when we fall. Up at the top now, I sit on the toboggan and down I go, out onto the ice. I look back, not bad. Puff, puff, puff, up the hill. One, two, three and I'm on the ice again. Puff, puff, puff, up the hill... you know, I spend more time, pulling this thing up the hill. "Hey, Brian! Let me try your plastic!"

Brian yells back, "No way!"

Cousin Joe is coming with a piece of cardboard, too. Trying something different, I lie down on the toboggan, head first and kick with my feet. Ooh, my head is bouncing on the toboggan, all the way down. Slowly, I slide to a stop. "Hey! this is great! Did you see me, Joe?" I pull the toboggan up the hill again. Joe is at the top waiting for me. "See, I'll go down again!" I gasp, puffing, out of breath. I lie down, but I'm not quite ready when Joe kicks my toboggan hard. I go shooting down the hill. I hang on for dear life on one end of the rope. I'm lying on my side now; then I hit a bump. I go flying and land with a thump on the ice and my knee comes up and hits me on the forehead. I see stars. I lay there for a minute feeling for any other pains. I turn and stretch on my back. I can hear Cousin Joe laughing.

Coming to a stop, Brian and Tony shower snow in my face. "Are you okay?" gasps Brian, big-eyed and panting.

I nod and sit up. Awwooo, my forehead! I lie down again. They've gone back up the hill. I study a dead branch hanging over the ice. Below it is a big thick snowbank. Feeling better now, I get up and walk to the tree. I climb up, sit on the branch and inch along till I am right above the snowbank. I jump. Oh, so soft. This is fun. Scrambling up the tree again, I can hear the boys behind me. Cousin Joe is the first one up the tree behind me. I jump and get out of the way, just as Joe lands beside me. We watch Tony and Brian jump. Then, systematically, we take turns, one after the other. My head still hurts, so I take time out to lie on my belly on the ice. I brush the snow away and lie there licking at the black ice, melting a dent with my tongue.

Suddenly, there's a scream. I look up quickly. Tony is swinging from a branch with arms and legs thrashing, hanging by the seat of his pants. I get there in time to hear a loud, 'rripp!' The tear in his pants is getting bigger; it's caught on a broken branch that's sticking out from where they were jumping. I glance at Joe and Brian and we burst out laughing. Tony stops struggling and hangs there by the seat of his pants, swaying back and forth, yelling, "Get me down. Get me down from here!"

Joe and I are the same height now, but we can just barely touch Tony's hands. I ask Joe, "How are we going to get him down, if we can't even reach him?"

Amused, Joe looks up at the branch. He climbs up the tree and along the branch. Then, bracing himself, he starts kicking at the broken branch that holds Tony's pants. "Get out of the way, down there!" he yells at me.

I jump back just as Tony falls head first into the snowbank. I grab his coat and pull him up. He sits there, gasping and wiping the snow off his face. Then he starts bawling his head off. Time to go home. I sit him down on the toboggan and Brian and I pull him home.

The smoke from the stovepipe drifts almost straight up; there is no wind and not a cloud in the sky. I can hear a handsaw slowly going chee-chaw, chee-chaw back and forth, back and forth, from Sarah's cabin. It must be her brother, Bobby, sawing wood.

He sits behind me in school and always looks over my shoulders to copy my answers. I always put down the wrong answers when I know he's looking. Then I erase them before I hand my paper in. He always asks me afterwards, how much I got on the test. I didn't have time to erase the wrong words once, so I just stroked them off with my pencil. Teacher asked me to stay after school and he wanted to know why I wrote words down twice after each question. So I said, "Because Bobby is too tall."

He looked at me for a moment. "Bobby?" I tugged and twisted the end of my scarf around my neck. "Go on, tell me." he said.

I felt like a squealer but I answered, "He copies all my answers on the tests. He just looks over my shoulders and he gets mad if I cover my answers. So I just put wrong answers down where he can see them." I bit my lip.

Teacher started chuckling, "You are a very smart girl, you know that? Now, go on home." Somehow, I felt proud. Something in his voice made me happy and proud. I ran home very happy… . Gee, the toboggan is heavy. I glance back. "Hey, Brian! Get off!"

He giggles, "Awww, come on! It's only a little way more!"

We get to the door with its new, white boards but it looks like the lid of a wooden box, with a big Z reinforcing the boards going up and down. I stand there looking at it, then I push — nothing. I pound on the door. "How do you open this door?"

It opens, pushing me aside. It opens to the outside. "But, where's the handle? How are we going to pull it open to get in?" I ask Mom.

"I was just finishing this. See? It's a leather strip that goes through these holes on the door, and we just leave the leather sticking out during the day for people to pull on to open the door. And at night, we just pull it in and push this bar through the loop. The bar fits over this big hook on the door and then over these hooks on each side of the doorjamb. What do you think?"

I stand there for a minute. "It's okay, but it's a backwards door. Whoever heard of a door opening backwards?"

Mom laughs at me, then her eyes follow Tony as he walks by her toward the bed, "What happened to you?"

I start to laugh and tell her what happened to Tony, when her hand comes up to brush my hair back from my face. She says, "My Gosh! You look like someone crashed a two-by-four across your forehead!"

Brian grins and says, "No, it looks more like you're going to have a big horn growing out of your forehead!"

I throw my coat at him, saying, "You shut up!"

Tony says from the bed, "Joe did it."

Mom's smile fades. "Joe did that to you?"

I shake my head, "No, I fell off the toboggan and my knee hit me on the forehead."

Brian, still grinning, says, "Joe kicked her toboggan down before she could lie down."

Mom sighs and turns toward the stove. "Sit down if you're hungry. There's some soup here. And Tony, if you rip those pants one more time, I'll sew on a bright red patch!" We snicker and dunk some bannock into our soup bowls.

Mom says, "Oh, the Joker came here this morning to tell us that Barbara had a new baby! It's a boy! She's coming to stay with us around Christmas time. The silly guy didn't remember to tell me till he was on his way out the door!" She chuckles.

A new baby. "What's his name? What does he look like?" I ask.

Mom smiles, "You'll have to wait till Barbara gets here to see what he looks like and I don't know what his name is either."

Oh, I can't wait. "Where's Jane?" I ask.

Mom turns from the stove to answer, "Oh, she said she's going over to see that old lady on the hill."

"Is the old lady's son home again?" I ask, glancing at Maggie, who's helping Tony out of his pants and we both laugh.

Mom stands there, looking at me, "What? Where did you hear that?"

I shrink into my shirt collar, "I was only teasing. That's what they were teasing Jane about at the store the other day." Mom is firing questions at Maggie now. Oh, oh, I think I said something wrong. What the guy has to do with Jane, I don't know. I don't understand. "Hey, pass me the bannock."

13

CHRISTMAS VISITORS

Winter 1962

Blowing white clouds from my mouth, I approach the school. Today is the last day of school before Christmas. It's very cold. The snow crunches dry and hollow beneath my feet. "Hey! What does the sign say?" I yell, as Ben comes around the corner of the school. Running up the wooden steps, I break into a grin. Teeth chattering with cold, I read the sign tacked on the school door: NO SCHOOL TODAY — STOVE GONE OUT. HAVE A NICE HOLIDAY!

"Oh, boy! No more school till after Christmas, Ben!" I sigh happily. Ben shrugs his shoulders somewhere in the oversized coat he has on. I stand around outside the school with Ben, eagerly waiting to tell the other kids. One by one the kids come and I sing out the joyful news even before they reach the school. Here comes Cousin Joe. "No school today. The stove has gone out again!" I announce.

Joe stomps up the steps and pushes me aside to read the note. "I can read, too, you know. And shut up. Stop yelling your head off. I could hear your stupid voice all the way down the road." he grumbles, glaring at me.

Beside me, Ben shifts his thin body in the dark coat and asks, "What's the matter with you?"

Joe spins around on the step and faces us again, "You mind your own business, you stupid flea bag. Your drunken father must have made a mistake and hung his dirty, old coat on you instead!" Cousin Joe snickers under his breath and turns to walk back down the path.

I sigh, trying to think of something to say. Ben jumps down from the steps and shoves his bare hands into the folds of the coat. "Joe is just mad 'cause he has to go home to his mother as soon as school is over," I say.

Ben shrugs and says, "I hope he doesn't come back. You think I could beat him up?" He grins.

Picturing Joe's tall, sturdy body compared to Ben's small, skinny frame, I shake my head, "No, I don't think so. But both of us could!" I grin.

Ben smiles back. "Okay. If he comes back."

I nod and Ben walks away. I chuckle, knowing that with both of us going at Joe, he'd probably just bang our heads together and knock us out. Brrr, it's cold. I'm going home, too. I jump off the steps and run back down the path on the shortcut home. Oh, my throat hurts. The air is too cold for running. I cover my mouth with the end of my thick kerchief. I'm so happy. No more school. Vera and Annie are home. We decorated the cabin last night, too. And Rosiak has puppies inside her doghouse. Mom heard the puppies when she went to feed the dogs this morning. She says there are six of them. Oh, I can't wait to play with them.

Hey, what's he doing here? I just saw the Town Joker coming from the back of the cabin and going inside. I run the rest of the way home and fling the door open. Annie just turned away from the door, puffyeyed and sniffling. She has one black puppy in her arms. Oh, there's Rosiak on a mat behind the stove, looking very nervous. I look at the Joker and Mom; they're looking back at me. Then Maggie and the boys burst in the door "Hey Mom! No school today! The oil stove went out again!"

I turn to go out the door.

"Hey, where are you going?" Mom asks.

"I have to go to the toilet!" I run out.

I can hear Mom yelling behind me, "Don't go back there!"

I run around the cabin. There's something going on. I run down the narrow footpath, skipping and hopping over the piles of snow and footprints. I stop dead. Five little bodies are hanging by the neck between the trees. Black, white, brown... the little tails with white tips slowly swaying. I can't see anymore. I rub a sleeve over my eyes and turn to run down the path to the outhouse. There, I sit and cry till I'm all empty. I knew it. Mom told us over and over, as soon as she noticed that Rosiak would have puppies. She told us that all the females would have to be killed and the males would be given away. So there was only one male then, that black pup inside the cabin. Maybe she'll let us keep him.

Oh I hate that Joker. Mean, evil man. Why did he have to hang them like that? He could have...well, how else could he have killed little puppies? I heard the Old Man next door kills his puppies by hammering them on the head—blood everywhere. Then there's that old lady at the point that drowns her kittens in a potato sack. Oh Geez, I'm crying again. Poor little things. Mom will get mad at me if I go on like this.

I remember once when we had a little kitten and it got under our bedding on the floor. We didn't have the double beds then, so we all slept on the floor. Anyway, the kitten got under the quilts and when Vera spread the blankets on the floor to sleep, she stepped on the kitten. Barbara made Tony and I go and throw it in the lake. Mom wasn't home at the time. The kitten's back was broken and it meowed pitifully.

Barbara came after us, yelling and threatening to beat us if we didn't throw the kitten in. I couldn't do it. Tony closed his eyes and threw it in. It was getting dark and the kitten kept paddling toward us meowing, meowing, and we had to push it out again with sticks, whispering, "Please, don't come back again."

We were crying like crazy and it kept coming back. We finally just pushed it out one last time and we ran. We sat crying in the dark bush for a long time before we went back inside the cabin. I kept thinking about it for days and days and I would find myself looking along the shoreline whenever I had to go for water. I couldn't go swimming at the beach.

I'm freezing; my nose is all plugged up and my face is all wet and cold. Mom is going to get very mad at me. I get out and melt snow in my hands and rub my eyes and face using my kerchief to wipe it off. My face feels like it's starting to freeze. I run back to the cabin and enter slowly. The boys are pushing each other on the floor, trying to get a better look at the nursing puppy. Rosiak looks content, lying on her side and chewing on a piece of bacon rind. The Joker is not here. Mom is on the bed sewing a pair of moccasins. Vera is curling her hair and Annie is reading a comic on the top bunk. My face is tingling from the heat of the stove. I pour myself a cup of tea.

I decide to dress up warm and go outside to play. Mom is humming a hymn as she sews. I step outside. The snow is very bright in the clear sunlight. There's not a cloud in the sky. I break off a huge chunk of icicle from the edge of the roof. Some of the big icicles almost touch the snowdrifts against the house. I wonder if those puppies are still there. I slowly walk down the path behind the cabin again. There is nothing there now. Not a trace of anything. I turn around and go to the pile of green wood beside the cabin. I tug and pull out a small log and drag it to the sawhorse. The log is about five feet long and I heave it onto the sawhorse. Next, I take down the handsaw off the nail on the tree. Oh, it's heavy. I have to hold it with both hands. The log keeps moving everytime I push or pull on the saw.

Tony comes out. "Hey, Tony. Come here! Sit on this log for me, okay?"

He shuffles over and scrambles on top of the log. I decide to saw the end off first. Back and forth, back and forth. About half way through, my arms feel like they're about to fall off. Huffing and puffing, I finally saw through it. With a sigh of relief, I wipe the sweat off my face. Tony is chatting away and laughing. "Move over a bit," I tell him.

He slowly moves over to the other end and sits there holding on to the frame of the sawhorse. "Don't saw it right through. I'll fall down inside!" he says.

Back and forth, I'm almost to the bottom of the log somewhere. "Sit still, will you? The log keeps flipping around. I can't tell how far down the cut is now!" I yell at him.

"Just stop right now!" he whines.

"And how am I going to break it if it's too thick? I have to saw it till it's thin enough to break off. Okay, that will do it. Now, move over on this side so I can cut the side you're sitting on." I say.

He looks at me for a minute before he jumps off and gingerly sits on the crack in the wood.

Then Mom comes out with the puppy under her arm and Rosiak behind her. I can hear her talking to the dog, as she ties her up again at her doghouse. Mom looks at us a moment and goes back inside the cabin. Feeling proud of myself, I start tugging and pushing again. The log is bouncing around quite a bit.

"Tony, you're not even sitting on it. Sit down and don't let it bounce around!" I yell at him.

His bottom lip sticks out in a pout. I'm about halfway through when, "Crack!" The log breaks where Tony is sitting and Tony and the wood blocks crash inside the sawhorse frame. He sits up bawling his head off, spitting out snow and sawdust.

I reach in to pull him up. "Tony, shush. Be quiet," I say, dusting some snow and sawdust off his head.

"Listen! What's that noise? That's an airplane coming!"

Everyone comes rushing out, still slipping their coats on. The airplane roars over our cabin, circles and disappears behind the island. The loud roar echoes over the hills as the airplane lands on the ice. Suddenly, it appears from the corner of the small island, making a wide detour of the rock and comes straight towards us. It leaves two deep trails behind it on its approach, and stops about fifteen feet from our water hole.

My heart is pounding with excitement. I can see someone moving around inside. Then the pilot gets out. Suddenly, there are people everywhere around me. Some come running along the ice trail, the rest come down the path leading to our place. Everywhere there are people, kids and dogs, all coming to see who is getting off the plane.

There's a dog beside the plane, barking incessantly. The pilot is calling for someone to take the dog away. No one moves to claim the vicious dog. Finally, the pilot opens the passenger door and out steps Barbara with the baby in her arms and little Cora. Mom is there now to grab the baby. Annie takes Cora's hand and Vera and Jane fetch the bags and suitcases. People are milling around us, talking and laughing. The dog is still barking at the pilot who gets back in. The propellers start, the wind blows and the airplane moves to turn around.

The dog is still running along beside the airplane, barking. With a loud roar, the airplane turns and the dog is almost invisible in the blowing snow. Then I hear a shout from one of the guys and I get shuffled out of the way when the group surges forward again toward the plane. The plane has stopped. I hear someone yell, "The props just chopped the dog's head right off! Who's dog was it anyway?"

I feel sick. I push my way through the people, back to the cabin. Mom and Barbara are already inside. Everyone is talking at the same time and there are lots of water puddles on the floor from the tracked in snow. I look out the window. I can just see the tip of the airplane wing as it is taking off again. The people are moving away, some coming in to see Barbara and the new baby. "The Owl is too busy looking outside to notice the new baby," says Mom.

I turn and see the smallest face I've ever seen poking out of a fancy bonnet. The mouth opens wide in a yawn — no teeth. It forms a bubble when the mouth closes again. The eyes are closed shut. "What's his name?" I ask.

Barbara smiles, "His name is John."

Amused, Brian shouts, "John! Couldn't you think of a nicer name? Who wants to be called John?"

Barbara laughs, "Better not let his father hear you say that. He named him."

The door opens and Aunty walks in. The voices burst out loudly all over again. I feel very tired. I crawl to the top bunk and lay there, watching them. Constant noise echoes within the cabin walls. Visitors continue to come in, tracking in snow till Mom's paper mat at the door is soaking wet and falling to pieces.

"Owl, eat something before I put the food away." Mom turns away from the bunk.

I rub the sleep from my eyes and stretch. It's lunchtime and I'm hungry. It is almost quiet with just the family inside now. Suddenly, an awful noise starts outside. It's so loud! What is it? I'm at the window in no time with the rest of the girls. There's the Town Joker with a hand machine with a long blade on it that seems to melt through the wood like a hot knife through butter! It is so noisy! But I smile, remembering how long it took me to saw up one log this morning!

I can hear Mom behind me, yelling over the noise, "That must be the power saw that John, across the tracks was supposed to have bought. I heard him sawing with it the other day!" She shakes her head at the growing pile of cut wood.

When the machine stops, I hear a ringing in my ears. The Joker stands, grinning at the pile of wood that would have taken us a week to cut with the handsaw. He's standing there, the machine at his hip, when suddenly, he drops it and starts hopping around, grabbing snow to rub on his pants and shove into his pocket! Everyone runs out the door and crowds around him as he starts to laugh. He pokes a finger through his pocket from a hole that was still smoking a bit. With a sheepish look on his face, he pulls out a handful of blackened, burnt matches from his pocket. We burst out laughing. I laugh till I'm bent over, holding my sides. He looked so funny. Then he comes after us for laughing at him. I get a handful of snow rubbed in my face before Vera, Jane and Annie pull him off me.

Back inside the cabin again, I watch the Joker gobble up the rest of the leftover soup from the pot before he leaves. Later we hear the machine at the old man's house down the path. "Mom, I'm hungry and the Joker ate all the soup," I say.

Mom laughs at me. "You're lucky, Owl. If you went to sleep too often during the day, you'd starve to death!" She gives me hot tea and a fried bologna sandwich made with fresh bannock.

I crawl to the top bunk again to get out of the way. Mom and Barbara are clearing out the storage room, trying to uncover Mom's bed somewhere beneath the boxes, clothes, snowshoes and paddles. The baby is crying and Vera picks it up. She looks like a mommy sitting there with the baby. Cora is always eating; she's at the bannock and jam again. She has baby fat cheeks when she smiles. She's cuter than a kitten. The boys are on the floor with a box of pinecones and rocks which they're pretending are cats and dogs.

The green and red foil decorations sparkle and glitter, as they hang crisscrossed under the ceiling beams. In the middle of the room hangs a big red and green paper bell. Oh, it's so beautiful. Mom says it's five more days before my birthday. I'll be eleven years old. And after that, it's Christmas Day.

I know some Christmas carols from school. We had a great time singing them yesterday. "Mom, do you know if Teacher got on the train today?"

Brian answers, "Yep. I saw Ben at the store; he told me. Cousin Joe went on the train, too."

Dreamily, I watch the large bell hanging, turning and gently swaying and I smile.

14

CHRISTMAS CANDIES AND BEAVER MEAT

Winter 1962/1963

I'm wide awake. All is quiet. The stove is making gentle popping sounds as the last of the ashes glow through it's air vent. In the dark room, I can see the light of dawn shine softly through the window.

I can hear the soft breathing from all the sleepers in the cabin. Bed by bed, I count the people. There are eleven of us again. Hey, it's Christmas today. I poke Maggie beside me and whisper, "Wake up, it's Christmas!"

Maggie pokes her head up and whispers back, "Gee, you can't even see a thing yet. Go back to sleep." She turns around and pushes her rear end against me. Oh, well, I can't resist. I give her a good hard pinch.

"Ouch! What did you do that for?" she wails.

I can almost feel the jolt, jarring everybody wide awake in the room. Instantly, everyone stops breathing, listening for the noise that woke them. Guiltily, hesitantly, Maggie says softly to the silence, "Uh, it was just me. The Owl pinched me."

I hear an annoyed "humph!" from Barbara's bed and the breathing resumes it's collective rhythm.

Then I hear Mom's footsteps on the porch. I didn't even hear her sneak out. Maybe that was what woke me. Quietly, she comes in and softly closes the door behind her. We giggle and she clicks her tongue at us, "Be quiet. It's still too early." She flips the stove lid up and throws in half a dozen blocks of wood, sending showers of sparks everywhere. She slowly lowers the lid back down. The stove breathes in and roars happily, as Mom pushes open its air vent.

Jane and Tony are awake now, too. Whispering and giggling, we watch the reflected light from the stove flicker crazily all over the room and across the ceiling. It flashes and teases the red and green tin-foil streamers from above. Then I remember something. I push the blanket aside and dive to the foot of the bed. There, sure enough, I find four small paper packages at our feet. Grabbing one, I rip it open. Candies. Every Christmas we find wrapped candies at the foot of our beds. I pop one into my mouth and jump back into bed, pulling the quilts over me. Maggie and Jane are rummaging around the bedding at their feet for theirs. Finding them, they quickly jump back into bed. The room hasn't warmed up yet; it's still pretty cold.

A light shines from Mom's room. Soon, she comes in carrying the lamp. Oh, she has a nice dress on. She looks beautiful. The whole cabin is now filled with laughter and everyone is talking. Tony jumps out of bed and runs across the floor in his bare feet to the next room and pounces on the bed with Brian.

Barbara giggles from the double bed in the corner; Cora is trying to shove a candy into the baby's mouth. From the bunk beds, Vera and Annie are giggling and exchanging candies. It's a little warmer now. Mom is chipping away the ice from the bottom of the water pail. I jump out of bed and put my jacket and boots on. Oh, look. "Hey, Mom, look what someone put in my boot. It's a bannock crust."

"Silly mouse. You'd think he'd find a better place to hide his food than inside your stinky ol' boot!" she smiles from the stove.

I laugh and push the door open. Oh, it's cold. The eastern horizon is tinged with red and the clouds hang very low. I breathe in the fresh, morning air mixed with whiffs of wood smoke. The sun may shine only a few minutes before it gets covered by those clouds. I have to hurry and get my face washed and hair combed. The old man across the tracks told us a story once, about a joker who pulled his pants down and bent over with his butt to the sun one morning, and how the sun got mad and zapped him on the butt so hot, he couldn't sit down for a week! Ha, ha!

The outhouse door squeaks as I pull it open. Brrr, it's cold! Coming out, I see steam coming out of the doghouses. Mom gave the new puppy away. Now we only have Jumbo and Rosiak again. I run the rest of the way and burst into the cabin. I feel a rush of warmth in my chest, I'm so happy. Mmmm, fried bacon with raisin bannock. Coffee is brewing on the stove, too.

Barbara and Mom are laughing and talking together by the bed with the baby between them. The gentle light of the coal oil lamp casts its glow into the back corner of the cabin, as the daylight creeps into the room through the two frosted windows. Vera pours out cups of coffee while everyone grabs a piece of hot raisin bannock and a slice of bacon. With my breakfast, I sit down at the foot of the bunk bed by the stove. I sit there chewing slowly, enjoying each moment.

It's daylight now and there's no sun. Mom blows the lamp out. I can smell the smoke from the lamp wick. Barbara is throwing more wood in the stove. Vera and Jane are washing the dishes. Another pot of coffee is bubbling on the stove. Too bad Aunty is not here. They've gone to visit their oldest daughter, Joe's mother, far away. I climb to the top bunk with my little hoard of candies and watch them cleaning the cabin. Mom's gone outside. I can hear her chipping at the water hole on the ice to make it bigger. Barbara is sweeping the floor. Annie and Maggie are folding up the quilts. The baby is asleep in its cradle board at the corner of the double bed. Cora is on the bed still filling her face with candies. Tony and Brian are getting dressed to go out and play. The sound of footsteps cross our porch. The door opens and Mom enters. Right behind her is John, the man who owns the noisy power saw.

"Merry Christmas! Merry Christmas, everybody!" he bellows in a crooked, drunken grin. He flops down on the bench. "Got something you can feed me, Delia?" he asks.

Mom laughs, "It's amazing your stomach still knows when it's hungry after all the liquor you must have put in there."

John chuckles, "I keep moving. That's why I still have some, see?" He pulls out a bottle of liquor from his coat and puts it on the table. It's still more than half full.

Mom clicks her tongue at him, "Put it away. I'll never get rid of them if someone comes in and sees that thing sitting on the table!"

Mom heats the leftover bannock and bacon and puts a plate in front of him. The man laughs, "I won't stay long. They're behind me somewhere. I just keep moving from house to house. You know, Delia, if I stayed in one spot they'd be all over me and this here bottle would be gone in five minutes. Well, that's okay, anyway. I still have four more bottles hidden at home." He chuckles again and shoves the bannock and bacon sandwich into his mouth.

Mom clicks her tongue again, "You'll kill yourself. Don't drink too much while you're walking around. You'll freeze if you fall outside somewhere."

John laughs and washes down the bannock with a cup of coffee. "You know Delia? You sound like my mother! Everytime I see you, you give me a lecture."

Mom shakes her head and refills his cup full of coffee again. "How many times do you figure the drunks have pestered your wife for your liquor since you left your cabin this morning?"

John laughs, "Oh, she can handle them. She's a strong woman, my wife."

Mom smiles, "Yes, I remember that black eye you had the last time you went on a big drunk!"

John throws his head back and roars, topping it off with a swig from his bottle of liquor. "Here Delia, have some! It's Christmas."

Mom smiles, "No John, I don't want any. Just remember me when you take the last gulp from the bottle."

John turns to Barbara, "How about you, Barbara? Drink one with me!"

Barbara glances at him and goes, "Humph!"

John picks up a cup and the brown liquor sloshes and gurgles from the bottle into the cup. He gets up. "You drink that, you hear, Delia? Merry

Christmas! Merry Christmas, everybody!" He staggers to the door, waves at us and goes out. Then he pokes his head back in, "Hey, Delia. Did you know that your door opens the wrong way?"

Mom laughs, "Of course, I know my door opens the wrong way! It's my door, isn't it?"

We can hear John's chuckling and his footsteps fade down the path. Tony and Brian are squealing and laughing outside somewhere. About five minutes later, a woman comes in. She's not too drunk and her teeth are chattering from the cold. She doesn't even have a coat on. She has an old blue sweater which she clutches at the front. She's from the west end of the village. "Did John come in here?" she finally asks.

Mom smiles, "Yes. He just left."

The woman is still by the door, warming her hands over the stove. "I've been going from house to house. I ran out so fast from my cabin, I didn't have a chance to grab my coat. My husband was going to beat me," she smiles. "Delia, would you give me some snuff?" Mom gets her snuff box and I watch the woman pack her lower lip. She turns, mumbling through the snuff, "Thank you, thank you. I'll go now. I've thawed out enough to reach the next cabin." She smiles and leaves.

Mom has just turned from the stove when the door opens again. Another woman comes in. She's the daughter of the Old Man across the tracks. Silently, she stands by the door, looking at us all. She may have been drunk before, but she isn't now. Mom says, "It's very cold outside this morning."

The woman nods and smiles shyly. After filling her lip with snuff, she stands there a few more minutes before she turns and leaves. This time it is almost ten minutes before we hear shuffling footsteps across the porch. Mom says, "I wonder just how long John's tail is this morning!"

We all burst out laughing, just as a short old man enters. He looks at us all for a few seconds before his grisly face breaks out in a toothless grin. He's slightly drunk and his beady eyes are twinkling as he stands there shrugging and laughing back at us. Oh gosh. He looks so funny, now everyone's laughing really hard! Slowly, the laughter peters out into smiles. Still not a word has been spoken. The little man stands there, nodding and grinning his toothless void several more minutes before he slowly turns to leave.

I decide to get dressed to go out and play too. I don't hear Brian and Tony anywhere now. Once outside, I can't think of anything to do. It is still very cold. The dark clouds hang low over the horizon. I hear dogs barking somewhere. Someone is hooting and yelling by the store. A few snowflakes gently fall down from the sky and disappear into the snow. I start down the path. I wonder if Sarah is home. A door bangs somewhere up ahead. I come around the corner of the footpath beside an island of tall pines.

Someone is coming. And he's very drunk. I look up at a large jack pine beside the road. Quickly, I step off the path and pull myself up the first branch and climb up fast and high as I can before the man comes near enough to hear me. About ten feet up, I stop and clutch the tree trunk. The man is really drunk. Staggering back and forth over the path, he stops and staggers back two or three steps before he bends forward and lunges ahead three or four steps, then his body lurches back again.

It's Sarah's father! He's about twenty feet away now. He has on only a thin summer jacket with no hat, no mitts, a moccasin on one foot and a black rubber boot on the other. Oh, oh, he's fumbling around with the front of his pants, he's going to pee. I turn my head. I hear a thud and I glance back. There he is, face down in the snow. I remain still; no sign of anyone anywhere. Another few minutes go by. What should I do? His face is plopped right in the snow and he hasn't moved a muscle. Briefly, I wondered if people can breathe in the snow. I scramble down from the tree and approach him.

I nudge his leg with my foot, my own muscles straining to run if he moved even one inch. No response. His left hand is buried deep in the snow. His other hand is under him somewhere. I can't even see his face. I pull his jacket at the elbow; his hand comes out of the snow. He still does not move. I pull his arm back hard and half of his face comes out of the snow. I step over his legs and peer at his face. The snow is slowly falling off his nose, but it does not seem to be melting off his cheek. He coughs and I jump a foot high. He still won't move, but at least he's alive. I notice a yellow stain in the snow under him. I turn and run down the path to Sarah's cabin. Maybe Sarah's home.

A couple of dogs bark at me as I approach the cabin. Tubs, snow-shoes, handsaws and dogsled harnesses hang along the whole length of the cabin wall. I push the door open and enter the dark interior; there is only one window. Something smells awful. As my eyes adjust to the darkness, I can see the mess. Things are scattered everywhere, like someone ransacked the place. The fat old woman is sitting by the table beside the window noisily chewing something from a pot beside her, staring at me. Groping around with her hand in the pot again, she pulls out a piece of meat which she hacks off with the knife in her other hand and then she shoves the greasy mess into her mouth, slurping and licking her fingers.

Suddenly, she barks at me, "Why are you staring at me for? You want some?"

"No." I quickly say.

"Here, take it!" she lunges toward me, shoving a piece of half-cooked beaver meat with yellowish-white fat clinging to the side of her filthy hand. I can see her dirt-ringed fingernails digging into the piece she shoves again at my face.

"Here! Take it!" she yells angrily. I'm scared and she knows I'm scared. Slowly, I reach for the yucky lump. My fingers close over the warm, slimy meat. It stinks; it's rotten. "Put it in your mouth! Go on! Put it in your mouth, I said!" she screeches at me. My heart is pounding very hard, as my arm slowly comes up. I close my nose at the back of my mouth and deposit the rotten meat inside. Her voice comes again. Satisfied now, she says, "There, good! Now, what do you want here? You can see Sarah's not here. Even if you seem to be the only one that plays with her around here. Does your mother know you're here?"

I shake my head. My nose is still tightly closed and I shove the rotten beaver meat to one cheek, before I say, "Sarah's father, he's asleep in the snow. He won't get up." A whiff escapes from my mouth and goes up my nose. I almost gag.

The woman gets up and goes to a bed where someone is sleeping. She yells, "Go get your father. The stupid fool has gone to sleep in the snow!"

It's Bobby. He must have come back from his trapping line yesterday. I see him swing his feet off the bed, as I dash out. Oh, I can't stand it any longer. My stomach is heaving so badly. I run as fast as I can on the path across the ice toward our cabin. About halfway, when I'm sure the woman won't see me, I spit out the wad of rotten meat. Eee-yuk. Yuck. I shove snow in my mouth and spit it out again and again, as I moan and gag all the way home. I can still taste it.

I run inside our cabin, grab the teapot, and pick up the first cup I find on the shelf. It has half a cup of black tea in it, so I just fill it up to the top. Quickly, I add sugar and milk, then I take a big mouthful. "U-u-gh!" I spit it out instantly, back into the cup. "What's wrong with the tea?" I yell. My mouth is stinging and burning real badly.

Then I hear Mom. "Holy smokes! That was the whiskey that John poured in that cup!" Her tongue is clicking pretty loudly now, "Spill it out! What's the matter with you anyway?"

I climb up to the top bunk and cram candies into my mouth. I begin to feel better as peppermint fills my mouth and nostrils. I tell Mom about Sarah's father and the old woman with the rotten meat.

The door opens and Uncle Daniel enters. "Hello, hello, hello! Merry Christmas!" He comes around hugging everyone. "There's the Indian Maiden. How are you, Indian Maiden?" he asks, beaming at me.

I answer, "Fine."

He chuckles, "That's good, that's good."

Mom dishes out stew for lunch. "Sit down, Daniel. I bet you haven't had anything to eat yet."

Uncle Daniel laughs, "No, I don't even remember leaving my home last night. I woke up at John's house this morning. I've been visiting everyone." He quietly sits down to eat.

I quickly eat my stew and scramble back to the top bunk. After lunch, Uncle Daniel holds the baby for awhile before he decides to lie down on the lower bunk. Mom pulls off his shoes. Soon I hear him snoring. For the rest of the afternoon Maggie and I sew up doll clothes for our dolls. My doll dress gets all bloody before I'm done. I keep pricking my fingers with the needle. Cora and the baby are asleep on the double bed.

Mom's frying fish for supper and it smells good. She keeps the fish frozen in a tub atop the woodpile outside. Everyone is getting noisy again, laughing and talking, because Uncle Daniel finally woke up. The boys are wrestling on Mom's bed in the next room. Mom's going to get mad. They're probably messing up the blankets on the bed.

Supper's ready and Uncle Daniel gets to eat first. His plate is piled high with fried fish, bannock, canned peas and mashed potatoes and he gets a big mug of tea. He's joking and laughing between each mouthful.

The coal oil lamp is re-lit. It's getting very cold and dark outside. After supper, Uncle Daniel picks up his cap, gloves and coat and waves from the door before going out. The stove is now roaring, glowing red around the airvent. The dishes clatter from the wash pan at the table. Barbara busily puts thick quilts over the windows to keep out the stinging draft. Vera and Jane brought in a big pile of wood. Since the baby's been here we've had to keep the fire going all through the night. Mom pulls out a big bag of nuts. Oh boy. She sits at the edge of the bed and we all crowd around her. She spreads a cloth over her lap and puts a block of wood between her knees at the end of the bench. Then, armed with the hammer, she proceeds to crack the nuts: Brazil nuts, walnuts, almonds and hazel nuts! Mom's telling us a story, interrupted occasionally when she cracks and pops a nut into her mouth. The stove is burning quietly. The lamp wick is set fullbright at the table. I lay back against the wall on the bed, smiling and munching on the nuts that are passed on to me. I pass on the walnuts; I don't like them very much. I nudge Tony; he loves walnuts.

A light tap sounds at the door. "You still awake in there?" It's the Joker! Annie runs and pulls the bar aside and pushes the door open. The Joker comes in, holding his nose. "I forgot the darn door opens backwards!"

We all laugh, as Mom says, "You should know, you're the one that made it like that!"

He stops abruptly in front of Mom. "What are you pretending to be? A giant Mama Squirrel?" We crack up! Oh, that is funny and Mom's mouth is so full of walnuts, she can't say anything, except make funny faces!

The Joker sits down in front of her on the bench and proceeds to pop the nuts into his mouth as fast as Mom can crack them. Their faces are about a foot away from each other. Suddenly, Mom shakes the hammer over his head and the Joker ducks back laughing, pleased his teasing is successful.

When the nuts are gone, we all have a cup of tea. Then the Joker departs, doing a tap dance on the porch for us before his footsteps recede down the path. We are all still giggling, as we get ready for bed. Vera and Barbara sort out the green wood from the dry wood by the door. I'm standing behind the stove when, suddenly, someone crashes against our door. We forgot to bar it after the Joker went out. Almost immediately, the intruder flings the door open with such force that it crashes against the outside wall. A man hurls himself inside the cabin and stands there blinking in the bright lamplight. It's the man who kicked the door down the last time.

I see Vera and Barbara on each side of him with blocks of wood still in their hands. Suddenly and simultaneously, they attack the man, striking him repeatedly on the head and arms as he tries to cover his head. Again and again, they pound at him with the wood. Their blows drive him back against the wall. Then Mom is in there with the thick broom stick, whacking it at his exposed midsection. Finally, as the man doubles over, she grabs his coat from the back and hurls him out the open door.

We hear him crash on the porch and roll off the steps. Mom steps out to pull the door closed. I hear her speak to the man, "Don't you EVER, EVER come around here again! I swear I'll kill you next time you bother me or mine!" She comes in, slams the door, throws the bar across and pulls in the outside handle.

All is quiet. I've just realized that I haven't moved an inch since the door first flew open. Now, I sigh as I feel my body relax. Then, a slow pressure mounts in my chest and I begin to giggle. Still standing around by the stove, they all look at me. Then they, too, start to laugh. That is all I need; I let my laughter go. Oh, that was so good to see. I feel like hugging them all. I look at them with love-filled, adoring eyes, my mother, my sisters… now I feel like crying. Oh, I'm so proud of them. The baby starts to cry. The spell is broken. Instantly, everyone rushes to the baby, exclaiming about the cold air that filled the room the few minutes the door was open. Vera and Jane fill up the stove and pull the air vent wide open. The stove belches a cloud of smoke before it roars to devour the gummy dry wood.

Finally, we're all in bed. Mom has closed the air vent on the stove again and blown out the lamp. Tony is already asleep beside me while Maggie and I are talking about the Joker with an occasional giggle. Jane is already asleep, too. Again I watch the lights flicker over the ceiling. I sigh; it was a nice day, a very nice Christmas day.

15

SPRING TIME

Spring 1963

My eyes pop open. I can hear Mom calling outside, all excited, "Come out! Come outside, everybody! Listen! Listen!"

Barbara, Jane and Maggie are out the open door already. I grab my blanket and jump off the bunk and land on the floor with a thump. Brian walks by me in his bare feet towards the open door, still sleepily rubbing his eyes and mumbling, "What's going on out there? Must be something very special. Better be!"

The stove is blazing hot, fighting its every morning battle with the open door. I slip my wooly socks on and rush out the door ahead of Brian. Mom is standing by the woodpile, pail and axe in hand. "Shh, shh. Listen," she says.

Then, "Caw, caw, caw," comes the welcoming sound, joyfully echoing its news of spring through the hills along the shoreline.

"It's a crow!" says Brian, beaming. Everyone is so excited and happy. They go back in, laughing and talking. Mom's ambled down toward the lake to get the water. I can hear the Old Man at the point, chopping wood. I jump off the porch, run across to the sawhorse and scramble up on top, pulling the blanket tightly around me. Huge piles of sawdust are all around the sawhorse. Some stick up like mushrooms where the snow has melted all around them, leaving the tops insulated from the sun with caps of sawdust. I shake my socks free of ice crystals and sawdust. Oh, it's such a clear, fresh morning. The sun is up about an inch on top the horizon already. Slowly, I inhale the fresh air, flavoured occasionally by whiffs of wood smoke from the chimney.

The Old Man's voice breaks the stillness. "Did you hear it?" he yells across the bay.

Mom is halfway to the island now. She stops and yells back, "Yes! The crow is back!" The Old Man's chopping has started again. I can hear someone else sawing some wood with a handsaw.

Mom is chipping away at the thin ice that formed over the new water hole she made the other day, very close to the island. She says all the dirt and filth that collected on top of the snow over the winter gets washed down to the lake when the snow melts. She says that from the highest ground by the railroad tracks, the little rivulets run pass the outhouses, garbage dumps and dog houses. Some run down our path into our water hole. And where, she says, do you think that water, which you have in your water pail has been? I smile. That's Mom. No one else would think of things like that. I watch her gingerly make her way back over the wet slippery ice with her pail full of water and the axe in her other hand. I giggle. She looks like the girl in the moon. That's a story she told us once about a girl who went out to get water at night and she was not supposed to look at the moon. But she stopped and looked at the moon anyway because she thought the moon was so handsome. The moon came down and took her away and there she was to stay for ever and ever, on the moon, with her pail still in her hand...

"I'm talking to you! When are you ever going to stop your daydreaming?" Barbara yells at me in exasperation.

"Huh?" I ask.

She sighs, "I told you to come in and pick up the blankets and hang them outside. Now!"

I sigh and look out at the snow-covered lake once more before I jump off. Rrripp! Oh no. My blanket gets caught on the sawhorse and there's a big hole in it now. Mom sees and hears it because she's shaking her head at me as she comes up the path. I grin sheepishly and kick hard at the sawdust cap off one mushroom-head of snow. "Ouch!" That wasn't snow under the sawdust; it was a block of wood frozen solid to the ground. I hop around gasping, holding my foot, tripping over my blanket and crash in the crisp snow by the path, right in front of Mom.

I sit up quickly and hold my foot, slowly massaging my toes. Mom puts her pail down, looks at me, then starts to laugh. She drops the axe and laughs harder, clapping her hands and rocking back and forth. I grin and struggle to stand up with the blanket tangled all around me. Mom gasps and, wiping her eyes, says, "That was good! That was very good, Owl! Honestly, the things that happen to you..." Reaching for her pail, she starts giggling. I dash into the cabin, pulling off my blanket and my wet socks. Mmmm, coffee and bannock cooking. It's very cozy and warm inside even with the door wide open; the stove won again. It's really springtime.

I rummage around in the clothes box from under the bed till I find some change of clothes. School day today, too. Oh, I wish school were over already. "Mom, what day is it today?" She's still laughing, telling Barbara how I looked with my blanket and hair flying everywhere.

"Friday! Don't you know what comes after Thursday?" says Brian.

"Oh, shut up! I just forgot what day it was yesterday, that's all!" I yell.

Barbara pokes me in the back, "Be quiet and get those blankets out! Now!" I pull my blankets off my bunk, gather up the others and stomp off the porch. I wish she'd go back to her husband. She came home at

Christmas time and never went back. I grunt and groan, working up a sweat, as I hurl the heavy quilts and blankets up over the hanging pole behind the cabin. I'm hungry.

Back inside, I stuff my face with bannock and jam, while Mom brushes and braids my hair. I hate braids. Bobby always dunks them in his ink bottle behind me or he spits on them. Oh, I hate him. He's back from trapping already and he'll go to school from now till the end of June.

I linger by the door as long as I can. Oh, I hate having to go to school today. Tony, Brian and Maggie are ready to go. I sigh and take off at a run down the path, past Aunty's house. Cousin Joe didn't come back with her after Christmas, although he'll probably be back in the summer. Passing the Catholic church, I slow to a walk and pull my braids apart and shake out my hair free over my shoulders. The snow is muddy from the exposed areas on the path. Everything looks so dirty; the path, dogs, kids with boots always covered with mud. Oh, glorious mud. Yesterday, Bobby packed a snowball hard and rolled it in the mud behind the school and hit Ben 'splat,' right on the back of this head. That was funny.

The kids are very noisy, laughing and chasing each other around as I near the school. Hey, there's Hanna standing by the trees with a pile of papers in her hands. Her father traps in the winter so they live in their trapper's shack in the bush all winter. She's lucky. She does her schoolwork at home. She comes to school whenever they come in from the bush. I stop beside her. She's shy. I smile. "Did you get all the work done?" I ask, indicating the papers.

She nods, "Yep. Some of them, though, I couldn't do. I got stuck in math lots of times."

As the bell rings or rather jingles, I glance up, just in time to see Ben swing the bell and clobber Bobby over the head with it. Clang. The teacher steps out, promptly taking the bell from Ben. It was supposed to be Ben's turn to ring the bell today. We giggle as Teacher rings the bell and Bobby and Ben have to stay outside with Teacher till everyone is inside.

A flicker of panic crosses Hanna's face as she sees everyone kicking off their boots. I kick mine off and wait as Hanna slowly removes her black rubber boots. Her eyes focus on the long string of safety pins on my sweater, then she pulls me to the side behind the stove. "Can I have one of the small safety pins? I have a hole on the heel of my sock!" she whispers.

I quickly pull off one small silver pin, hand it over and try to block her from view. The others push and jostle each other by the door. "Okay, I'm ready," Hanna whispers behind me.

Following behind her, I'm very conscious of the metallic "click, click,

click," of the pin on her heel with each step she takes on the tile floor. I can feel a familiar, overwhelming pressure fill my chest and begin shaking in my throat. I pull at her elbow and we lean against the black board as I hurriedly whisper, "I can hear it!" The giggle comes up my throat. She nods and we both burst out laughing silently. I have my hand over my mouth, as I follow her to our seats. She takes the empty seat in front of me.

When Teacher has everyone quiet and working, he comes and picks up Hanna's papers. Hanna works in her new notebook which the teacher gave her when he took her papers.

The sun streams through the windows making the small kindergarten kids squirm uncomfortably from the heat. Teacher motions for Hanna to come forward. Oh no! I hold my breath, as Hanna stands up and walks, "click, click, click, click," all the way to Teacher's desk. Sure enough, the titters turn to giggles from the kids in the whole room. Hanna's face is all red as she stands beside the teacher's desk. Teacher raps a ruler on the desk and all is quiet again. I look at the clock over the teacher's head—five minutes, ten minutes, fifteen minutes then twenty minutes. Hanna is switching from one foot to the other. Finally, she gathers the papers and comes back to her desk, "click, click, click, click." The long held silence erupts into loud grunts and hissing which echoes through the room from the many suppressed giggles and laughter. My eyes and throat hurt as I swallow my laughter and tightly clench my teeth. Teacher goes to the windows and pulls down the shades and the room is quiet again, broken only by the normal rustling paper and pencil tapping. When the sun arches high in the sky, we break for lunch. After, we play in the snow and mud and troop into school once more. I wish I were outside.

What a long afternoon. It seems like ages since we had lunch. It's recess soon and it will be another long period before school is out for the day. Desperately, I wish it were time to go home already. Sighing, I look out the window. The window shades are open again and the sun now reaches only the back cupboards. Hey, there's Mom. She's on her way home from the store with a paper bag under her arm. Teacher is at his desk, looking at me. I duck my head into my book and continue sketching Jumbo under a pine tree.

Yesterday there was no school so I was able to go with Mom to check the rabbit snares deep into the bush on the other side of the tracks. Oh, it was so nice. We left right after lunch. The sun was shining, the air was fresh and clean, the snow was melting, and the birds were chirping. I walked behind her and the small tobaggan she pulled, ducking branches and twigs, on a narrow path through the dense bush. We found three rabbits in the snares. Then we came upon a lake and Mom chopped two holes in the ice while I broke off pine branches for us to sit on. She pulled out fish lines and bait from the little sack on the toboggan. There we sat and fished, facing each other about twenty feet apart. She told me stories about Indians of long ago and the magic people who lived inside the rock cliffs. Mom caught three large jackfish and I caught one. Oh, that was great. Afterwards, we built a fire and had some tea and bannock and jam sandwiches before we headed back home. The sun was almost down and it was quickly getting cold. I could tell because the ice glazed snow was cracking louder and louder under the toboggan. We came home with three rabbits and four jackfish. Mom was so happy and I was really proud of us.

Pausing at my desk, Teacher whispers in my ear, "Hey, wake up! You're daydreaming again!"

I can feel my face turning red. This is ridiculous. I don't know how many times Teacher has told me to wake up today. I hunch my shoulders forward. Everyone's restless and just busting to get out.

Teacher's voice rings out from the front, "All right, books away! Let's call it a day but you have to work harder on Monday!"

'Yaayyy!" comes a chorus of voices, followed by talking and laughing. The big clock at the front says two o'clock. He's letting us out at recess time. Half the class is gone already by the time I finish putting my books away. Hanna already has her books under her arm. I grin at her and say, "I didn't laugh at your stupid sock!"

She looks at me. "Why not? I just about died laughing!" she declares and walks away.

"Is anyone going to help me put this stuff away?" Teacher calls out from the back of the room where the vitamin cookies and milk stand on the table. The mugs were already laid out for the after-recess snack. Hanna's gone. Rita, Sarah, Maggie and I volunteer to put the things away. In two minutes, we're the only ones left in the class. Teacher chuckles from the window, looking out at the kids squealing and the snow balls flying.

Everything is all put away and Teacher comes outside with us. He hasn't got his coat on. We start playing tag. Laughing and running with Teacher behind us, we scatter everywhere around the school. I dodge around the fuel oil drums behind the school and there I get tagged by Rita. I race around the corner and right into Teacher. I tag him, slapping him hard on the chest over his shirt pocket and my finger stings. Blood is all over my hand. I've hit a sharp pencil he had sticking out of his pocket. He puts his handkerchief over my hand and leads me inside the school with Rita and Sarah behind us.

At once he washes the blood off my hand at the sink and puts a bandage on my finger. I'm all fixed up again. I giggle, tag him and make a dash for the door. His hand closes over my arm before I can reach it and Rita and Sarah run out laughing and squealing. I hear their voices fade away toward the store. Laughing, Teacher sits down on the edge of the counter by the door. Still holding my arm, he pulls me and starts tickling me. I begin struggling when he pulls me tight between his knees. Suddenly, I see I'm alone in the classroom,. Something is wrong; he's pulling me tighter, holding me closer to him. I don't know what, but there's something wrong. Quickly, I push him away and I'm out the door in three seconds. There is no one around outside the school now. With my heart pounding, I dash through the bush on my shortcut home. My knees tremble. I slow down to catch my breath. I can hear the other kids yelling and screaming by the store. I slowly start walking again. What was it that scared me? I should tell Mom. Tell Mom what? I shrug... I don't know.

Our door's open and there's Mom frying something on the stove beside the door. I run and pounce on the porch with both feet. Mom yells, "Not so fast! Barbara's scrubbing the floor. What are you doing home so early anyway?"

"School's out for today! I saw you going home from the store. Can I have something?" I ask.

Mom smiles, "Big eyes! Can't hide anything from the Owl!" She digs around in the food box under the table, then into her sewing box on the top shelf. She turns and hands me an orange and a chocolate bar.

A chocolate bar! I tuck the orange in my pocket and go out to the steps to eat the chocolate. I hear Barbara scrubbing the wooden floor inside. Sometimes wood slivers pierce her hands. I get up and stand by the door to watch her. Sweat drips off her nose and her dark curls are plastered around her face. A folded cloth is under her knees and her hands are already washed white and wrinkled from the hot Javexed water. She leans back and brushes the scrubbing brush over the yellow bar of soap, spraying suds over the floor. I study the floor space left to do — about three more squares. She does it in squares as far as she can reach and backs up toward the door. Already the wooden floor is drying a clean pinkish-white at the back of the room. Mom does the floor when Barbara's not here. Sometimes Vera does it, too. Maybe I'll go see Hanna for awhile. There are three cleaning things I hate. First is laundry-day in the winter with wet floors from splashing wash tubs, strong Javex smells and pails and pails of water to lug from the water hole on the lake to be heated up on the stove, and sitting everywhere with melting ice floating around. Such a cold damp mess. Second is dishcloth and towel stain-removing day. Oh, the stink of strong Javexed water steaming on top of the stove — I get very sick. Third is floor-scrubbing day. Once or twice a week, winter or summer, rain or shine, the floor has to be absolutely, cleaned white! And we have the strong Javex smell again and the "stay off the wet floor!" screeches. Hey, I'm so busy thinking, I suddenly realize, I've almost eaten all my chocolate. There are only two squares left, and I don't even remember eating it. Feeling cheated, I save the last two pieces and carefully push them into my pocket.

Mom finishes making bannock and sits down, pulling her feet up on the bed. Barbara is doing that area now. I don't have to do all that stuff. But I have to get the water sometimes or pour it out, if I'm around. I usually make myself scarce.

Brian brushes by me into the room and instantly Barbara screeches, "Get off the wet floor!"

Time to go. I race down the path, past the large clearing by the shore, up the hill... Oh, I forgot, Hanna has company. Some of her relatives got off the train this morning to visit them. I slow to a walk and eat my orange. I hear some commotion inside her cabin as I push the door open. My eyes fall on the back of a woman; in front of her lies a child about four years old. The woman is pulling out a wiggly live white thing out of the child's rear. There are piles of moving white flat ropes on the floor beside her. I feel my stomach come up my throat and I fling the door open to dash back outside. I stand there gasping. The door opens behind me. Hanna comes and stands beside me. I look at her and whisper, "Are those things the same kind of worms that hang out of dogs sometimes?"

She nods, "She'll be okay." Then looking at me, she begins to giggle. "Oh, you looked so funny! Your eyes popped out and your mouth fell open! You looked so funny."

I don't feel like laughing. "Come on, let's go to my place," I say. "Barbara must be finished scrubbing the floor by now."

As we near the cabin, I see Mom by the stove again; this time, she's frying the fish. It looks so good. Mom gives Hanna an orange and we play on the top bunk with some paper dolls, cut out from an old catalogue.

Hanna's paper doll has just lost a foot when, suddenly, all heck breaks loose. Barbara is screaming and pointing to the floor]. She lunges forward at the passing Tony, clamping a hand on his neck, jerking him off his feet and hurling him out the door. Tony lands on his feet outside on the porch. Then I notice the brown smudges on the clean freshly-scrubbed floor, as the smell reaches us. Dog poop! Hanna and I bury our faces in the pillow and kill ourselves laughing.

Hanna's gone home for supper. She's going to ask her parents if she can come and sleep with us tonight. Mom says she can sleep on the empty bottom bunk. Mmmm, the fish is delicious! I can't wait till tomorrow; right after breakfast, Hanna and I are going to the island and clear out the snow in the clump of cedars to build a nice home for our dolls.

16

FIRE

Spring 1963

I skip through the open door.

"Where have you been? Hurry up and eat your lunch. The church bell will be ringing soon," says Mom, as she turns from the mirror above the sink. Nicely dressed, she has just finished combing her hair into smooth rippling waves. She stands there scowling down at me, "Tsk, tsk, look at your shoes. They're covered with mud!"

My face cracks into a big smile, "Oh, we were at the little stream. There are lots of little suckers there. I caught two and I gave them to Rosiak. Bobby says there's a bear there. Do you think a bear would come to the stream? Bobby says his father saw some bear tracks there. Do you think there's a bear there? Huh?"

Mom shakes her head and says, "I don't know. If so, it's probably hungry and I'm sure he likes eating those suckers you're talking about. Don't go there anymore. If Bobby's father says there's a bear, then there's a bear."

After a mouthful of rabbit stew, I pause, then ask, "Why does it have to go there, anyway? We were there first!"

Mom laughs, "Would you like to tell that to the bear when you meet him on the path to the stream?"

I shovel another spoonful into my mouth. "Where's everybody?"

Mom sighs, "I don't know. We'll probably see them at the church. Even Jane hasn't been around for lunch yet," she trails off.

I scrape off the last bit of stew from the bowl with a piece of bannock and mumble through my mouthful, "I saw Jane going up the hill with the old lady, back to her cabin. The old lady's son was outside splitting wood." I wipe off my mouth with the back of my sleeve.

Mom sighs and orders, "Go change your dress. You're wet and muddy all over! Look at your elbows!"

I brush by her to the back room. Rummaging around in the clothes box, I grumble, "Well, I had to lie down on my belly by the stream to grab the fish, didn't I? How else do I catch suckers with my hands, huh? And my shoes, well, I can't help it if the ground is muddy, can I?" Still grumbling under my breath, I pull my old dress off over my head and yank on a clean one. All my dresses look the same. I hear "ding-dong, ding-dong." The church bell is ringing. I run into the next room yelling, "The church bell! Church is ringing!"

Mom attacks my hair with her comb. "I heard it too. Stop yelling!" She picks out a couple of twigs from my hair and pulls the comb through. I wince and watch the comb growing hair by the hundreds.

Suddenly, she raises her voice, "What are these little, white specks in your hair? My God! You have lice in your hair! Have you been inside Sarah's cabin again?" She clicks her tongue rapidly and pushes my head back. "Now, I'll have to delouse your bunk and check everyone's head too. Where did you throw that dress you took off?" She's screeching now, "Go get it and put it outside by the woodpile. I'll deal with you when we get back!"

I run and pull my discarded dress off her bed and dash out the door to the back of the cabin to fling it over the woodpile.

Mom has just hung the padlock on the door as I come around the corner. She glares at me. "I expected you to carefully roll up that dress and carry it outside, taking care not to drop any lice if there are any on it." she hisses at me.

Meekly, I follow behind her, feeling like I've got some filthy disease.

Down the path and across the clearing, people are coming from every direction, all heading for the little red Anglican church as its bell tolls a second time.

My lice are quickly forgotten when I see the ladies dressed in all colours with many rows of ruffles on the gathered skirts. The ladies comb their shiny smooth hair down the sides of their heads, pinning their hair down with glistening rows of hairpins, some studded with sparkling glass and sequins.

There's Maggie with Rita. Hanna is waiting for me by the birch tree beside the path and she falls into step beside me. Tony and Brian come running down the hill from the store.

The sun is shining hot and not a cloud is in the sky. It's such a beautiful day. Mom stops to chat with some ladies beside the church. Dogs are everywhere, all heading for the shade under the church.

"Hey Mom, how come white people always build their houses so far up off the ground?" I ask.

Brian pipes up, "That's so they can put stairs going up, dummy! Ever see a white man's house with no steps?"

I reach over to pinch his neck. "Yawooo! Mom, she pinched me!" he howls. Mom glares at me; she's mad! Embarrassed, I glance at Hanna and we giggle. Up the six steps and into the crowded church, we rush for our seat in the fourth row.

There are about ten long benches on each side. Some chairs are stacked behind the wood stove at the front. On the raised floor to the left behind the stove, is a high table where the minister stands when he talks. To the right is a bench for the minister to sit and kneel. At the very front stands a shiny, gold cross on top of a long table covered with green cloth with gold trim and designs on it.

It smells like musty bibles in here. There's a big picture of Jesus on the wall beside the door; how peaceful his eyes are, his face so gentle, his mouth slightly curved in a smile. His hair looks so soft as it comes in gentle, brown waves down the side of his head. I poke Mom who's beside me now, "Hey Mom," I whisper, "look. Did you know Jesus has hair just like yours?"

Her eyes widen. Then she glares at me before she turns away. Oh, oh, she's really mad at me now.

The church is full. People are whispering everywhere. Nobody talks in church. We all have to whisper when we come in. It looks like the whole community is here. The storekeeper and his family sit on the bench behind us. The only ones not here are the four Catholic families. Their black-clad priest comes only once a year, in the springtime, mostly.

The minister comes out of the little room at the back in his black and white gown. We stand and sing our first hymn. Hanna and I nudge each other about the upturned toes of the minister's shoes. He must kneel a lot to make his shoes permanently fold up like that. Suddenly, a dogfight erupts outside, underneath the church. Some men rush out to stop the fight. It's quiet again. Collection time comes and Mom puts in five dollars and all of us kids get a quarter to put in. There are lots of ten and twenty dollar bills in the plate. I have never seen so much money. Piles of it. Hanna says the old man by the lake and the man across the tracks always try to outgive each other.

We sing another hymn. Someone opens a window and we can hear the birds singing outside. The minister is talking. A train is coming and a kid is crying outside by the store somewhere. Another hymn and church is over. Everyone smiles at each other when we line up to go to the door where the minister shakes each person's hand as we go by. The sound of laughing and talking gets louder from the people outside. The men stand around at the foot of the steps either watching or waiting for the brightly dressed young ladies as they come down the steps, one by one. I shake the minister's hand, too. His blue eyes are twinkling and his white hair is neatly combed and parted at the side. His top gown is very white and his curved shoes stick out beneath the black gown. Hanna pushes in beside me and we jump to the ground from the top steps. I'm already skipping off with Hanna toward the store when I hear Mom calling me. I forgot about the lice on my head. I have to go home with Mom so I wave back to Hanna and run after Mom who's already going down the path toward home. We meet Jane by the Catholic church.

Jane smiles, falls into step beside Mom, and says, "The door was locked when I got home."

Mom glances at Jane and says, "You didn't come to church." Jane says something which I don't hear and then Mom says, loudly, "He's Catholic!" Suddenly, she spins around and yells at me, "Go and play for awhile but don't go far. Come when I call you!"

I stop and watch them talk, getting farther and farther till I can't hear them anymore. Suddenly, a head pops up from the sand bank along the shore. It's Ben. I run towards Ben, skipping over the tall grass and weeds.

"What are you doing?" I ask. Ben looks up, smiling. He's squatting on the sand, picking up small, flat rocks he is trying to make skip along the surface of the water. "They won't skip; the water's too choppy. I just came from church; how come you didn't go?" I ask.

Ben looks down at his calloused, bare feet and his faded tattered pants rolled up to his knees. His old shirt is full of holes. He plunges his hand into his pants pocket and holds out some matches. "Let's make a little camp fire and roast this!" He picks up a stick with a minnow impaled at the end.

"Okay. We'll pretend we're Little People!" I beam. We run around gathering twigs and sticks. Stopping at a flat rock by the clearing, we pile the twigs. Soon we have a good pile about four inches high. Ben pulls up a small roll of very fine, dry grass which he shoves into our miniature fire.

"Okay, we're ready." Ben strikes a match on the rock and it flares up. He shoves it under the small pile of twigs. It goes out. He strikes another match and this time our campfire comes to life. Ben holds out his fish over the flames and yells, "Get me some more wood. It's burning fast!"

I run to break more twigs. I can see the back of Aunty's cabin about fifty feet away. I tug at a dry branch. A lot of dry bush has been piled here when they cleared for Aunty's new outhouse. I turn back with a handful of twigs and see Ben hopping around.

"What are you doing?" I yell. Little flames are leaping everywhere all around the rock.

"My fish stick caught on fire and I was trying to shove it in the ground to put it out. It lit the dry grass instead and fire keeps springing up everywhere! Hurry! Help me!" he babbles, panicking and gasping, as he leaps about stomping on the flames with his bare feet. I feel myself moving to join him in his weird dance around the flat rock. Suddenly, Ben dives at my legs, nearly knocking me down. He's bunching up my skirt together at the back! He yells, "Your skirt's on fire! Oh no! Look!"

The fire is now burning into a circle, like a big tent. Helplessly, we stop by the rock as the fire spreads in a complete circle quickly widening away from us. Soon the fire is a four-foot wall all around us, getting higher and roaring louder every second. Figures appear from all directions, yelling, screaming, and running. In two minutes we have the whole community right there in front of us. The men quickly stop the grassfire by the path. But now, a six-foot wall of fire has risen to our right, as it greedily consumes the nearest pile of dry brush cuttings. People are running toward Aunty's cabin. Already, men are lined up, passing the water buckets as fast as they come. Other men are throwing water over the flames and on the other brush pile.

Ben and I are still standing on the blackened rock and I notice his bare feet. "Did you burn your feet? I can't see; they're all covered black with ash. Do they hurt?" I ask.

Ben smiles at me before he answers, "No. I didn't burn my feet. They're probably thicker than your shoes!" He chuckles, "Come, I'll show you." I follow him to the lake where he splashes around in the water before he lifts a foot. "See?" he says.

I look at the brown, scorched soles of his feet. "You sure it doesn't hurt? How about your hands?"

He washes the soot off his hands and turns them over. "Not bad. My right hand hurts a little between my fingers but it's okay." Then he laughs and sprays my face with water. "You look funny. Black smudges over your nose. You going on a war path or something?"

Mom's calling me. I run to her, yelling, "Hey, Mom! Ben's feet didn't even get burned. He has very thick skin on his feet." My yakking is cut short when she clamps a hand on the back collar of my dress. I almost stumble, as she propels me along in front of her. The fire is out now; the brush pile is charred black and dripping wet. The men are standing around in front of Aunty's cabin, talking and laughing. I feel so embarrassed as Mom pushes me along right by them. They chuckle and laugh at me. "I didn't start the fire!" I protest at Mom, as I try to pull my hair. out of her grasp. "Awwoo, you're pulling my hair!"

Mom pushes me in through our door, hissing, "Shut up! Take off that dress and change into another one!" Oh, she's mad. I look down at two pairs of eyes.

"What are you staring at?" I yell at Brian and Tony, stomping by them toward the back room. I pull the dress off over my head. Oh my, there's a big burn hole in the dress, right up to my butt! The charred hem is hanging down at the back. Mom comes and yanks the dress out of my hands and shoves the whole thing into the stove! I sink down on the bed and pull out another dress from my clothes box. Mom stomps around, banging pots and lids. Brian and Tony are quietly sitting by the table when I come out. They're waiting for something worse to happen—the brats. I stick my tongue out at them.

"Come outside with me." Mom orders. I follow her out the door with the boys a few feet behind me. At the woodpile, Mom pulls out the coal oil can. "Bend your head over here." I walk slowly to her and she pushes my head down to the ground beside her. The cold stinky oil flows over my scalp and onto the ground. Then Mom works the coal oil into my hair, rubbing it all over my scalp.

"Mom, it stinks!" I protest.

"I checked the dress you took off. I didn't see any lice on it," she says. She puts a piece of canvas over my shoulders. "Go and sit by the lake till it dries off a bit," she orders.

The wind blows cold over my head. The evening train is coming. The minister will get on it. Brian and Tony follow behind me. I whirl around and hiss, "Go away!"

Tony kicks at the ground. "Why? She put that stuff on my head once, too. Remember?" he smiles.

"Do you think they're dead, yet?" Brian asks.

Puzzled, I shake my head and ask, "Who's dead?"

"The lice! The lice on your head. Mom says your hair could have caught on fire from the flames when your dress caught fire. Hey, then your lice could have burned to death instead! Eh?" he laughs.

"Oh, shut up! Just go away!" I yell.

Brian stops and his lips press into a thin line. I stomp off and jump on a rock by the lake. Brian shouts at me, "I could put a match to your head!"

I jump up and shake my fist at him. They take off through the bush back to the cabin. I sit down again, trying to ignore the stink of the coal oil.

Seagulls are everywhere; bright, white and flashing against the evening sun. The birch and poplar trees are tinged with a pale shade of green. The leaves are brand new and yellow buttercups are budding along the muddy shore. My brother's dog, Rocky, was tied to the tree behind me. That's the one that was shot last summer. The blackbirds are squawking, a long continuous noise from the island.

I yawn and sprawl back on the rock, resting my feet up on another rock a few feet away. I have to cross my feet otherwise my right foot will fall in the water. I open my eyes and Maggie is standing on a rock beside my feet. She nudges my foot and it slips and splashes into the water up to my knee. I sit up yelling, "Hey, why did you do that for?" I stand up shakily. My leg has fallen asleep. That's why it just fell in the water like that. Maggie is giggling with her hand over her mouth. "Help me get off this rock. My foot's asleep and now it's being attacked by millions of invisible needles!" I groan.

She pulls me onto the ground and sits down beside me and says, "Jane is gone."

"What do you mean, gone?" I ask pouring water from my shoe.

"She went with the old lady's son on the train this evening."

I pull off my stocking and wring it out. "You mean for good?"

Maggie nods, "She told me last night that he was taking her with him."

I look at her. "Mom didn't know?" I ask.

Maggie looks down at her fingernails, "Jane told me not to tell. She was scared Delia would get mad and not let her go because he's Catholic. And anyway, he doesn't go to church and doesn't believe in getting married in a church."

I shrug and smile, "Can you just imagine yourself running off with someone like him? Anyway, now you have lots of room on the double bed."

Maggie grimaced and said, "Your head stinks."

"You think Mom will wash my hair before we go to bed?" I ask.

Maggie shrugs, "Well, if she doesn't, then she'll have to wash your blanket and your pillow tomorrow. I'm hungry. It's suppertime."

I put my wet sock and shoe back on and say, "Race you home!"

17

DOG DAYS

Summer 1963

It's hot. Bugs and grasshoppers are popping up and twirling all around me. The blueberries I'm picking are very dry. I blow on a handful. No good, the berries just fly off my hand.

"Where are you? We're going now," someone calls.

Oh, good. I wipe the back of my hand over my forehead. Barbara and Vera are already running down the sandy hill ahead of me. I glance at the graveyard at the far end of the clearing beneath a tall stand of pine trees; I don't like this place much. I run after Barbara and Vera, showering sand and stones over their shoes. Barbara glares at me, "Here, take this bowl and don't spill the berries."

Handing her my cup, I take the big bowlful of blueberries and walk carefully behind them. I can feel the sweat trickle down the side of my ear. My nose is itchy. I try to hold the bowl with one hand but it's too heavy. My hands are sweaty and my nose is really itching. I stop and gently rub my nose against a twig from a nearby bush. Ah, good. "Come on, hurry up! There's a train coming. Let's cross the tracks before it gets here," yells Barbara.

Half running, we scramble up the sandy bank to the railway track. Annie and Maggie are laughing and racing down the path on the other side already. I can hear the train coming. I jump over one rail, then I trip. The bowl goes flying, hits the other rail, and blueberries bounce and roll everywhere. I glance up in time to see Barbara's murderous eyes on me. I scramble up and run away as fast as I can down the middle of the railway tracks. I can hear Barbara behind me. I glance back. She's yelling at me and getting closer. I try to match my steps to the railway ties down the track. I can still hear Barbara almost breathing down my neck, still screaming at me. I'm scared she's going to beat me this time. Oh gosh, she's going to catch me and I make a last desperate lunge. I feel my foot hitting the gravel between the ties. My ankle! Then I feel Barbara's hand clamp down over my shoulder and jerk me clear off the track. I practically fly over the side gravel, my feet touching the ground beside Barbara's when the train screams by, roaring in earth-shattering closeness. Its wind whips my breath away as I scramble down the sandy bank behind Barbara. I stand, trembling from head to foot. Several yards ahead of me, Barbara sways, bending over, gasping for breath.

The train rattles by and goes around the bend. Barbara fixes a strange look at me for a second before she turns away without a word and walks through the bush towards our cabin. Neither of us speak, while I follow several yards behind her, all the way home. The other girls are already home and I hear Mom's raised voice as she comes running out to meet us. Barbara starts to say something to Mom but it comes out in a painful whisper; she's lost her voice from yelling so hard. They're really mad at me. I move away and walk toward the lake. Hey, Wess is over at the point. I take off at a run down the path that goes around the lake.

I emerge from the path slowly. He stands there, very slim and tall. His curly brown hair lies neat and shiny on his head. He came back from the sanitorium just the other day. His face is so white without his tan. He turns and smiles, "Come here. See if you can hit that piece of metal by the shore across the bay." He holds the gun out toward me. Hesitantly, I take the gun. I've never held a gun before. This is the .22 that Mom usually has hidden under the bed.

My heart starts to pound as I lift it to my shoulder. Following his instructions, I make sure the sights are lined up right and hold my breath. Then closing my eyes, I pull the trigger. My eyes pop open at the crack of the shot. "Did I hit it? Huh? Did I?" I ask.

Wess chuckles and says, "Did you hear it hit since you had your eyes closed?"

"No," I answer.

"Want to try again? Why are you shaking?" he asks.

Handing the gun back, I ask, "Did you hear the train whistle?"

He takes the gun and aims. "Yeah, I heard it. Long whistle at the wrong place. Kids maybe," he says, and shoots. The shot hits its mark. We both hear the metal.

"That was me on the tracks." He looks at me a second, then stands to aim at the metal again. "I dropped the blueberry bowl and I thought Barbara was going to hit me, so I ran away. I forgot about the train coming. She pulled me off the tracks."

Crack, another hit on the metal. "So, you figure everyone's mad at you over there, now?" he chuckles and turns to look at me. Miserably, I nod. "Go home," he says, moving away as if he has completely forgotten about me. I stand there a moment before I turn and slowly walk back home.

I approach the cabin quietly. No noise. The door is open though. I stop at the door. Mom turns from the window and slowly looks me up and down. There's a strange expression on her face. Then she says, "Why are you standing there? Come in and have your lunch."

I'm hungry. I smell the oranges as soon as I enter the cabin. "Mom, when did you go to the store?" I ask, eyeing the loaves of white bread, cookies and oranges on the table.

"While you girls were out picking berries. Sit down and eat your lunch first," she says, filling a bowl of stew.

"Mom, do you know what the storekeeper said to me yesterday? He asked, "How old are you, eleventeen?" I giggle until I realize that Mom doesn't understand the joke. Oh well. "Where's everybody?" I ask.

"Gone to the store," she answers. She takes up her sewing on the bed by the window again and sighs.

Wess comes in and I watch him put the gun away. "Shoots good. Nothing wrong with it. Just needed some cleaning. Get the tea pot," he says to me, sitting down on the bench beside me.

I jump up and get the teapot from the stove and carefully put it on the table in front of him. I sit back down on the bench beside him. Thud! I land right on the floor with all my weight on my seat. He's moved the bench away. All right, so I forgot. He's killing himself laughing at me and Mom's shaking her head at him. Smiling, I get up and tightly hold the bench to sit down again. Wess helps himself to a bowl of stew and conversation starts up again.

The girls are coming back; I can hear them from a long way off. Soon, their laughter and merry voices vibrate the wall of the cabin while they eat their lunch. I grab an orange and decide to go look for someone to play with.

Looking from the highest rock along the shoreline, I can see a kid with a stick at the end of the dock. It's probably Ben. He always hangs around there. I take off at a run dodging low branches and watching for roots and rocks on the path. I'm puffing and sweating when I arrive at the foot of the dock. "What are you doing?"

Ben looks up and says, "There's a pot down there in the water that looks like it doesn't even have a hole in it. Maybe my mother could use it." After many attempts, he finally throws down his stick. "Forget it, it keeps slipping off. I'll get it later. Come on, I want to show you something."

We run up the path from the lake, to the railroad tracks and over, pausing for breath. We near the stunted pines, growing in the sandy soil, then turn towards an old abandoned cabin further into the bush. Approaching the old cabin, I hear a squealing noise. The door and windows are open holes, though the roof still looks solid. Ben drops down on his hands and knees beside the broken porch steps. There's a hole underneath. I drop down beside him. That's where the noise is coming from. Ben turns, "There are puppies in there. I heard them yesterday morning. I waited and waited for the mother. She's gone. See? I left this string across, so I'd know if she came back. She'd knock it down but it's still here. I have to get them out." He wriggles under the steps. Puffs of dust and rotten smells rise. Then Ben's hand comes down his side and he pushes a little black puppy down his leg till I can reach it. The puppy is very dusty and dirty. Ben is wriggling out now, bringing out another one, it's black and white, and cute! The stench is so strong now.

"Let's go," he says, as he sits up, "there's something rotting in there. I couldn't see—too dark. Maybe it's the mother or some dead puppies. Here." He hands me the black and white puppy. "This is a male. Maybe j your mother will let you keep it." He takes the black one from me. "This one is a female. I'll try to find someone to take it. My dad would kill it if I took it home. I have four dogs already. One had puppies and my father killed them all." His voice trails off while he looks around, thinking.

The puppy is trying to suck my fingers. "I have an idea! Uncle Daniel, he'll help us! At least, we could wash them there, eh?" I suggest. "Come on."

Back down the hill, along the sandpit by the railway tracks, past the C.N. water pump and up the path we go. Oh good, Uncle Daniel is outside sitting in the shade at the corner of his cabin, smoking a cigarette. We run up breathlessly and drop down beside him. I ask, "Uncle Daniel, can we use your tub, some soap and an old rag to dry them? These puppies are filthy!"

"Well now, where did you get these pups from?" he chuckles and runs his hand over my puppy's head.

Ben fills him in while I get a pan and soap. Soon we are scrubbing the puppies in the tub and drying them off with an old shirt. They are so thirsty, they lick the water that splashes on their noses. After much encouragement, they began to lick the water off our fingers. Uncle Daniel figures they're much younger than we first thought. They will not be able to drink or eat on their own yet. They are so thirsty and starving that they hardly move. My puppy, content with a warm bath is asleep in my arms. Uncle Daniel offers to keep the other puppy in the house providing Ben comes by every day to look after it.

Problem settled, Ben walks with me with a big smile on his face, back to the store, where he turns off towards his home. Slowly walking home, I croon to the warm little puppy in my arms. Poor puppy, I'll look after you, play with you, feed you and love you lots. You will be all mine. All mine. My very own dog. I'll give you a nice name, too. I'll take you home and put you to bed. But when I reach the door, Wess stands there. He doesn't look too friendly. "Where did you get that? Turn around and take it back. Mom will never let you keep it. You wouldn't look after it!"

I feel my arms stretch out, holding up my treasure and I hear my voice say, "Here, he's yours. It's your puppy. It's a male."

Wess stares at the pup and his face softens. Reaching out to cuddle the pup to his chest, he whirls around and I hear him order, "Milk, syrup and some warm water."

Barbara's voice comes, "It's not even weaned yet! Wait, I still have Cora's old juice bottle with a nipple on it." I'm hit by a pile of questions about the puppy.

Later that evening, we sit around talking after supper, and Wess starts playing his guitar and singing a song we always hear on the radio.

Annie and Vera put a white sheet over the doorway to the back room. They get Wess to straddle the bench with his guitar. Then they stand behind him with the coal oil lamp and Wess's shadow is on the sheet. Slowly moving, rolling, like a cowboy on a horse, he sings a song. Riding along, like in the western movies. Oh, that looks nice. Mom claps her hands in delight. When he's done, we all yell, "Wess, sing another cowboy song!"

When he's halfway through another song, Aunty comes in and sits down beside Mom. We all ask for more songs. Vera and Annie are taking turns with the lamp. I pick up the clean puppy with the full tummy from his soft warm sleeping box and cuddle him. Then a man and his wife stop by. They were passing by and heard the singing. They smile when they see Wess. When the song ends, the woman whispers, "We heard him singing from the road. Oh, he sounds just like the singer on the radio!"

Wess turns and a look of surprise crosses his face when he sees the unexpected number of people he has for an audience. Smiling, he slowly stands up and says, "Show's over, folks!" Then he ducks into the room behind the sheet curtain.

Giggling, I gently put the puppy back in its box.

18

JUST TAGGING ALONG

Fall 1963

When are we going home? I'm hungry. I glance at the cabin again for the sixth time. Mom is in there cleaning up the cabin for the new widow. Her husband died the other day. There are boxes and boxes of the old man's things piled beside the door. When Mom's finished cleaning up, other ladies will come and take whatever they need of the old man's things from the boxes.

"Come and get something to eat," says the old lady, sticking her head out the door.

Freddy says, "She looks like a witch. Her hair's all over the place. Father always wanted her hair nice. Now, look at her!"

What a weird thing to say. He's sixteen years old and he seems okay. We've been shooting birds with his slingshot. He thinks I'm a pretty good shot, for a girl.

"I don't even remember when my father died," I offer. "I remember when I use to sit on his knee by the wood stove, but I just don't remember the day he died. Or the funeral. Or anything." My voice trails off.

He shrugs, saying, "You were only a little kid then, but I have to look after a mother and little sister now, don't I?"

I shrug and both of us shuffle off towards the cabin, not knowing what else to say. I don't want to enter a room where someone has just recently died. But his mother is at the door, handing us a bowlful of creamed corn and a slice of bread. I take the bowl and think, "Yuck! Of all the things on the shelves at the store, the one thing I cannot eat is creamed corn." Sitting down on the steps beside Freddy, I stare at the bowl in my hand. I'm so hungry! I dunk the bread in the corn and take a little nibble. Not bad. Then I'm gulping it all up and mopping the sides with the last of the bread. Boy, that was delicious. I grin at Freddy, "You know? That was the best lunch I've ever had."

He shakes his head at me and laughs. "I saw a partridge up on the hill yesterday. Want to see if we can find it?" he asks.

I follow him towards the hill behind the cabin. It's cool here in the shade of the dense bush. Leaves rustle under our feet. There's no sun. Orange and brown leaves flutter occasionally overhead. Birds chirp to the left. The air is heavy with rotting leaves and damp earth. The ground is getting swampy here. "How do you know where to look? It could be anywhere now," I say.

"They don't usually go very far in one day unless something scared it off," he says.

I stop. I don't like this place. It's dark, cold and damp, and my runners are getting wet.

Freddy stops and turns, "What's the matter?"

"My feet are getting wet. You going into the swamp?" I ask.

Freddy starts walking again. "No. We'll veer off here and up the hill. It's shorter this way."

I follow, keeping up with every step he takes. Twigs tug at my hair, slap my face and scratch my cheeks and ears. I'm getting mad. We're continually going uphill now. My heart pounds in my chest from the exertion. I jump over a fallen log and duck under overhanging branches. Moss slips off the rock under my feet. The ground is starting to level off now. Lonely pine trees stand tall and sparse with fewer, longer branches on them. A light drizzle begins. What a miserable day. Suddenly, Freddie stops, lifting up a hand for silence, then he's walking again. My shoes are wet and covered with dirt and twigs are clinging to my socks. This is just getting ridiculous. "Hey, I'm turning around." I stop.

Freddy beckons me forward and points up a tree. There it is, the partridge. Freddy looks around at the little trees and branches on the ground. Finally, he picks out a dry skinny tree, about two inches wide and very tall. He breaks off the top and pulls out a small rabbit snare wire from his pocket. Quickly, he ties it to the tip of the pole. The partridge is still up there, turning its head occasionally. Slowly, Freddy extends the pole. The loop is now nearing the partridge. He misses. Slowly, the pole inches towards the partridge again and misses again. I sit down on a stump. Amid a flutter of wings, the partridge lands on another tree. Slowly, we approach it again. Again, the loop misses the head. I begin to feel a chill creeping up my back. I'm getting cold. The drizzle doesn't stop and my head is getting wet. My sweater is also wet across my back. Switching from one foot to another, I wait. Freddy doesn't move except for his hands holding the pole so steadily. Oh look, the loop has slipped over the partridge's head! Immediately, the pole comes down with the partridge and Freddy pounces on it! Wings thunder and beat frantically all over Freddy's arms and face. With feathers flying all around him, he does a dance and whoops and shouts while I laugh and clap my hands in delight. I've never seen anything like that.

The wings are still now. Freddy is holding the partridge by the feet, extending it to me. Blood is dripping from the beak. I take it and feel its warmth under the feathers which I start plucking. "Do you come here often?" I ask.

Freddy pauses a moment. "I started coming here when Dad got sick."

The partridge skin is ripping, shucks. The skin is always so thin on the back. Leaving the feathers on the ground where they fall, I throw the defeathered partridge back at Freddy. He spins around in time to catch it and laughs. "I'm getting cold. Let's go," I say.

Back down the hill we race. It seems like a shorter distance coming down than it did going up. We are back at his cabin already. I race by the cabin and down the road waving my hand. I glance back. Freddy is still standing by the doorway holding the partridge. I run on.

As soon as I come through the door, Barbara yells at me, "Where have you been? It's evening and Mom hasn't seen you since you left this afternoon with Freddy!"

I'm puzzled. "We killed a partridge on the hill."

She throws a towel at me which misses my head and continues to yell, "You may be eleven years old but you sure don't look it. Just you remember that."

What's going on anyway? What did I do wrong? What's she so mad about? She gone crazy or something? And what's my age got to do with anything, anyways? Oh shucks, forget it. Mom is sitting by the bed sewing with the beads, making such a nice pattern. Why doesn't she say something?

She glances up at me. "Annie went on the train this afternoon to see your brother, Dave. I thought to send you, too, but you weren't here."

I feel like crying. I turn around and go back out the door. I jump down off the porch. Is it fall already? Annie. Annie is with our oldest brother Dave now. When he comes, he always takes her away with him. Sometimes when he comes to visit, he makes a mistake and calls me Annie. "Thanks, Annie," he says when I rush to do something for him. Annie. Always Annie. She spends a lot of time with Wess now, too. Mom wants her to go to school with me in the fall because Vera is in the sanitorium with T.B. now. I go back inside and scramble onto the top bunk. At least this bunk is mine when she's not home.

Third month into the school year and the thrill and excitement is still there. Annie dresses me with her spare clothes and lets me tag along with her and Rita. Come to think of it, she's taken all my old friends, too, and now I'm always just tagging along, but I don't mind. She's shown me all kinds of things with clothes and hairstyles that I didn't know before. I didn't even know what a hairstyle was.

Wess comes home once in a while. He works on the railroad now. He tried one of his tricks once when everyone was getting ready for church. He saw blouses hanging freshly ironed and starched all ready to wear to church. Thinking they were ours, he grabbed one and blew his nose on it. It turned out to be one of Mom's. Boy, she was mad. I loved it.

Then one day he put on Mom's black dress when she had gone to visit next door. The dress hung on him like a minister's gown. Folding a long white scarf, he draped it around his neck with each end hanging down on each side of his chest. Very solemnly opening one of Mom's bibles, he stood up on the bench and had us all seated on the floor in front of him. Clearing his throat, silence fell on his eager audience. He was right in the middle of a heated, loud, hell-fire sermon when Mom walked in. Oh boy, he scrambled off that bench pretty fast. Mom screeched at him something awful for playing with the sacred image of a minister. I laughed. Oh, never will I forget that!

On cold autumn days, Annie, Rita and I would wet our hair over our foreheads and push it back into a wave and walk out into the freezing mornings. By the time we got to the front door of the school, our hair was frozen into shape and white with frost!

Then would come mornings when I didn't want to go to school. Those were the times when Wess was home and he would have to push me all the way to school, every step of the way! One morning, after pushing me all the way to school, there, tacked on the school door was a sign saying: "Due To Oil-Stove Freeze-Up, There Will Be No School Today." Laughing, I chased him all the way home.

A duck fell in our school chimney this fall, too. Everyone wondered what was making all that noise in the chimney till the teacher opened the air vent and banged the chimney and out fell a duck. It flew away into the woods when Teacher took it out. All we saw was a black bird with a duck's bill and webbed feet. We never knew what colour it was supposed to be or what kind of duck it was.

Last week, Annie and another girl drank some wine at the girl's house when her parents were drunk. I got there just as Annie and the girl were locking the door after her parents were asleep. Annie and I slept at the girl's place that night. The next morning we saw some police standing around at the store. So Annie and the girl decided to run away till the police left. They thought the police had come to get them because of the wine they had drank. I followed them off into the bush, across the swamp, over the hill, out onto a bay and across the lake to an island. I nearly froze my toes.

That was around the time they stopped handing out the vitamin biscuits and introduced large, red, oblong vitamin pills. Everyone gagged and couldn't swallow them. It got to the point where the whole classroom demanded that the teacher's kids take their's first. The new teacher had three kids, and much to our delight, all of them couldn't swallow the inch-long pills. We were forced to accept one teaspoon of cod liver oil a day instead. All the kids grumbled again. We eat a lot of fresh fish every week and we still have to take a teaspoon of rancid, rotten fish oil. That's just plain craziness. Rotten fish grease!

Annie's been ordering things from the catalogue ever since she's come home. A couple of weeks ago, another one of Annie's orders came. It was linoleum in a lime green design. We all had picked that particular one from all the others in the catalogue. So, one afternoon, Mom came home from the store with the roll of linoleum over her shoulders. That night, when we laid it out and nailed it down on the boarded floor, quite without warning, our door flew open and in sailed the Joker. He landed flat on his back, sliding across the floor and half disappearing under the double bed in the corner of the room. We all roared, laughing hilariously. I never saw anything so funny. My tummy hurt.

Mom quickly put a rug by the door and warned anyone coming in to be careful. Snow-covered moccasins were especially treacherous on the new linoleum floor.

19

NEW EXPERIENCES

Fall 1963

One day, the way-freight delivered two big boxes marked: Indian Day School. The boys lugged them to the school and we all held our breath when the teacher slowly cut the box tops open. What are those? Shoes? No, they've got blades on them. Skates. Skates for us? Where did they come from? Who sent them? Suddenly, the room explodes with giggles and laughter. Runty Ben stands clutching a pair of fourteen-inch long men's skates to his chest. His eyes glow and a wide smile lights up his face. The teacher takes the big skates away from him and places a shiny black pair of boy's skates in his hands. Then the room vibrates with running feet, squeals of delight, when the girls discover some ladies' skates at the bottom of the last box. I stop to watch all the kids going crazy until the teacher says to me, "Don't you want a pair? Better hurry."

I run to the box and find myself digging with Brian and Tony. All the girls stand at the side, each holding a pair of skates. Finally, Brian says, "Ain't no more girl's skates here. Take a pair of men's skates. You got big feet."

I feel my eyes smarting. Then I find a large pair of lady's skates. These are soft, brown leather so well-worn that they are flat to the heels. But at least they're women's skates. I grab them and stand back in line with the girls. Class is dismissed and we all rush home with our treasures. I clean my skates and pack the four-inch space at the toe with a wad of paper and shove cardboard paper around the ankles. That evening everyone is out on the ice shovelling back the snow to form endless circles and wavy roads around the island and clear across the lake. My legs hurt, my feet hurt, my ankles hurt — all my muscles are sore. Ben comes up beside me by our waterhole. Slowly, we walk up the path to our cabin helping each other over the steps and into the cabin. Mom glances up with a grin on her face, "You guys look like you've travelled many miles. Warm up and have a cup of tea. Looks to me like you two spent more time on your hands and knees or flat on your backs, than you did on your feet." Then she begins to giggle.

Grinning at Ben, I pull off my skates. It's getting dark out there. I can see flashlights out there on the ice from the bigger boys still shovelling. Even the fathers are skating around out there or shovelling the snow for the skaters. Ben looks up from his teacup, "See those clouds over there? Hope it doesn't snow."

I hadn't considered that possibility. I don't want snow falling now. I wish someone could stop the snow, change the weather. All my life, the weather came and went. We took what came and never gave it a thought. I look at the clouds and think, "Go away! Please don't snow." In the summer, when it poured rain, we found shelter. If we happened to be out on the lake and the wind came up, we simply pulled into a bay until the wind died down or until the canoe could take the waves. If we were out in winter and a blizzard hit, we found shelter and stayed there till the storm was over. I turn to Ben and grin, "Well, if it snows, we'll just have to shovel it aside, again."

Ben smiles and says, "Well, I better go home. I'll come here first tomorrow before I go skating."

I return his smile, "I'll be ready."

Mom says from the bed, "Remember, tomorrow's a school day." Ben leaves and I pull off my four pairs of socks, moaning, "Oh my butt hurts, my elbow hurts, my knees hurt, my hips hurt and I think I have a large lump on my head."

I crawl into the top bunk. Brian and Tony are arguing in the next room. They didn't last out on the ice very long. Tony's skates hit Brian on the forehead when he went flying off his feet, and now Brian has a bandage on it. It's just a small cut. Annie and Rita are still out there somewhere skating with Ross and Jed.

The next morning before the sun rises, I'm up with Mom and gobble down my porridge. I repack the tips of my skates, pull on layers of socks and wait for Ben. I'm drinking my second cup of coffee when I hear his footsteps cross the clearing outside. The boys are already up, too. Brian's bandage is stuck to the cut and he screams before Mom even touches it. What a spoiled brat.

I'm pulling on my skates and tying the long laces when Ben slowly pulls the door open. Mom glances at him and says, "Sit down and have something to eat before you go out there." Ben doesn't hesitate and sits down at the table to make short work of the steaming bowl of porridge, dunking a large piece of bannock with each bite. I sit and wait for him, just busting to get out on the ice again. Finally, out we go, slipping and sliding unsteadily down the lake. The ice swishes beneath our skates and down we go. By the time the sun is an inch above the tree line, we're skating confidently, back and forth. We discover a bend of the shovelled circle is quite close to the rink we'd made. Walking across in the snow, we find it is the tail end of the swirls and curvy trails the shovellers created last night. We follow the ice trail around behind the island. Two more complete circles and we reach the other end of the island.

Exhilarated and beaming, we're now skating quite well. We're even getting fancy, walking around the curves. Suddenly, Ben says, "Let's go, fast. School."

We take off, full speed, interrupted occasionally by undignified falls. We come around the island, just as Mom comes out of the cabin. We can hear her clearly in the morning stillness: "Come inside now. Get ready for school!"

Ben stops by each morning for breakfast and a quick skate before school. On weekends, he doesn't come inside. Sometimes, I don't see him all day. I learn later, that's when he has to cut and split wood to last all week.

Later, something else comes out of a box at school. First, Teacher lugs in a pine tree, sticks it into a pail and braces it against the corner. The kids laugh. It kind of looks ridiculous a pine tree in the corner, stuck in a water pail. We think the teacher's gone crazy. Who would ever bring a pine tree inside a room and stand it in a pail in the corner of the room? Wait till I tell Mom when I get home; she'll kill herself laughing. Now, the teacher's pouring water in the pail. Oh my tummy hurts from laughing. Does he think he's going to make it grow? Everyone is whispering back and forth in our language, watching Teacher's every move, laughing and giggling at each new action. Satisfied that the tree is secure he pulls out a box from behind his desk.

We wonder what he has in there. Now I know what he's doing. He's making the kind of tree that's in our books, the kind white people stand around at Christmas. A Christmas tree. But I hadn't thought those trees in the books were real. I poke Ben and say, "It's probably a Christmas tree. You know, like the ones in the books."

Ben looks at me doubtfully, then says, "The ones in our books have all kinds of things sticking to them or hanging on the branches. And besides, the ones in our books are just made-up trees, not real ones like this one!"

The box is open now and we all stand around waiting to see what the teacher will pull out. First comes wads of newspaper stuffing from around the sides, then a box. Teacher opens the lid. We all gasp, when he picks up a shiny, glistening, glittering ball. There are others, red, green, yellow, blue; they're so beautiful. Teacher hands out the balls, one by one, to the girls, instructing where they are to be hung on the tree. Strings of glittering foil and tinsel that shimmer and sway with each movement are handed out to the boys. Laughing and giggling, we decorate the tree with great respect. For the tree is no longer an ordinary outside tree, it's now a real Christmas tree.

That evening, we set out to cut our own Christmas tree for our home. We place it by the window. Mom looks at us but doesn't say anything.

We string up colourful materials such as strips of shiny, colourful foil wrappers from candies and we cut designs from shiny coffee liner bags. Our tree looks great: not as good as the one at school, but it is beautiful just the same.

Some of the parents peek in the school windows to see the Christmas tree. Then on the last day of school, Teacher walks in with a bag over his shoulder and puts packages under the Christmas tree. But we can't touch them. That evening, all the parents are called to the school and, there, the teacher hands out the presents to the school kids and candy to the little ones. Mom and the other mothers ask where the gifts came from and we learn they came from the churches in a city somewhere. I get a doll — such a beautiful doll, with yellow hair and it has on a beautiful blue dress, just like her eyes.

I'm getting sleepy. I yawn, snuggling deeper into my blankets and hugging my doll closer to me. She is now wrapped tightly in a moss bag which laces up the front. Slowly, the lights sway and flicker across the ceiling — reds, greens, blues and yellows from the tree's decorations. Every crackle of the roaring wood stove sends more lights through the holes around the airvent which reflects off the Christmas foil stringers on the ceiling to every corner of the room.

Tomorrow is Christmas. I am twelve years old now. And we'll find candies at the foot of our beds in the morning. Slowly, I fall asleep to the sounds of people breathing softly and the flickering lights from the wood stove.

All the young people and grown-ups are out on the ice. Some are skating, some are just walking around while others are still shovelling the snow, making new trails. The sun has gone down and it's getting cold. I wrap another scarf over the other one before I push the door open. There stands Ben and we head down to the lake. People are everywhere. Hand in hand, we start out, pulling each other forward alternating left and right, round and round, then left and right again, along the curved trails. Some trails are zigzags which are quickly being rounded out by the skaters who can't quite make the sharp corners. In the middle of the joining trails stands a huge snow pile. Ben and I scramble up to rest. We glance at each other and begin digging and piling the snow. When we are done, we climb down to look back up at our work. There stands a giant throne. It's a big chair which can seat four people and it has a backrest, too. We skate around the chair and decide to check out the crowd behind the island. As we approach, we see a long string of people skating, each holding onto a scarf or rope from the person at the front. Oh, that looks like fun.

“Here, I have a scarf. Grab hold and I’ll hang onto the person at the end,” I yell. Men, women, boys and girls are swishing by us laughing and squealing. As the end of the long line comes in sight, we get ready.

Maggie’s at the end. She whips out her belt and yells, “Grab on!”

I grab it and feel the pull that nearly knocks me off my feet. I struggle to maintain my balance as I fly behind the long line. A straight stretch gives me a breather, long enough to remember Ben. I glance back. He’s skating flat out, yelling at me for my scarf. I still clutch the end of it so I fling it out to him as we sweep around another corner. I glance back and Ben is still trying to grab it. Finally, he’s got it. I feel the added weight behind me and, immediately I feel stable. But Ben’s got problems. Here comes a zigzag corner. Oh gosh, we’re going too fast. Ben and I find ourselves upside down in a snowbank.

My arm hurts, my head hurts and I think my left foot hurts. I can’t tell. Maybe it’s frozen. Ben scrambles over to me, peers at my face and asks if I’m hurt. His toque has come off and his hair has chunks of snow stuck on it.

Giggling, I shake my head and answer, “No, I’m okay.”

He lays back down beside me and we look up at the moon. The clouds are gone. They’ve got another line going again and some of them have flashlights. The beams are streaming about on the ice. It sure looks nice. “I’m getting cold. Let’s go to my cabin and get something to drink. I don’t know if my foot is frozen or not.” I scramble to my feet. About halfway across the lake, we decide to take a shortcut across the bay, past Sarah’s cabin.

Bobby’s coming across the lake with a flashlight. “Here, grab on,” he says, flinging the end of a coiled rope, draped over his shoulder. I pass the end to Ben and we hitch a ride home. Bobby isn’t skating too fast, just warming up, he says. It saves us a walk and we let go when we pass our water hole. Bobby waves and skates back out to join a double line now forming by the island.

They’re really making a lot of noise out there. The whole community must be out there. As we approach my cabin, the door opens and out comes Barbara, Annie and Mom — on skates. Being supported on both sides, Mom comes down the path, slowly and carefully. Well, we can’t miss out on this. Ben and I scramble out of the way and get ahead of them onto the ice. We skate circles around Mom, as she stands there teetering on her skates. Everyone is laughing while Mom tries to move her feet forward without them taking off on their own. I come skating up behind her, when suddenly, her great form escapes the supporting hands and down she goes right on top of me. I feel the jarring impact on my back when I hit the ice and lay there quite stunned. She sits up to examine me. “Are you all right?” she asks.

"Yeah, I'm okay," I say shakily and try to back it up with a laugh. I sit up. Ouch! I gasp and roll over onto my belly. The others manage to get Mom back on her feet. She decides she has done her best and wants to get back inside before anyone else sees her with her feet up in the air.

Ben kneels down beside me and asks, "You got hurt, didn't you? Your leg?"

I shake my head. "It's my back. There's something wrong with my back. I can't sit up!" I gasp, rolling over to my side.

Ben sits and says thoughtfully, "I don't think you could move if you broke your back. You know, my mother fell down the steps once and she said she broke her tail."

I started giggling and say, "People don't have tails! What do you think I am, a dog?"

Ben looks at me with a straight face. "Of course not! You're not a dog! I know for sure you're an owl!"

I start to laugh. The pain is slowly receding. Maybe it will go away and I'll be all right. "Here, give me a hand. I'll stand up." On my knees and up I go. There's a throbbing pain in my lower back, right where I sit down. "I think I may have hurt the last bone down my back," I say.

Ben giggles and says, "That's what's called a tailbone. I'd say you broke your tailbone." He grins.

My face becomes grave. "Was your mother all right the next day?" I ask.

Ben looks at me. "I don't think you'll be able to skate for awhile. You may not be able to sit down at all tomorrow or for awhile after that."

I gasp, "What do you mean? You mean I have to lay down all the time? And how long is awhile? What about our skating tomorrow?"

Ben shrugs, "I don't know. Go and ask your mother."

We trudge up to the cabin in silence. When we enter the cabin, Mom is putting the skates on Barbara. Oh, I would dearly love to see this. But my tail tells me differently. I sit down on the bed and shoot up with a gasp. Gosh, that hurt. How am I going to take off my skates without sitting down? Ben is at the table, filling his face with bannock and jam and a cup of tea, so he can't help me. I gently lower myself down on the bed and stretch out on my tummy. That's much better. Then Mom is tugging at my skates, pulling them off."My goodness. You're feet are soaking wet! These soft leather skates are useless. You'd do better if you cut the blades off and tied them on your own boots! That's what people use to do long ago, you know."

Ben is grinning at me from the table, when I roll over to my side. He stands at the door pulling on his mitts before he goes out to join the merry band of skaters. They are still hooting and hollering out there.

Mom fills up the teapot again. "This is the third pot of tea I've made this evening" she says, glancing at me. It's a big pot and it's never empty during the day.

I smile and say, "That's because our cabin is the closest one for those skaters out there."

Mom turns from the window facing the lake, laughing. "I don't know if Barbara is having a better time at it than I did. Every time I look, she's just getting up!" she says, throwing more wood into the stove. I can hear people coming again and soon our cabin is filled with freezing, laughing, talking people. Some warm their hands at the stove and others light up cigarettes or snap open snuff boxes. I lay on the bunk, smiling and listening, thoroughly enjoying our unexpected company of skaters. The cabin is slowly filling with cigarette smoke and the steam from the six pairs of mitts by the stove. Then they're gone again, voices trailing back toward the lake. Mom mops up the melted snow by the door and refills the sugar bowl. There's another crowd coming. It's Barbara this time being helped up the steps by four other people. Soon, voices and laughter bounce off the walls again.

They keep coming, in and out, even after we're in bed. The door is left unlocked and the lights on since Annie and Maggie are still out there skating. Each time a group comes in, Mom just calls from the bed, "Make yourselves some tea," or, "Throw a couple of logs in the fire and have some tea."

And our outhouse is kept just as busy as our cabin!

One evening, with my tailbone sufficiently mended, I head out with Annie and Maggie when they go off to skate at a pond about a mile north of the railway tracks. They chase me off. "Stay home. You're too young; you'll get too tired. Go home!" they yell, throwing snowballs at me. I go home crying. They're going skating with all the teenagers and don't want to be bothered with me.

Well, I can just as well skate around here, I guess. Ben comes over and we skate backwards full speed and do figure eights on the ice till we're very tired. I crawl into bed totally exhausted. Mom is still sitting by the lamplight sewing beads on moccasins.

I've already drifted off to sleep when there's a knock on the door and the storekeeper's son pushes Annie inside. Annie walks like a zombie; she's very pale and she keeps swallowing and can't speak. She stops by the bed and sits down but doesn't say anything. Mom sits up from the bed and asks, "What's happened? Is she all right?"

The storekeeper's son answers, "She'll be okay. She's just very scared. We saw something out there in the sky. Goodnight." He leaves and all is still.

Mom gets up and throws some logs in the fire, then stops in front of Annie. Where's Maggie? I glance at the double bed by the window;

she's there sleeping. I didn't even hear her come in. Mom is helping Annie off with her jacket and sweaters. After handing her a hot cup of tea, she sits Annie down by the bed and asks again, "What's the matter? What was it you saw?"

Annie looks around the room and finally her gaze comes to rest on the basin. She points to the washbasin.

"Mom, pick up the basin and turn it over." Mom hesitantly crosses the room, spills out the water in the basin and turns it over, obviously puzzled. Then Annie says, "That's what it looked like! And it had lights, all colours of lights going around in circles, all around it."

There's a pause and Mom asks, "But where did it come from? This thing you saw?"

Annie stares at the basin again. "I was down on the ice, trying to break through with my skate to get some water. I could hear music from Liza's radio. They had a big fire, too. Then the radio went off. When I lifted my head, I saw this thing hovering over the ice. All the kids ran into the woods. I lay still. I couldn't move. It landed on the ice. The lights kept circling underneath the rim of the basin. Then, after awhile, it went up and paused a moment, then it just zipped across the sky and it was gone. When I was able to move, the fire was all burnt out — nothing but ashes, where the big bonfire was. Then all the kids started coming out of the bush. Liza was crying hysterically. Then we noticed the radio was on full blast again. I was so scared. Just so scared."

Mom looks at Annie a moment, then sighs, "Better get to bed; get some rest. Since you weren't the only one that saw this… this thing, then we'll probably hear all about it in the morning. Maybe they'll tell you what it was on the radio if you listen. They always know about these things on the radio. Probably some new airplane the white man's come up with."

Annie looks at the basin again. "It wasn't an airplane, Mom. White men didn't make it!"

I was lucky I wasn't there, but I would have loved to have seen it, too.

The next morning Annie rushes to the store, but comes home kicking the snow. There's no word. The storekeeper had called the nearest airport base to find out what it was the kids had seen, but there was nothing. They never saw anything there. Nobody knew anything about it.

We begin hanging around with Liza and Rita. They live close to each other. Sometimes we sleep at Rita's and other times we sleep at Liza's house. Liza's parents drink a lot, though. One day, we find a full bottle of wine. Liza takes a big swallow and passes it to Annie. Annie swallows quite a bit, too, and hands it to me. I take the bottle, hold my breath and swallow a couple of times. Yuck! It tastes like sour grape juice.

Again, it's handed to me and I swallow, just a little this time. It sends shivers down my back. After several more rounds, I'm barely taking sips, when the bottle is finally empty. My head feels funny, but otherwise, I feel fine. They find another half empty bottle and pass it around. I don't like this. I pass it to Liza, then it goes to Rita and on to Annie. Then Hanna comes in. They're getting really noisy now. I'm getting scared. There's something wrong here. The girls decide to go to Jed's house. Hanna says Jed's parents got off the train with wine, too. That's where Hanna got hers, from Jed. So off we go. Hanna isn't walking straight. She's falling down. Annie and Liza are laughing really hard and staggering and they pull Hanna along behind them. I follow behind. This is really wrong. I'm scared. Hanna won't get up. It's very cold. She doesn't even have any mitts on! Then Rita says, "Let's take Hanna home. I don't feel like dragging her all the way to Jed's!"

Agreed, we veer off toward Hanna's cabin. We open the door, trying not to be too loud. They leave her on the floor and we go back out. I'm still walking behind them. They're singing and laughing so loud. When we near Jed's cabin we stop. There's a big fight going on in there with loud voices arguing and screaming, breaking glass and crashing wood!

We decide to duck inside Uncle Daniel's cabin; he's not home. He's probably drunk somewhere. We sit there for a minute, when the door suddenly opens, and in walk Mom and Barbara. I'm so happy to see them. I smile and babble, "They're having a fight over there! We don't know where Uncle Daniel went." My hiccups are becoming annoying. Barbara is very mad and starts giving us a lecture and firing questions. I try to defend myself, "I didn't drink..." I hiccup.

She whirls around at me, declaring, "You didn't drink, eh? And you hiccuping like a drunk! Humph!"

I meant to say that I didn't drink very much. There's nothing wrong with me at all. My head has long since cleared. It's just these hiccups, that are causing me all the trouble. Anyway, I'm branded guilty along with the rest of the group. I may as well have finished the whole bottle myself. What's the difference? Well, the difference is that I knew it was wrong and I stopped.

All next day, they make fun of me, saying, "There was The Owl, hiccuping and saying, 'I never drank.' Hiccup!" They giggle and laugh. I'm mad. They don't say anything about Annie, Rita or Hanna or anybody else — only me! I stick out my tongue when no one's looking.

There's one thing I like about Sarah even if I don't particularly like the company she keeps on her scalp. Sarah always has a box of snuff in her pocket. I love it now and we both stick wads of snuff inside our lips every chance we get — recess, after school or anytime I'm with her. Her mother buys the snuff for her, but Mom would kill me if she found out I was taking it! It's much more interesting, that way. Everytime Mom gets after me for something, I go to Sarah for a chew of snuff and I feel good stuffing a wad under my lip thinking, "Okay, Mom, watch me!"

One thing I find unsettling is that I'm now towering five inches taller than Annie. I'm proud to look down my nose at her, but sorry to miss wearing all the clothes she's out-growing. I wear altered clothes from Mom and Barbara. And my feet — I'd hide them if I could. When I walk they stick way, way out in front. With each step I see my bony knocked-knees, then my big feet. How embarrassing. My legs are very long. My upper body hasn't grown much though; my chest is still flat and my waist and arms are still the same size. But from there on down, I'm all legs and feet. Yesterday, Mom noticed my bottom lip sticking out when I was pulling on my pants. After several questions, I finally answered, "My legs are too long!"

She laughed and said, "Well, don't worry. Your upper body will catch up soon!"

That was comforting. I won't be a kangaroo forever. But that still didn't make my long legs and big feet disappear.

Anyway, it's almost spring now. You can smell it in the air. The snow is getting soft, the birds are singing everywhere, the wind blows warmly from the south… . "Owl! I'm talking to you!" That's Mom, yelling at me through the door. Washday. Oh, I hate washdays. Javex, Javex, Javex! "Hurry up and get that pail of water I asked for!"

I grab the pail off the porch step and run to the lake. Hurry, hurry, get it over with, then it's all done. More time for fun. Run, run as fast as you can — each step with a word to match. It's great to be alive, breathing in all that fresh air!

"Owl! Get that pail of water up here right now!"

20

THE OUTHOUSE GANG

Summer 1964

Rita whispers, "Shhh, here she comes!" I part the tall grass and see Rita's mother outside the store. A beam of light from her flashlight passes over us and disappears down the path. Boy, it's dark tonight.

"Oh, look! It's Mom!" whispers Annie, beside me.

I can see a swinging light coming down the path through the tall stand of pines. Rita's mother has stopped at the corner of the store and stands there waiting for my mother. Together they walk to where light glows from the store window. Of course, we can't hear a word for right behind them is the constant putt-putt of the store generator. There's a scurrying movement behind us, then a tap on my shoulder. We fall face down flat on the ground, holding our breaths. Footsteps are approaching from up the path, swift and even. With whistling breath and swishing jacket, the person walks by, two feet away from our heads! The black shadow of the person nears the light at the store window and I know who she is. "Hanna, it's your mother!"

Three of our mothers are now standing around by the store window, talking. They're out there looking for us.

After a tug at my elbow and a hiss in my ear of "Let's go", I edge back into the dark bushes behind us. The mosquitoes are murderous! My ear feels really hot and swollen. I forgot to put some mosquito repellent there. My ankles are really stiff from a million lumps, too. Silently, we run and group together at the sand pit. Are we all here now? Yes, we are: Annie, Rita, Hanna, Maggie, Sarah, Liza, me, Freddy, Ross, Jed, Ben, Joe, Ted and Little Tommy. Ross tells of their escapade while we were lying in the grass waiting for their return. They had strung a rope outside the old white man's door and lifted his outhouse to set it back down on the other side of the hole, so he'll fall in the hole before he reaches the outhouse door. I giggle with the others but feel a bit guilty. The boys are getting nasty.

First, we rolled small rocks over the rooftops, making a lot of noise and waking the sleepers inside. Then we'd run when someone came to see who was doing that. A few times we put a pan or two of water outside a doorstep and waited for someone to finally come out for a trip to the outhouse. Then we'd take off, laughing our heads off. Imagine stumbling into pans of water in the dark when you're half asleep. Of course, we constantly raided the gardens too. We took carrots, radishes, turnips and rhubarb. Then we'd have to get sugar for the rhubarb, either from Rita's or Liza's place.

The moon comes out from behind the clouds. We're standing around talking and laughing, when someone notices Little Tommy and says, "Oh, my goodness! Would you look at the size of his right eye?"

"Can he see anything?"

"No, it's swollen shut!"

"Why did you rub it like that when the mosquito bit?"

"Probably got it several times by the looks of it!" We're really rolling with laughter now. My sides hurt. Gasping for breath, we flop down on the sand. Cigarettes are passed around. I take a pinch when the snuff box comes around. It's quiet. The generator has stopped. Frogs are chirping and crickets are buzzing; the night sounds are loud. "Why would they shut the generator off when the train hasn't come yet?" someone asks.

It must be very late. I bet it's way after midnight. But where's the train? It usually comes around eleven o'clock. No one has a watch. Ben used to bring a clock in his pocket but it ticked too loudly and one time his alarm went off and just about got the whole lot of us caught. "Let's sneak to Rita's cabin and see what the clock says," I suggest.

"Shhh!" someone whispers.

Sounds of rocks crunching come from the direction of the railway tracks. We can't see anything; the moon has gone behind the clouds again. It's very dark. There's more than one person. Someone whispers, "Hide!"

We all dash into the bushes, just as the moon emerges from behind the clouds again and shines full and bright on a huge black form coming down the path from the railroad. Totally immobilized, my face starts to tingle. Then suddenly, the shape changes. It's collapsing in the front. Then two pairs of legs are kicking in the air and curses and laughter erupt as the back end of the "bear" piles on top at the front, exposing another two pairs of legs from the tangled mass of black covering. Muffled voices from the unfortunate ones beneath are cursing. Annie grabs my arm and we sneak away quietly through the underbrush and down the other path. Once in the clear, we run all the way down to the lake, past Rita's house. I can feel the wind blowing through my hair. The thunder of our running feet dies when we near the big dock where we flop down and immediately burst out laughing. What are they going to think of next? They can't catch us so they tried to scare the heck out of us. We figure those were the young men who are supposed to put a stop to all the pranks we are playing on people.

Hey, where's Little Tommy? Oh, no! Who saw him last? Where is he? He was still running with us by Rita's house. Maybe he went home from there. He lives close by. We really have to watch that kid; he could tell on us. So far, nobody has seen any of us. They don't know for sure who's playing all the tricks on people. We just pretend we don't know when the older guys ask any of us anything. We shrug and say innocently, "I don't know." Some even think that people from the next town are sneaking around here to scare us.

I yawn. Rita yawns, Liza yawns, Hanna yawns and Annie and Maggie yawn together. We're wondering what happened to the train. Someone suggests, "The light is still on at your cabin, Rita. Why don't you go home and ask whoever's up why there's no train yet?"

Rita gets up slowly, stretches and yawns again. I get up, too. "I'll come with you. I'm thirsty." We walk slowly up the path. The moon is gone again. We hear voices. We stop together. Someone is by the outhouse. No, there are two people. It's the Town Joker and one of the young ladies. Who would have believed it? He's saying very embarrassing things to her. She's giggling.

"Let's go!" I whisper, on the verge of bursting into laughter. Hold on. Run, fast. There's the door and we run into Rita's cabin. The room is filled with cigarette smoke, people are sitting around a blanket-covered table playing poker. We rush to the bed and yank a blanket to our mouths to muffle our giggles, rocking back and forth, laughing, till our eyes water.

"What did The Joker say again?" I ask, and we cover our mouths again. Oh, my tummy hurts. Where's the water bucket? I'm thirsty. We sit down at the sidetable. Rita is eating a piece of bannock. I get a second cup of water. The door opens and The Joker walks in, alone. Immediately, water sprays from my mouth, all over the table. In surprise, I watch Rita wipe her face, then suddenly her mouth opens and out comes, a wailing screech before her voice breaks into laughter. I grab her arm and push her out the door and we lean against the wall outside, catching our breath. I can't stand this, not being able to laugh out loud. Suddenly, Rita yanks me around the corner of the cabin. Footsteps slowly approach and the door creaks open. We go to a window and look inside. It's the girl who was with The Joker. She's sitting quietly behind her mother who has a large stack of coins in front of her on the table. Where's The Joker? Oh, there he is, his back to the lady. He's laughing with one of the guys and watching the card game. Let's go tell the others. Wait, we're supposed to find out about the train, remember? Can we face The Joker and the girl without laughing? Not really, eh? Look. Someone is coming down the path from the store. It's an old man, probably coming to play cards, too. We wait by the door and ask if the train has come by yet.

"No. No train tonight. There was a train derailment far away. Probably won't be any trains tomorrow, either." He goes in.

We run down the path toward the lake. The moon is out again and the lake glistens like a sparkling, living thing. When we approach, we see a red tip of a cigarette. The low murmur of voices indicate the presence of... what did the teacher call us this spring — the Outhouse gang? Anyway, when he heard about the fall-in-the-toilet-hole trick, he said, "Someone must do something about the Outhouse Gang."

We played a couple of tricks on him, too. There was the one when he found female panties hanging on his clothesline which we had taken off someone else's line.

Giggling, we approach the group. Wait till they hear about The Joker. We sit down together in the middle of the group and ask for a pinch of snuff from Sarah's bottomless box of snuff and settle down to give our information.

We don't like going home until after the train has come and gone. So I guess we should go home since there's no train coming. One by one, we get up, each going off in different directions. Annie, Maggie, Sarah and I take the path along the lake. Oh, no. That stupid dog by the minister's house is barking his head off at us! The dog comes bounding down the path in front of us. Sarah steps off the path and we stop in the middle. Here he comes heading right for us. Sarah's foot shoots out. The dog whirls around and yelps in pain. Sarah got it right in the ribs. Giggling, we continue past the dog's territory. What a stupid dog. The same thing happens almost every night. He gets a kick in the ribs and he turns to run back home to the minister's porch.

Suddenly, Annie yanks my arm back. "Listen!" she hisses. We stop dead still. Someone's snoring. What's someone doing snoring by the lake, in the bush? "Shall we walk by or turn and go around?" comes Annie's whisper.

Maggie says, "There may be more than one person sleeping there."

Sarah suggests, "Let's see who's there with him."

Maggie says, "What if they wake up as we walk by them?"

I ask, "What if they're drunk?"

They all turn and look at me, "Oh course, they're drunk! No one sleeps out in the bush when they're sober!"

We all agree to backtrack a bit and go up the path, the dog's path, passed its porch and down the path by the Catholic church to our place. The moon is gone now and we can't see a break in the clouds anymore. Sarah grumbles at the total darkness. A distant thunder is rumbling across the lake. "Oh boy! Did you see that lightning over there?"

The dog remains quiet when we walk by. I'm glad we are going home. I'm very tired. We start running softly, feet falling on the side of the road on the soft grass. There's our cabin. Sarah continues on toward her cabin. She still has a way to go. We walk noiselessly across the porch step and slowly ease the door open. One by one, we sneak in. The smell of mosquito repellent spray hangs in the room. We gently close the door again. I hear Annie slowly lowering herself into the bottom bunk. Maggie and I feel our way along the length of the double bed by the window. "Did you lock the door?" I whisper.

Maggie stops. "No, I forgot." Slowly, she makes her way back to the door and slowly pulls the bar over the hook, securing the door shut. Slowly and softly, we pull our shoes off. Oh, what stinks? Maggie's feet always stink so bad. The bed creaks as Maggie crawls over the sleeping Tony. I lay down on the edge. Oh, it feels so good! Now, I can hear everyone's soft breathing. Barbara is gently snoring, Vera is softly breathing. She just came home this spring.

It was on that day, Annie, Maggie, Sarah, Rita, Hanna and I had skipped school. We decided to go catch some suckers at a little stream which runs under the railway tracks about three miles away. Oh, we had a lot of fun. We never even noticed the teacher coming down the tracks till he was upon us. We just stood there looking up at him on the tracks. All around us suckers were flipping. We were down by the culvert. I thought for sure we were going to get it. He stood there looking at us, then smiled, "Annie and you…" He pointed a stick at me. "I came to tell you that Vera got off the train, today. Now, don't forget, it's a school day again tomorrow."

Then he continued down the tracks. Oh boy. Vera was home. "I'm going to run home right now," I yelled over my shoulder, scrambling up the gravel shoulder to the tracks.

I ran, first trying to match my steps to the tarred ties. It didn't work. I tried to run on the sandy shoulders, but that was very uneven and sometimes not there at all. Finally I found a spot, just at the tip of the ties. My sides started to hurt. Passing the rock cut, the pain in my sides slowly receded. My breathing was coming very hard, hurting my throat. I passed the switch and neared the other rock cut. It was very dark, deep and gloomy there. I couldn't hear any trains coming. It seems like there was only about a six foot space between the rock cliff and the tracks. Finally, I was out in the open again. My breath was coming easier. My legs and feet were going at a steady pace, not breaking stride. Gee, this was a wonderful, strange feeling. I was almost comfortable. My breath was coming evenly. I could see the train station about a mile and a half away. I watched the ground blur by beneath me. I had to change my stride for up ahead I could see that my running space was gone. When I broke the rhythm, I had to struggle again. The road shoulder had very soft sand with a few tufts of weeds growing here and there. I was almost home.

Soon I passed the section house, then the station. Next I passed the store and the Catholic church where I began slowing down. Slower still by Aunty's cabin. Her door was wide open and I slowed even more. I headed for the tree by the lake and threw myself down on my back. My legs were trembling. My heart was slowing down but still pounded loudly in my ears. Voices were at the door of the cabin. There was Vera, coming out with Barbara.

Springing up, I ran to them, exclaiming, "I ran all the way from Worth's Trail. Three miles! I didn't even stop at all!"

Barbara elbowed by me, "Get out of the way! Where's Annie and Maggie? You girls weren't at school today!"

Vera smiled at me. "Do you realize we're both the same height now? Good Lord! Look how you've grown!"

Barbara pointed at my feet and laughed. "About the only thing I see that's grown are her legs and feet!"

I ran inside the cabin. I was very, very thirsty.

Well, I am very itchy from a million mosquito bites. I shut my eyes tight.

21

THE LAST ROW

Fall 1964

Mom hums under her breath. It's very calm on the lake. In the evening sun, the lake shines like a mirror. I can see the clear reflection of trees on the island. Smoke from the camp fire gets in my eyes. Mom always lights the fire in the evening. She's drying trout over the open fire by smoking the fish, which she'll pack away for later. We have only one dog left, Rosiak. The man across the lake needs a lead dog on his team and has been asking Mom for her. Mom says that this fall she'll let him have her. She says we can't afford to feed her anymore. Rosiak lies on her side occasionally flicking her ear against the flies which continually buzz around her head. Laughter erupts from the cabin again. We have a record player now and there's music in the cabin most of the time.

Vera is in there with Greg. They're getting married in the fall. Wess has already married Laura and she's at his side most of the time when he comes home. Annie's gone with Barbara and her husband, Allan, to a place down the tracks where he works. Maggie's gone to live with her mother. The only ones left here now are Brian, Tony and me. I find myself spending a lot of time with Mom which is strange but nice. I help her with the fishnet that she's making, sew the beads on the moccasins she's sewing, scrape the moose hide when she gets too tired and clean the fish for her while she starts the fire. I never realized that fish could be cleaned in so many ways.

Mom pokes me and says, "Here he comes again!"

I look up to see Greg's friend, Jere. Whenever he finds out that Greg is here, he comes down to see him from where he works. He hung around Annie quite a bit but she didn't like him. Annie likes Ross now or maybe has as long as I can remember. Anyway, Annie was always running away from Jere. Now she's gone and he still comes. Mom smiles at him and says, "They're all inside."

Jere walks by. His hair shines light brown in the setting sun. He looks nice. I've never noticed that before.

The fish are all done and Mom goes next door to see Aunty. I sit down on the swing. The knots up on that branch don't look too secure so I scramble up the tree, edge along the branch and tie several more knots. I slide back down and jump the last four feet to the ground. I hear a chuckle from the open doorway. It's Jere, looking at me, smiling. I sit down on the swing again feeling suddenly quite shy. Imagine him watching me when I thought there was no one around. The music in there is still quite loud. I don't bother going in when they're in there. Suddenly, I feel a pair of hands grip the seat of the swing and pull back. Released, I sail away, free and far only to swing back to the same pair of hands. I giggle and glance back. "Higher!" I yell.

He laughs again and pushes harder. Away I go, higher than the branch that holds me. He comes around the front and watches me sail by. Then I become conscious of my long feet sticking out in front of me. Oh no. I jump down and run away, toward Aunty's cabin. I don't look back. How embarrassing. He must have seen my long feet. Oh, he must think I'm crazy, dashing off like that. Mom and Aunty are talking about going camping with the Widow. I think of her son, Freddy. I don't talk to him very often. They went away for awhile this summer and it's almost fall right now. Our Out House Gang is quite broken up, too. Well, maybe it's for the best; the guys were getting out of hand. The conversation catches my attention, just as Mom is saying, "I'll ask her tomorrow if she'd like to come with us for the weekend."

I can't wait. I dash back toward the cabin again. No one is around. The record player sits quietly in the corner. They probably went to Greg's place. Vera practically lives there now, anyway. Greg moved into the empty cabin on the other side of the tracks when he came into town last year. He's really nice. Our gang used to go there often just to listen to his records. None of us had a record player then, just radios. I wish everybody was still here. I get bored quite often. Rita and Hanna hang around together all the time now. Sarah is still my friend but her brother Bobby is getting strange. I've been hearing stories of his weird behavior like torturing animals and always being mean.

I never liked him for as long as I can remember. I have a very bad feeling each time I see him. That strange look on his face — he stares at me in a way that makes my skin crawl. So I only play with Sarah when she comes here but I never go to her house anymore.

I hear a loon calling out on the lake. The smell of pine needles fill my nostrils. I love waking up in the tent. We always put a layer of pine branches on the ground and load down the sides and corners of the tent with rocks. Someone is breaking branches. I poke my head out from under the blanket. Mom is gone already. That must be her out there. No matter how early I think I wake up, she's already out there. I kick off my blanket and crawl out of the tent. Where are my shoes? Mom clicks her tongue at me from over by the fire. "You should have taken your shoes inside the tent. What if it had rained?"

"But it didn't rain," I smile, before running into the bushes on our side of the camp. Deep into the bushes I walk. The ground is very spongy with moss. There are some holes at the base of the pine trees. Squirrels? I wonder if I'd catch anything if I put a snare over that hole in the ground. Well, I don't need to catch squirrels anyway. Not much I could do with a squirrel; besides, they're full of bugs in the summer. I find a good place to squat. Oh, look at the bright pink Lady's Slippers over there. They're so beautiful. Mom gets mad when I pick flowers for her. She says I should just tell her where I saw them so she can see them again and again. I always figured that it's funny how wild flowers die when you touch them.

On the other hand, the teacher got off the train once with flowers he wanted to show us. And they lived for a long time. Are white men's flowers able to live longer than our wild flowers? The ones Teacher brought were big, bushy, white flowers. When I asked Mom why his flowers lived so long, she just got mad at me for asking so many questions. I wish I could move some of the beautiful wild flowers and put them all around our house.

I'm almost back at camp and I smell bacon frying. Mom must like frying bacon when we camp because she doesn't buy it very often when we're at home. I see Freddy coming up from the lake with a dripping face towel. Oh, he looks so fresh and clean in the morning. Mom is giving me a strange look and Freddy openly smiles at me, teasing. I get uncomfortable; I don't understand something here. I duck into the tent. My heart is pounding as if I'd been running. Why? I don't know and I don't care. I'm hungry. I rummage around the packsack for a clean pair of socks.

I kick at Brian's feet, sticking out of the blankets. "Wake up, sleepy heads! Always sleeping in," I tease, as Brian rubs the sleep out of his eyes. Tony stretches and his feet stick out. I slap at his feet, muttering, "Keep your stinking feet under the blanket." Giggling, I crawl back out.

Oh, it's such a beautiful, bright, fresh morning. I dash over to Mom by the camp fire. "Need some water?" I ask. She shakes her head and hands me the towel. I take it and run down to the lake. The surface of the water is smooth, showing a crystal clear reflection of the trees along the shoreline. It's going to be hot though, if a wind doesn't come.

Whenever we put face soap in the water, the bloodsuckers come by the dozens. I wonder if they come because of the soap or because of the water disturbance? I see a hook go sailing up and over in a graceful arch and plop into the water. That was a beautiful cast. I toss the towel on the rock and skip over the boulders till I come to the point where Freddy stands. He looks so beautiful to me this morning. He reminds me of Tarzan in Annie's comic books. He pulls out a cigarette and lights it. I watch the smoke drift into the still morning air around his head. He offers the package to me. The package is white and blue. I don't see those at the store very often and I've never smoked them either. I shake my head. Suddenly, his fishing rod jerks and he quickly holds out his cigarette to me. I take it while he starts reeling in the fish. Oh, it's a beautiful fish, a pike and it's a big one! I find myself giggling in delight while he reels the fish in. Suddenly, the fish is flapping back and forth on the ground behind us. On impulse, I throw my arms around him. Then I remember the cigarette in my hand and also, that this is Freddy. I should not be doing things like this anymore. He's laughing at me, his arms tight around my back. I pull away to cover my embarrassment. I put the cigarette to my mouth and puff. I make a face and hand it back to him. He throws his head back and laughs. I like the way he throws his head back to laugh. His eyebrows go up and he softly says, "Remember the partridge?"

Then I remember the partridge he caught last summer. I nod and run back, skipping over the rocks, back to the campsite. I stay with Mom all day, drying fish while Freddy and his mother paddle over to the point to check the fishnet. They return with another tub filled with fish. We clean and dry the fish over the open fire; some to be smoked, the rest to be made into pemmican. Mom doesn't like fish pemmican too much, so we're making it all for the Widow. Freddy's little sister just sits by her mother. She won't play with Brian and Tony. But then, those boys are always gathering rockfish that live under the rocks and pebbles on the shore. I carve out little canoes and paddles for them to play with. I make a miniature birchbark canoe for the little girl, but she doesn't want to play with anything. I think she's sick.

In the evening after supper I'm sitting on the big rock by the shore, when a whiff of cigarette smoke reaches me and I see Freddy. He comes to sit down beside me. I point to the bearskin draped over the back of the overturned canoe. "That would look like a bear to someone across the lake, wouldn't it?" I ask. The canoe is green. Set against the green bush background, the black fur is draped over the front bow of the canoe.

Freddy whips the skin off the canoe and walks to a shield of roots from an old windfall. It is about six-feet high intertwined with numerous roots holding the soil and Freddy drapes the bearskin over it. I giggle and energetically fashion a dark head and legs for our moose. We stand back and admire it. Yep, that looks like a moose all right. I grin up at him and share a newly lit cigarette. We settle down to talk about the coming fall and the possibility that Freddy will be going away to school. Suddenly, his mother sets up a cry for my mother to come quick and look at this thing the kids have made. "Who did this?" the Widow demands.

Sheepishly, Freddy and I walk to the camp fire. Our "moose" has his skin unceremoniously yanked off his back and shoved under our noses by the Widow. She yells, "What's got into your heads? Don't you realize this is where the Americans are hunting now? They'd think nothing of riddling our camp with a million bullets trying to kill that thing you put out there. We'd all be dead in a few minutes. What's the matter with your brains?"

Freddy and I look at each other. Gee, I never thought...

The next day, we prepare to go home. We've had a nice weekend. Freddy says that in a couple of days, they will be taking the train back to his aunt's place in the next town. He will be going to school from there. I'm getting to feel quite lonely already.

Sure enough, in the following weeks, Annie, Jere and Freddy go off to school far away. Tony and Maggie have been sent away to boarding school too, because their real mother wouldn't look after them. Barbara, Cora and the baby have gone away again to live with Allan. Even Aunty and her family have gone to live with her oldest daughter in the next town. Of the whole busy household, only Brian, Mom and me are left.

We have another new teacher with a family. The kids like him so far. Mom likes the teacher's wife. She always comes over to visit, talking and laughing with us since Mom doesn't understand her. Hanna is off to the bush with her parents again this year. Rita isn't in school either. I don't know what she's doing at home. Only Sarah and I walk to school together now, except when her brother, Bobby, is with her. Then I usually wait till they go by before I start off to school. He has me really scared.

I'm the only one in the grade six row this year. That's the row that's always empty for fear of being sent far away to school. Hardly anyone has the guts to sit there all year. I'll be leaving next year. I have gone from the grade one row, one row each year, and now I'm in the last row of the school room. I feel at times like I'm sitting on death row. I get to thinking — where do all those people go who go away on the train? Where does the train go? What's it like where Annie is? I would like to see what's out there. All I've seen so far is from the occasional hospital trips. Then, I'm usually too sick to care. What will it be like when I go off to Boarding School?

Vera lives in another town too. She and Gary got married last month. Wess and Laura live somewhere else. I hear they are going to have a baby by Christmas time.

Jed is turning out to be the town drunk. I don't even talk to him anymore and Ben is back again. He was gone all summer to the bush with his parents. He's still in grade four. He keeps failing his grades. Maybe he does it on purpose so he never gets sent away.

Maybe I can go visit Vera and Greg sometime. Yeah, that's a good idea. Tomorrow is a school day and I feel like everyone's gone and left me all alone.

It's hot so I kick off my blankets. The top bunk squeaks under me. Yeah, I'm back on the bunk again. Brian sleeps beneath me and Mom has the whole double bed to herself in the corner. We've curtained off the little room at the back because it gets too cold in winter. Mom has put the extra double bed back there. I yawn. Mom doesn't even feel like telling nighttime stories, anymore. Nothing's the same.

22

LOCKED OUT

Winter 1964/65

Oh, it's so cold. The frost just about freezes my breath in my throat. I run as fast as I can, but my throat hurts. About ten inches of snow is on the ground right now and it squeaks with each step I take. I have my books and paperwork clutched under my arm. There's our cabin. No smoke from the stovepipe. No fire. Oh, please God, not again. My feet slow to a walk as I approach the path to our door. She's gone. There's the padlock on the door. Where am I going to find her now? I feel like crying. Where do I put my books? I look up at the roof but there's too much snow; that's where I used to put them before the snow came. It's a good thing I don't come home with schoolwork very often. There's the washtub hanging against the side of the cabin. I shove my books in there.

Now, where would she be? Maybe at Sarah's. I run down the path. I feel like bawling. Oh, I hate this. Why did she start drinking so much, anyway? When did it happen? I love my mother very much but why is she doing this? Nearing Sarah's cabin, I can hear the drunken noises. Oh, it's all her fault — Sarah's mother. If she had left my mother alone, she'd be home right now. Oh, I hate Sarah's mother.

I push the door open. It stinks. The room is filled with cigarette smoke and bodies. People are crammed around the table and on the bed. Some are talking and others, with elbows on their knees, sit with their heads hanging down. There's Mom. She's singing one of her favorite church hymns quite loudly, swaying from side to side, a high-pitched voice, totally oblivious to everything and everyone around her. I walk across the floor and shake her by the shoulders. "Come home! Right now!"

She manages to focus her glazed eyes on me for a second then slowly, her arm comes up and brushes my hand off her shoulder. "Mom! Get your jacket on! You're coming home with me. Right now!" I grab her jacket and roughly shove her arm in it. Pursing her lips, she clumsily tries to put her arm into her other sleeve. She begins to sing her church hymn again. I growl at her, "Shut up! And get your stupid arm in the sleeve!" I can't believe I said that.

Suddenly, she grabs my arm and pulls me down, glaring at me, almost cross-eyed.

I nod, "I know, I know. But you make me so mad! Why did you drink again?"

She pushes me away, grumbling, "Never mind! It's none of your business what I do!"

I look at her a minute. Then swallowing the lump in my throat, I manage to get her right arm in her jacket. All right now, next. I've got to get her to her feet. "Come, stand on your feet and we'll walk to the door. Put your arm over my shoulder. Come on now."

She takes one big breath, arches her brows way up on her forehead, looks down her long straight nose at me and says in an almost sensible manner, "Why, I don't feel like going anywhere at the moment."

I shove my short, stubby nose between her eyes and hiss, "You are coming home right this minute. If I have to drag you home, I will! Now, move your feet. Right now!"

She blinks several times at me very slowly and, very slowly, she nods her head. All right, one left foot forward; she's swaying badly. I'm beginning to have my doubts about this. I've never seen her drunk like this before. Oh God, I hope she doesn't fall. She's much too heavy for me. Here's the door; hang on, one step over. Okay, great. Around the corner of the cabin, not bad. Now up the little hill; oh no, she's coming backwards. I push forward with all my might. Okay, whoa, too fast. Now, she's going sideways. Just a little faster, get a good momentum. Boy, we're sure coming down the path at a pretty fast pace. I hope she doesn't stumble. I'm puffing very hard and I can feel beads of sweat down my back. "Don't fall! Careful! Careful!" I groan, because she's almost leaning her full weight on me.

Then she starts to giggle. "Owl, will you remember your mother when one day, you'll be so drunk, your kids will have to carry you home?"

I glance at her sideways. "Me? I will never get drunk! My kids will never have to carry me home!" I say with such force and confidence that Mom starts laughing out loud. She laughs and yahoo's, like it's the best joke she's ever heard! I pull her up against me and say, "Just you watch! It's quite easy, you see? I just let everyone else make the mistakes then all I do is learn from them. Like you. You've just taught me what it feels like to have a drunken mother!"

I feel so much more free to talk to her about anything when she's drunk. This is a lot better than talking to myself or maybe it's because I know she won't remember the conversation in the morning. "I found out Liza is pregnant. I didn't know she was old enough to have a baby. Now, Liza's taught me something. I know a man slept beside her so now I know not to do the same thing," I trail off, for Mom is laughing at me again.

"Wise Owl, it seems so easy to you because you still don't know anything. You think you have everything all figured out, but you still don't know anything! You're really quite a bird-brain, you know?" She looks at me and continues to laugh. "We'll see what you have to say when you're all grown up." She giggles again.

When is that suppose to happen? "Do I have to be a certain age to be grown up?" I ask.

Her head comes up: "Huh? What are you talking about?"

Forget it. That's the only problem; she doesn't stay on one topic very long. Her mind flies every which way or sometimes, she's in limbo, not thinking about anything at all. Most times, she just cries. We're almost home. "I forgot to check your pocket. We'll have to stop at the door. I need the door key. And stop slapping my hand away. I have to dig in your pocket for the key!"

She stands against the wall, swaying, "I'll get it, I'll get it!"

Sighing, I say, "If you drop it, I might not find it again!"

There, she's got it in her hand. Actually, the string on it is looped over her little finger. Lucky! We stagger across the porch together. I yank the key out of her hand and open the padlock. Then we lurch through the door quite fast and I throw her onto the double bed in the corner. She just lies back and closes her eyes. Now I have to light the stove. A bit of coal oil should do it. There, I have the fire going. I'll make some macaroni with tomato sauce and bannock with tea for supper. I'll let her sleep.

Brian bursts in through the doorway, "Gee, it's cold in here! I can see my breath in here. See? Hhh-hhh."

I hiss at him, "Shut up! I just got her home. Let her sleep. Maybe she'll be sober when she wakes up." Then I add, "There's no wood for tomorrow. I'll have to stay home and get some wood. Mom was supposed to get some today but she got drunk instead. Now, she'll be sick in bed all day tomorrow. Would you tell the teacher not to come looking for me? Tell him Mom's sick and I have to get some wood."

Brian is looking at me with big round eyes. "Okay. But how do you know she's going to be sick tomorrow?" he asks.

"I just know, that's all. She always gets sick the next morning, remember?" I'm thinking that since I got her home early today, maybe she'll be okay tomorrow. But just the same, I want to be out there on the lake all alone. If she sleeps in, I can be gone by the time she wakes up.

We have macaroni and tomato sauce, bannock, with tea — a good supper, a regular supper. Brian is teasing me about my bannock; it came out a bit flat.

The lights go out; it's time to sleep. Mom gets up, goes to the pail by the door, rearranges her bed and crawls in under her feather blanket.

This time doesn't turn out too badly. She didn't get up and try to go back to the party. And she didn't sit up and start singing. Maybe it's because she's more drunk this time. I yawn. I'm so tired.

The next day, I get up very early before the sun is even up. There's just a pink tint on the horizon when I start the fire. There are only a few pieces of wood left but perhaps they might last till lunchtime. I break off a piece of bannock and stuff it in my pocket.

Dressed nice and warm, I get a fresh pail of water from the lake. I turn down the stove and go out, closing the door softly behind me. With a light heart, I kick the sleigh over, banging it loose of the snow and pull it behind me. It's a crispy clean fresh morning. I follow a narrow path which runs clear across the lake in almost a straight line. Whoever goes in that direction usually uses one path. The path branches off to our woodpile we left there last week. It's the green wood we need. We still have piles of dry wood behind the house. That will last us until summer. The sun is well up over the horizon, when I reach the hill where the wood is piled. I'm puffing, as I pull the tobaggan up.

I dig up a couple of logs, five all together, pile them on the sleigh, and tie them crisscrossed with a rope. I pull the sleigh to the top of the hill. Mom usually walks the sleigh down by holding it back with the rope behind the sleigh. I don't think I can hold back this load all by myself. I know what to do. I get the sleigh into position, directing it by pulling it left, then a touch to the right. I get it lined up straight, making sure it will go right between the two pine trees at the bottom of the hill. Then, with a gentle push, I release it. Down goes the sleigh gathering speed. Then it hits a bump and veers sharply to the right and then crashes into the tree. The logs fly and scatter all over. I race down the hill. What a mess. The left runner on the sleigh is splintered. I haul the sleigh out of the snow-bank. Sure enough, the runner is broken, but it will get home okay.

After much huffing and puffing for another hour, I manage to get all the logs on the sleigh again. I tie a knot on the broken rope, shake the snow off me, wipe the sweat off my forehead and now I'm ready to go. I pull the sleigh over the bank of the shoreline and onto the ice. Back on the path, the load is quite heavy. Maybe I just got myself too tired out back there.

Halfway across I stop. I rummage around in my pocket. There was something I didn't forget this morning. I pull out one wrinkled but still whole cigarette. I then pull out a match from the pocket on my shirt. I lay down on the ice, strike the match on my zipper, blow a long stream of smoke into the air and stare at the sky. I smile, thinking of when I saw Uncle Daniel, slightly drunk, at the store yesterday. Asking what I'd like, I said, "One cigarette."

He just looked at me and chuckled, then pulled out his package of cigarettes and gave me one. I didn't think he would give me one. I was just joking, half hoping he would.

I prefer cigarettes to snuff . Snuff is too messy. Suddenly, a song wells up in my chest and I sing out loud, "If I was a speck of dust on this huge white ice, Lord, would you see me?" The sky has gone blurry. Tears are in my eyes, flowing freely, over my cheeks and wetting my ears. I must be crazy. Who ever heard of anyone crying, lying flat on his back in the middle of the lake? I start to giggle. When did I start thinking about God anyway? Well, maybe it was when we got confirmed by the Bishop. He came here last spring. I like Jesus from the Bible. I wonder what He would be like if He came by and sat down beside me, right now. He would probably smile. What would He talk about? He can understand anything, everything which even Mom doesn't know. When everything goes wrong, Jesus would be there. Actually, it's quite comforting to know that there is one person stronger and more dependable than your own mother! He will always be near me — yesterday, today and tomorrow and all the days after that. Whereas people may be nice yesterday, drunk today and maybe dead tomorrow. Oh, why am I thinking like this? Do I really need Mom? I can be on my own, can't I? Why not let her do as she pleases and I can do as I please? I can look after myself, can't I? Seems like I spend more time running after her these days. She's like a little kid when she's drunk. And Brian? I have to look after Brian too.

I find myself at my father's grave more often these days. I just stand there wondering what it would be like if he were alive. Then I start remembering all my friends' parents fighting, their fathers beating up their mothers. I don't want anyone beating up my mother. I don't want anyone touching my mother. I guess that's why I have to drag her home whenever she gets drunk. Maybe it's better that my father isn't around. But then I've never heard any stories of my father beating my mother, have I? What was it the old lady said once? If you're good, God will take you before you turn bad. If you're bad, He'll wait till you repent and become good.

But that's not fair, is it? But then, what's fair anyway? Seems to me, I'm always suffering for something I didn't do and feeling guilty about something I couldn't do anything about. Well, all I can do is go about my own business and to heck with everybody else and their opinions about what I should do or be. I put my cigarette out in a neat little hole in the ice and stand up slowly. I put the rope over my shoulders and pull the sleigh again toward our cabin. The smoke is still coming out of the stovepipe. I hope Mom is feeling better. There she is standing by the woodpile, looking at me.

A week later, on a clear cold moonlit night, Mom is drunk again. It's the day before Christmas — my birthday. I'm thirteen, I think.

"Shhh, don't move!" I hiss in Brian's ear. We're hiding behind our woodpile. Everyone in the community has gone nuts. They're all drunk. Mom is senseless drunk inside the cabin and here we are, hiding from that crazy Bobby. Someone's coming up behind us on the ice. "Up the tree! Quick!" I push Brian up the first branch and scramble up after him. The tree branches are frozen solid and the needles are stiff and sharp. I feel sticky blood on my hand. Higher!

It's the old man from across the tracks. He walks by us toward the cabin. I can hear the door open and close. Now I hear Mom singing her church hymn inside. Where can we go? Where can I take Brian? I ran out of the cabin when I first heard Bobby coming. Then after he went in, a crash sounded and Brian had come running out of the cabin, crying.

Oh, Mom! I practically pushed her all the way home, this time from Rita's cabin. What am I going to do?

"I'm cold!" says Brian, shivering up there.

I whisper, "Hush, be quiet!" I hear the door opening again. There's Bobby, coming around the comer of the cabin, toward us. He stops right below us. I hope he doesn't look up. Presently, he leaves, staggering and stumbling down the path toward his cabin.

I hear Rita's mother, still in there. She came after us when I had just gotten Mom in the door. She wanted Mom to go back to the party. I am so angry and stupid tears are rolling down my cheeks. "Come, let's go down!" I pull at Brian's leg. Slowly, we climb back down the tree, onto the woodpile and jump down to the ground. I'm cold and Brian is shivering badly.

We run back inside the cabin. Rita's mother and the old man are sitting on Mom's bed. Mom is down on the floor. I nudge her, "What are you looking for?"

"I can't find my snuff box. Brian, find it for me." she mumbles.

Brian makes a face at the spit-covered floor. He looks at me sadly, "I'm going to go to Tommy's house. He has a back room that we can stay in and lock it so no one can bother us."

I nod, "Okay, but come back early tomorrow morning. Be careful." He turns and runs out the door.

I pull Mom back up on the bed. "Oh shucks! I forgot to lock the door!" I mumble to myself.

Jed comes staggering in. He looks like an old man with his floppy pants and greasy hair hanging over his eyes. He's drunk, filthy drunk, with spittle running down the side of his mouth. "Hi there, Delia! You know, you have a very pretty daughter here. Another year or two, she'll be a beautiful young lady, the prettiest girl in town!"

A sneer stretches my lower lip. The stupid idiot. He's putting a hand on my arm and to my waist. I whirl around knocking some cups off the table and hiss, "Don't touch me! Keep your filthy hands off me!"

"Hey, what's the matter with you? I didn't say anything wrong. Why are you mad at me for anyway?" he shoves a lop-sided grin at my face.

"Just get away from me." I walk around him picking up the cups that have rolled across the floor.

"Listen, you're pretty miserable right now. But look at that body you got there and that pretty face, I'll wait for you! I'll wait till you're grown up in about a year or two, then I'll come get you!" he says, laughing.

I'm really mad now. "Nobody is going to come and get me! I wouldn't go with anybody around here, especially with the likes of you!" I yell. I hear a voice breaking, in the echo around the room — my voice!

Mom lifts her head and focuses her dazed eyes on us. "Hey you, Jed, you leave my daughter alone!"

Jed laughs. "How are you going to keep all the men off her when she looks like that, eh? In a couple of years, you'll have all the young guys at your door. How old are you now anyway? Eh? Fifteen? Sixteen, eh?" He's breathing down my neck again!

I move away. "Just leave me alone and shut up!"

Mom laughs from the corner of the room. "Jed, leave her be. She's just a little girl. Thirteen years old she is today. You'd never get anywhere with that girl, anyway. Even if she was a young lady already. Come here, Jed. Tell me where you came from when you got to our door?"

I grab the broom from the corner by the door and start to clean up, sweeping and mopping around everybody's feet. Finally, the old man leaves. Rita's mother goes, too. Jed has gone to the door four times already and always comes back to say something more. Filthy beast! I am so tired! It must be way after midnight. Oh, I hope Brian is all right.

Finally, Jed steps across the doorway. I bang the door right behind him and quickly bar it. I sigh and lean against the door.

Mom is snoring on the bed. She still has her shoes on which I pull off and cover her. I blow the lamp out. It's getting cold, since I've let the stove go out. I'm always afraid a drunk might fall on it and start a fire. I've seen some people burned. I crawl to the top bunk and close my eyes. I pray, "Please Lord, protect our cabin. Put a shield around our cabin."

23

THE LONELY TIME

Spring 1965

When I'd say, "Please Lord, let her be home," she most often wasn't home. So I figured maybe if I thought, she won't be home, she probably would be.

Whenever I need her to be home, to show her something I've made at school or just to come home all happy and normal, she's never home. So now, I'm thinking, "She won't be home. She won't be home…"

As I near the cabin, my heart sinks. I can see the sun reflecting off the silver padlock on the door. I feel like bawling. Approaching the door, I drag my feet slowly. Where will I find her now? I stand around at the locked door for a second. I wish I had a second key because I know they come with two keys. I've seen those padlocks at the store but she must have long since lost the other key. I wanted to show her the painting in my hand. I had finally painted the island across from our house, not as good as Wess can. Well, maybe I'll never be as good as Wess, but it was the best I've done yet. I was so glad when Teacher said we could paint anything we felt like. I look around but the washtub is not hanging where it was before. I walk around to the back of the cabin and finally settle on shoving my papers between the piles of wood. I sigh and lean against the woodpile. Brian has gone to a friend's house. I doubt he'll be back till bedtime. Sarah's mother was at the store today so she's not drunk. So where can Mom be?

I heard Hanna's father got off the train today. That's probably where she is. I take off at a run, past the Catholic church, down the long tall stand of pine trees to the left down a path to the cabin where Hanna's parents live. I hear the noise of the drunks in the house. Things are crashing and people are yelling and laughing. A dog snarls at me and crawls under the steps with his tail between his legs. Filthy beast, I think. I walk in. Right away I spot Mom with her head hanging between her knees. I head straight for her when a hand closes around my arm. I look up. "Freddy! What are you doing here?"

He has been drinking but he doesn't appear to be drunk yet. "I never went back after Easter break, I'm working on the CN, now," he says.

I smile. "Oh, here? Where's your mother and sister?"

Freddy looks at the floor for a moment. "No, I won't be working here. Mom has decided to stay there. And my sister died last week."

I reach over and put a comforting hand on his shoulder. Bad mistake, for his hand instantly covers mine. A bad feeling swells up in my throat. "Let go, Freddy. I have to get my mother home."

Roughly, he pulls me over to his side. I see anger cross his face, before he smiles. "Leave your mother be. She's not a kid. She's been a widow for such a long time."

I yank my arm free. "You've changed, Freddy. I'm taking my mother home like a kid. And don't ever speak to me or touch me again!" I hiss and I quickly yank Mom to her feet.

She seems surprised to see me but reluctantly she lets me put her arm over my shoulder. I step over someone's vomit but Mom splashes and slips through the mess, as I pull her to the door. I want to cry so badly. I don't know what hurts most; having to get Mom home again or seeing Freddy end up like all the rest. What a totally rotten world. What a damned hopeless life. Mom suddenly lunges forward. I grab her by the collar. "Don't you dare throw up on my feet!" I yell. She mumbles something and we continue down the path. I keep thinking, I hate this. I throw my head back and I feel and hear my voice, screaming, "I hate this!"

Mom puts her head up. "Huh? What's that you said?"

I feel tears streaming down my face. "Never mind, Mom. I love you. Don't worry, I'll get you home. I'll get you home everytime. Don't worry..."

She gets away on me several times before I get her to bed for good. She's that determined to get back to the party for another drink. Brian never came back. Maybe he tried before I got home, but the door was locked. I finally go to bed when I determine that Mom isn't going to try to sneak out anymore.

Suddenly, I'm awakened by cold hands rubbing my shoulder. It's Freddy. "How did you get in here?" I yell.

"Sh, sh! Your mother let me in. It's all right. Sh, sh. She knows it's only me," he whispers.

I slap his hands away. "Just don't touch me!" I hiss.

He giggles and brushes the hair away from my forehead as I try to scramble up. "Sh, sh! Did you know that my mother and your mother made an agreement long ago, that I would take you for my wife when I could support a wife? Well, I've loved you since you were a little girl. Now you're a beautiful young lady and I'll have you. I'll love you and look after you."

How dare Mom do that. How did Freddy dare to come in here expecting to collect someone he thought had been promised him? My God, this isn't ancient times. I have a right to say something about which drunk will beat me practically half to death each time there's a party. In any case there wasn't going to be one tonight. How dare Mom let him in. I jump out of bed and kick the table bench over. It vibrates with a crash in the empty room and I scream at the top of my lungs, "Get out! You get out of this house and don't ever come back! No one has the right to claim me, do you understand me?"

I've the notion that I grabbed Freddy by the collar and threw him out the door. Suddenly, I'm leaning against the barred door, breathing heavily and I hear the scuffling noise of someone staggering away. I feel like I'm going crazy. Tears are streaming down my face and I stagger to my bed. Oh Freddy, what made you end up like that? You were such a nice person. I sob till I fall asleep. Why, Mom?

Brian never showed up at all, so I walk to school alone. Mom is still sleeping. It's such a beautiful morning, the birds are singing, the sun is hot, and the snow is melting along the paths more and more every day. I can smell the fresh moist spring air and the pine scent when I pass the stand of pine trees. By now, I've noticed that the other children don't seem to be affected in the least, even if a drinking party has been at their house. And here I am, feeling like I'm ready to die each time I have to drag, push or pull Mom home from someone's party. Maybe it's because they have both parents and they don't have to worry about them. I only have Mom and it's up to me to make sure she comes home. I yawn. I hate having to go to school today but, at the same time, I wouldn't want to stay home if you paid me. Mom will probably sleep all morning, at least.

After school, Brian and I race home. I win, of course. He always sniffles when I do. What? The padlock is on the door again. Oh no. "Brian, is anyone drinking today?"

Brian shakes his head. "I don't remember anyone saying their parents would be drunk tonight!"

We sigh and sit down on the porch steps. Oh, it's getting cold too, in spite of this being a spring evening. Wait. I run to the garbage dump on the other side of the path and start kicking aside several cans. I finally find a Klik can with its key still attached. I pull the key-shaped clip off and run to the door. As I grab the lock, I notice it hasn't been clicked shut. I laugh. "Brian, it wasn't even locked! It's just hanging there!"

We enter. It's cold inside. I pull the stove lid up. There are a few ashes glowing. Maybe there's enough to start a fire. I throw some wood in and blow through the air vent. Nothing. I shove some paper through. It burns but goes out again; the wood doesn't catch. No fire. I get the coal-oil can, spill some inside the stove and close the lid. There's lots of smoke, but no fire. I blow at the air vent again. Nothing. I pull the lid up and bend over to look in. Suddenly, flames explode in my face. I spin around to the sink behind me. Glancing in the mirror, I check to see if my hair is on fire. Then I slam the stove lid down, as the stove roars to life. I push the door open to let the smoke out. I examine my face and find that my hair is singed around my face. Brian starts giggling beside me. "You even got curly tips on your eyelashes. And look at your eyebrows."

In spite of myself, I start to giggle. I do look funny. But at least the stove is going now. I put the teapot on the stove. Suddenly footsteps cross the porch. It's Mom.

Full of relief and joy at seeing her sober, I stand there by the stove with a big smile on my face. She enters and dumps a sack full of twigs and rolls of birch bark on the floor. "What's so funny? Smells like coal oil smoke to me," she says, glancing at me.

Brian busts out laughing and says, "Look at her! She's got curls on her eyelashes! The flames came out and exploded right in her face."

Mom glares at me. "You know better than that. What's the matter with you? You could have set the house on fire and yourself as well."

Feeling like a worm in the mud, I ask, "Where did you go?"

She rummages around in the foodbox for our supper, munching on a piece of bannock and says, "Well, I fished a little but it was too late in the morning. Maybe we'll go there tomorrow. I set some muskrat traps in the bay at the portage. We'll check them tomorrow. Now, how come the tea isn't hot? I'm starving!"

I giggle. "We sat around for quite awhile outside before we discovered that the door wasn't even locked!"

Brian scoffs, "Well, the dummy never even checked!"

I throw my mitt at him. "Oh, shut up! You'd still be sitting outside if I didn't open the door for you!"

Mom sighs. I look at her, slumped at the end of the bench. She sighs again, looking at me, then back to Brian. "Don't you kids ever stop arguing?"

Brian whirls to look at her, totally puzzled and asks, "Why for?"

I look at Mom. She shakes her head. "Never mind!" She takes a pot off the shelf and begins supper.

I sit down and try to figure out something here. But I'm hungry. I think maybe I'll just bring in some wood to make the time go faster and maybe make that nasty little pest help. "Come on, Brian, help me get the wood in for tomorrow, or else I'll punch your ears out!"

The morning sun is out bright and crystal clear on the shimmering sheet of spring-melted snow that now covers the ice on the lake. I breathe deeply and thank the Lord for such a beautiful morning.

Mom says behind me, "Honour the Sun for shining on your face and pray it will acknowledge you and bless you each morning..." Quietly, her voice fades. She's distracted by Brian's yelling.

"Owl! You stole my clean dry socks! I saw them hanging there yesterday! Give them back!" he howls.

I whirl around and shout, “They are not your socks! Those were mine ’cause I hung them there myself! When was the last time you hung your socks up?” The Sun and God quite forgotten, I stomp around, grab my mitts and scarf. I reach for all my property within the immediate vicinity. That includes my chipped tea cup with the spotted black and white dog on it. A spray of liquid spills on the stove and steam hisses. I hadn’t realized there was anything in it! Sheepishly, I fill my cup with steaming coffee to cover my embarrassment. Brian giggles. I feel like kicking him. What a nasty little excuse for a kid he is. I turn to the table for the sugar and milk, stopping to observe his light-brown curly head bent over a book at the table, trying to read the last page by the light of the coal oil lamp. My heart melts and I long to wrap my arms around his little body and hug him. Then Mom says, “Blow the lamp out. The sun is bright enough if you move to the window.”

Crunch, crunch, crunch, crunch. The snow squeaks under our boots and I look occasionally when I feel safe that a branch isn’t going to slash me across the face. We cut across the tracks and enter deep into the woods, walking for maybe two miles. Finally, there’s a lake. I examine the shoreline and recognize a boulder at the far end. “Mom! This is the lake halfway down the portage road!” I exclaim.

She rolls her eyes upward and sighs, as if to say, “Of course. What other lake can it be?”

I smile. Anyway, at least I know where we are now. It feels kind of strange walking deep in the woods and not knowing where I’m going. I wonder how she finds her way around the bush when there are no footprints.

It’s late afternoon and we still haven’t caught a fish. Mom finally pulls her line in and says, “Let’s go. We’re not going to catch a fish this morning. Let’s check those traps I set yesterday.”

I scramble up as best I can on a foot that has gone to sleep. The little rascal of a brother is eyeing me with obvious delight already. Little weasel. I’d belt him one if I had the time to make a snowball. I watch him dash into the woods way ahead of us.

“Mom told you to make the sandwiches for us, so where are they?” Brian rummages and dumps our packsack upside down on the snow and out roll our sandwiches — one, two, three. “Is that all?” he demands. “I could eat all of them myself and still be hungry! Why did you make just three sandwiches?” he yells at me.

Mom is upon us at that moment. She has one muskrat in her hand. She glances at the three sandwiches. “Is that all you brought?” she asks.

I nod. I just thought three sandwiches for three people. But I’m so hungry, too, that I can eat all three and still be hungry like Brian said.

Silently, I watch Mom peel the skin off the muskrat, clean it and poke a stick through it to anchor it over the open fire.

"It's quite good when it's cooked over the open fire like this," she says.

We have no salt. For the first time I've been responsible for the lunch and I've failed. I look at the pile of muskrat guts in the snow, still warm when suddenly, Brian kicks them over my foot! "Gee whiz! Knock it off!" I yell, scrambling to my feet.

Brian dodges into the bush on the other side of the fire. I hear him tramping over the crusty snow. I stand looking at the fire. I've felt like crying so many times these days. I feel so angry. Mom watches me and I sit back down. The blood drips off the muskrat and sizzle into the fire.

"Always listen to the silence. When you feel your emotions all in turmoil inside you, listen to the silence..." Softly, Mom's voice trails away, as if she were only thinking out loud. How do you listen to the silence when silence doesn't have a noise? Or does it? I sit and listen. I can hear my heart beat, my breathing, a bird chirp from across the bay, Brian breaking branches somewhere, a slight wind overhead above the trees, a train coming, a dull hum in the air, and always my heartbeats. I smile at Mom. Yes, it is very calming. But now I also hear my stomach rumbling and growling in hunger. I slowly sip my cup of tea.

The muskrat is quickly eaten. It tastes like roasted rabbit. I sigh and lean back on the snowbank with another cup of tea. The smell of wood smoke gives me much comfort.

"Pig, you got the last cup of tea!" Brian yells at me.

I smile and close my eyes. He stomps away into the woods again. Soon Mom begins putting the teapot back in the packsack with the muskrat skin. She'll probably stretch it tonight on the muskrat board before she goes to bed. I kick snow into the fire to put it out.

We are very quiet all the way home, following behind Mom and trying to match my steps to the railway ties. I kind of forgot the world around me. I'm always so worried or angry about one thing or another. It's kind of peaceful when it's quiet. I see Brian's foot cross mine just in time. I jump over and he dodges to the other side of the rail. I continue walking.

"Hey, what's the matter with you?" Brian asks.

I glance at him and smile. "Nothing." He looks at me then runs ahead of Mom.

It's hard to break a habit, a reflex, an unthinking response but eventually I no longer retaliate in kind to Brian's tricks. During a loud drinking party, I listen to the spring rain falling softly against the window pane. During the loud arguments of beligerent drunks, I strain to hear the wind in the trees outside the cabin and shut everyone out. More and more, I spend time sitting by the woodpile, listening to the silence. The ice melts on the lake, the grass turns green, the leaves come out, the flowers bloom. I look over the land and feel peaceful and happy. I rarely talk to anyone else outside the family and I never go out to play.

Then, Barbara comes home one day for a visit. After studying me for a moment she approaches me and touches my shoulder. I'm flustered and totally surprised. I tense. Then she pulls me to her in a hug. She has never done that before. I find my arms come up and around her. I can feel her shaking against me and my eyes are filling. I smile and in a shaky voice, I say, "How come you are so short now? You must have shrunk at least four inches since I saw you last."

She begins to giggle and stands back to look at me again. Mom comes in and I notice the two kids, Cora and John, standing by the door. I run to them, hugging them. Oh, it's good to have a family again. A heavy weight lifts off my shoulders.

24

WELCOME CHANGES

Summer 1965

My heart is pounding so hard and I'm terrified. I must be dying or, at least very sick. I stumble out of the outhouse in a daze, still clutching my swimming shirt under my arm. I can hear Annie and the other girls screaming and splashing in the water at the beach. I come around the corner of the cabin. Barbara is hanging clothes on the line. I walk very slowly and carefully into the cabin. Mom isn't home. I walk toward Barbara, feeling very sure that I'll be dead soon. I hang my shirt at the far end of the clothesline and hesitantly approach Barbara. She glances at me. "What's the matter? Don't usually see you out of the water first."

I take a big swallow before I find my voice. "I'm sick. There's something wrong with me..."

She takes a closer look at me and picks up another shirt to hang on the line, "Well, what's wrong with you? You don't look sick to me."

I take a deep breath. "There's blood coming out of me. Lots."

She pauses then slips the last clothespin on and looks at me. Then she starts to giggle. I feel my mouth stretch open. I'm dying and she's laughing at me. With trembling lips I snap my mouth shut. She takes up her paper box basket and turns to the cabin. "Come on, I'll give you something. You're just starting your periods, that's all."

I follow her. "My... what?"

She looks back at me. "Monthlies. Every lady gets monthlies."

I sigh apprehensively. "How long does it last?"

She says, "One week or four to five days. Depends on the person." I'm relieved. Maybe that's not so bad. Then she continues, "One week every month till you're old and grey."

My mouth falls open again. "What? All the time? Every month? That's not fair! I won't get a chance to do anything! Go swimming or ... or anything!" What a thing to happen to a person. Good Lord. I can't go walking around if I'm bleeding. What is a person suppose to do then? Lie down for a whole week?"

Then Barbara digs out what looks like a slingshot strap and hands me a box. It has clean pads in it, all smooth and white. "Hey, I remember Mom got mad last summer when she caught me using these as beds for my paperdolls. Remember? I never did figure out why she kept them."

Barbara sits down and starts laughing again. Snapping the strap, I ask, "What's this for?"

Barbara says it's a belt and pad and shows me how they're used. I dash out to the outhouse, relieved that I'm not dying after all.

I return to the cabin and find Barbara cooking outside on the wood stove. "I have one more question," I say.

She waits and says, "So, ask."

I shift my foot. "Why does this happen? What is the blood for? Do boys get the same thing? You only said ladies."

She giggles and shakes her head at me. "Of course, boys don't bleed. They're not the ones who have babies."

Now, I'm really puzzled. "Babies? What's this got to do with having babies?"

She takes a deep breath. She's getting annoyed with me. "When the blood doesn't flow, it stays inside waiting for a man to start a baby in you. When no man goes inside you, then the blood will come out again. But if a man enters you where the blood comes out from, then you will have a baby. And the blood will not come out again because the baby will be using it until it's born. Then it will flow again, until you get another baby."

I stand there for a minute. "Oh. But how would a man get inside me?" I get an awful thought of a grown person… "Come on! You're kidding!"

Barbara giggles at me again. "Yes, when you are grown up, married and have a husband then you'll have a baby."

I look at her from the corner of my eye and make a face. "I'll never get married. I won't ever need a husband because I'll look after myself!" She laughs out loud this time and I dodge around her to go back to the beach.

What's all the commotion inside? I can hear Mom's voice, loud and angry. I jump over the steps, landing on the porch and skip inside. She's still going on and on about something. I drop down on the bench and throw one leg over the side. Suddenly, her screech centers on me, "Look at her. Straddling the bench like a kid. Get off that and sit properly!"

She just about backhanded me off the bench. What the heck did I do now? She keeps at me. "You're only thirteen years old and you're a woman already. It's not normal to be having your periods so early. Put that cup down. You're suppose to be unclean at this time. Women used to wash everything after they touch things. I did not have mine till I was almost sixteen and I had to go sit in a little wigwam so that I didn't contaminate anything in the house… now, look at you. Your body is already ready to receive a baby!"

I jump up and run out the door. I run to the lake and stand there. I wonder why she never said anything to my other sisters. Tears drip off my face and land on my shirt. Well, what the heck can I do with my body to make the blood stop? Actually, I had already forgotten about it. It's not particularly uncomfortable. Maybe Vera can explain it to me. She wouldn't mind if I ask her questions. Why didn't Barbara tell me Mom would get mad? What could I have done to make the blood come? I shut my eyes, praying, "Oh Lord, I don't ever want a baby. Please make it stop and never let it come again." I hear footsteps behind me. I wipe my eyes with my sleeve.

Annie jumps on the rock beside me. "Barbara says, Mom's mad because you were the last of her baby girls. You're growing up too fast."

I look at her, "You never wash everything you touch, do you?"

She laughs, "No."

Silence, listen to the silence, I think. I hear seagulls and Annie breathing beside me. I grin at her. "You have a whistling nose."

She giggles and rubs her nose. "Look, Sarah is waving at us, there at the point!" We jump off the rock and run along the path by the shoreline.

We've been camping for a whole month already. It's very hot; the sun is beating down on our heads. Gently the canoe glides over the waves. I look back at Annie at the other end of the canoe and smile. Brian spends his time playing with Cora and John, leaving me and Annie free from his pestering. "Let's turn around here." I swiftly pull my paddle back as Annie swirls her paddle around and we are now heading back to camp. Smoke drifts over the bay where our camp is. Barbara and Mom are smoking moose meat.

I couldn't believe it when Mom shot and killed that moose with the .22 gun. We were setting a sturgeon net when the moose emerged from the bushes along the shoreline. We've been eating quite a bit of moose meat before it gets rotten. The rest is all being cut up and dried. Pretty soon in the evenings, Mom and Barbara will pound it into pemmican. We were running out of sugar and planning to leave before she killed the moose. She decided to take some meat to the old hermit who lives on the island to trade for a bag of sugar. We had to stay and look after the kids as only Brian went with them.

Annie speaks behind me, "Do you realize we'll be leaving in two weeks? You'll be able to come and visit me once in awhile wherever I'll be living. They'll let you leave the residential school overnight to visit me. It'll be great!"

I'm scared but I'm also looking forward to leaving home. I hate it at home now. I have nowhere else to go. I feel like Mom doesn't want me around anymore. She rarely talks to me directly so I avoid her as much as I can. I hardly ever talk to her anymore and she acts as if I'm already gone. I asked her if I could live with Vera but she wouldn't let me go and I don't have any money of my own to get on the train by myself. Anyway, it's a lot better with Barbara here all the time.

"Sh, sh. Listen!" I say. We sit still. "There! It's Mom!" I hear Mom yelling for us. Nearing the bay, we paddle faster. What's she yelling about?

As we jump out of the canoe, she comes to scoop a pail of water. "Barbara has cut her hand very bad! That darned moose hide! Look after the kids till I get her hand cleaned and tied up."

We scramble to pull the canoe up. Brian and the kids are standing, staring wide-eyed at the blood on Barbara's shirt. She's laying in the shade with a towel wrapped around her hand soaked with blood.

One morning a week later, Mom and Barbara are sitting by the fire talking when I overhear them. Mom sighs, "I guess we'd better head back home. They'll be leaving for school in a few more days."

Barbara nods, "Yes, my hand will be no problem paddling. It's pretty well healed by now."

I take off at a run. "Annie, Annie! We're going back!"

Annie looks up from the pool of minnows by the shoreline. "Good, I'm getting bored!"

I can't believe how nervous and scared I am as the departure date nears. Finally, it's the last day. I dig out an old suitcase of Vera's and wipe it clean, shaking out the dust. I gather bits and pieces of clothing and I clean my only pair of shoes. They're called penny-loafers, something like that. The sole of the right shoe flaps loose at the toe. Maybe I can sew it up. I sit down on the steps and sew it along the ridge. Then I sit on the little suitcase to close it enough to push the clasp on. Barbara pushes me aside. "Let me see. That's not how you pack things!" She smiles.

I stand and watch her neatly folding my two shirts; a sweater, a pair of pants, two pairs of socks, two panties and my old little Bible. She looks at it a minute before she shoves it under the clothes again. A couple of shiny rocks, a pinecone and a mallard tail feather, all wrapped in a piece of paper, pop out from a pocket. She frowns and shakes her head. "Can't take these! What are they going to think, you carrying around things like these? White people are going to be looking after you where you are going, you know?" I watch my treasures clatter across the floor to the corner behind the stove to be swept up into the garbage later.

The moment has come. The train is stopping and it's late afternoon. Sniffling, Barbara hugs me and kisses my cheek. I return her hug and for a moment I wish I weren't leaving. Then Mom is kissing Annie and I stiffen when she turns to me. I put my head down and she brushes my forehead and then she's gone. I follow Annie onto the train. When we are all seated, I feel the train moving. Everything is moving away. Quicker by the minute, the island goes sweeping by. The creek, the little portage, the big portage, the rock cliffs and then all is strange. I have never walked beyond the cliffs. Will anything be the same when I get back? Will I change while I'm gone? I have a tremendous urge to get off at the next stop and take the next train back. But I can't do that. Where would I go? I angrily wipe the tears off my cheeks that escape from my eyes.

25

CHRISTMAS AT HOME

Winter 1965

It seems so very, very long ago since we came this way. The hills are now covered with thick snow. The train thunders through the cliffs, sending swirls of snow across the window. I lean forward, recognizing landmarks now. The big portage, the little portage, the lake, the point and there's the island, all sparkling in the early morning sun. The sky is clear blue. I turn and smile at Annie and Ross sitting across from me. Jere has gone home ahead of us. He had to get home a little early to see his parents. I hear the train whistle blowing far up ahead, then the screech of brakes and hissing when it comes to a stop. The conductor is banging and clanging the door open. My heart is pounding and my knees feel shaky and weak. I reach for my suitcase and a bag and follow Annie down the aisle. Mom and Barbara are waiting for us.

Barbara takes me to her home. They've finally moved here or, at least, she's moved here. She now lives in the empty house beside the Catholic church. She says Allan comes home only on weekends and holidays. I guess he really had to move far up north in the bush now to work for a paper company. Oh, I'm so happy. There's even a room for the kids to sleep. In the corner by the table is a single bed where I will sleep. It is so cozy in here. Cora and John were all over me for the first couple of days.

Then Allan walked in on Saturday morning and the children forgot about me for a while. Barbara just leans back smiling as the kids climb all over their father for a change. I usually go over to Mom's place when I finish here. I help Barbara with the meals, wash dishes, clothes, and watch the children. Usually, when it's quiet, I run down the path to Mom's to see Annie. Mom says Barbara isn't feeling well. She'll have a new baby in the summer before we come back.

Listen, always listen, I must never forget because I'm really afraid of Bobby now. He's nuts. I've been dodging him since I got back. Everyone use to laugh about that last summer. No one is laughing now; he's taken it into his head that one way or another, he's going to have me. I wish he'd just marry someone and stop pestering me. I had to stand inside the closet for about an hour yesterday at Barbara's before he got up and left. When I hear him coming, I just slip out and run the other way. Yuck, it's sick.

Barbara has just come out of the kids' room and smiles at me. The dishes are done and the kids are asleep. "You go now. See what Annie is up to." she says.

I pull on my jacket, boots and mitts. Allan is sprawled on the bed with a cigarette in his hand. He'll be here until after Christmas, then he'll be leaving too, to go back to work. It's very dark already. I see the light from Mom's cabin. Approaching, I also hear loud talking. Mom's drunk but I don't feel anything anymore. I enter, Annie and Ken are playing cards at the table. Sarah, Ross and Rita are sitting by the stove, talking and laughing.

Ross smiles as I close the door behind me. "There you are. We were just about to come and get you. Okay, let's go!" he says.

I look at all the people in the room. Mom is sitting with Sarah's mother, the one who brought the bottle. Even Ross's mother is there with Hanna's father and Uncle Daniel. Smiling, I rush over to give him a quick hug and kiss. Then I'm grabbed by Ross's mother and she gives me a wet kiss, murmuring, "There's my Ross's girl!" I glance up in time to see Ross's face turn red. I giggle. I don't know when I became Ross's girl but at the moment I don't object. He looks so handsome standing there by the stove a little unsure of himself. I smile.

The door opens and Jed walks in followed by Freddy. There's a tense undercurrent, as we file out the door. Amid the jokes and laughter, I see all the toboggans on the porch that I hadn't noticed when I came in.

"Someone planned all this!" I laugh.

Ross grins, "Well, of course. Just like the good ol' times, right?"

Annie joins in, "Like, what was it, the Outhouse Gang?"

Right across the lake is a large hill we used to slide on when we were kids. Kids are there already with flashlights streaming down the hill. The snow crunches under our feet as we follow the narrow path across the lake.

Finally, we race up the steep hill. Ross grabs my hand and starts pulling me up to the top. In the confusion of setting our toboggans down at the top, I find myself beside Freddy. "Come, get on!" he laughs.

I can't just turn and walk away so I lower myself between his legs and I'm immediately enveloped in his arms. With one lunge, the toboggan slips over the hump and down we go. Over a hump, into a dip and over another large hump. We slide out onto the ice. Immediately to the right of us a toboggan comes to a stop. It's Ross. He pulls me up as he grabs his toboggan and we run up the hill again. Freddy lags behind us, dragging his toboggan. I feel really awful. Oh, Freddy, I'm sorry. I know it looks bad. I just want to have fun. Why does it have to be with one person? Cigarettes are glowing in the dark as a cloud covers the full moon. Ross slips and falls, pulling me down with him. Laughing, we push and pull each other up the hill. My boots are very slippery, too.

Just as we make it to the top, I see a hand reach down to pull me up. I grab it and come face to face with Jere. "Hi! When did you get here?" I ask.

His teeth flash white in the moonlight, "I came up just as you came sailing by with Freddy. That you, Ross?"

Ross comes up beside me, chuckling. "Hi!" He slams his toboggan down. "Come on." He pulls me and I nearly fall across his lap. I scramble to get myself turned around to sit between his legs and hear him yell back at Jere. "Got to be quick around here!" Down the hill we go, laughing. About halfway down the hill, we shoot out of the dip, suddenly go off balance and over we go. I get a mouthful of snow and find myself sitting on Ross's chest. I get up in time to see a toboggan heading right for us. Someone is yelling. I grab Ross by the arm and pull as hard as I can, just in time. A toboggan swishes by a few inches from his head. I roll out of the way on his other side.

Jere comes scrambling up the hill toward us. "Are you hurt?"

I shake my head and say, "No. Ross, are you okay?" Ross is still leaning back on his elbows.

Jere kneels down beside him and asks, "You hurting anywhere?"

Ross smiles, then laughs. "I guess I've had it. My ankle must have got twisted." Turning to his side, he winces. I pull his toboggan toward us and we roll him onto it.

Jere and I pull him across the toboggan run, dodging screaming riders, to a house nearby. A deaf man lives there. He's very nice; always keeping a fire going for the sliders. Come to think of it, I saw him sailing by us on his own toboggan when we first got here. We enter and find him sitting by the stove, smoking. He smiles and ushers us in and we all kneel and examine Ross's ankle. It's a little red on one side but otherwise, it looks okay to me. "Go on! Take my toboggan, Jere!" he says.

Jere cracks a big grin at me. I look at Ross sitting by the stove. I feel something again. There's some kind of undercurrent here. It's not a tense feeling like when Freddy is in the room. Rather, it's like a comfortable, friendly feeling. I can't figure out what it is yet. Right now, I want to have fun. So I say, "All right, Ross, since you got hurt and insist that we take your toboggan, fine, we'll go and have a good time!"

I feel like I'm being whisked out of the cabin and back up the hill. Then I settle in front of Jere. He even asks for assistance to be pushed off the hill so he can keep his arms around my waist. I glance back with a smirk on my face. Then down we go. When we get to the bottom of the hill, he doesn't let me go.

I turn my head back. "Don't you think we look silly sitting here in the middle of the ice on a toboggan that isn't going anywhere?" I ask, laughing and kicking us over sideways. We wrestle in the snow before I get loose and head back up with Jere coming up behind me with the toboggan.

Then Freddy is there, instantly grabbing my arm to plunk me down in front of him. He pushes off. Gee, my right leg isn't even on the toboggan yet. I scream when we hit the dip and sail clean off the snow before pounding back on the hard hill with a jolt. When we get to the bottom I'm laying on my stomach over his knees with my feet up in the air. I raise myself on my hands and knees and get ready to say something when he suddenly leans forward and kisses me roughly on the lips. I freeze. Then I quickly jump up and run up the hill as fast as I can. People are continually going down, four or five toboggans, all on the hill at one time. I make it up the hill, puffing and out of breath. Freddy's scaring me. That's the first time anyone's ever kissed me. I feel like he could have at least asked. I have to be very careful around Freddy.

An arm comes around my shoulder, turning me around. "Are you all right?" It's Jere.

The moon has just come out again. I can see his eyes shining. "I'm okay." Slowly, leisurely, we settle down on the toboggan. Again, he asks someone to push and down we go. I roll off as soon as the toboggan comes to a stop, just in case, but there's no need. Right beside us, Little Tommy comes to a stop all by himself on a long toboggan. Laughing, I pull him up. "How come you're all by yourself on such a long toboggan?" I ask.

He giggles and yells, "They all fell off behind me!" I flip his toboggan around and help him pull it up the hill again. I see Jere making his way toward the deaf man's cabin.

I sit down and pull Tommy on my lap, as the rest of the space behind us is filled by Rita, Sarah and Jed. Down we go. When we are walking up again, I think to check on Ross. I push the door open in the cabin and find Jere sipping tea with the man but no Ross. "Ross went home," says Jere. He doesn't seem to mind.

I smile, ducking back out the door and running up the hill. There sits Freddy with a smile on his face. I barely sit down before we are flying down the hill again. We come to a stop right beside Ken and Annie lying on the snow. I yell, "Are you okay?"

Freddy yells, "At least roll over out of the way, will you?" I hear them giggle.

The crowd has thinned out quite a bit. I'm getting cold. Ken and Annie have gone back home. Sarah and Jed are gone, too. Screaming, Rita goes by in a cloud of snow. She must be going down the hill sideways. I giggle when I hear a break in her voice as she hits a bump. We're on top of the hill now. Jere puts his arms around me from behind. I can hear him breathing in my ear. "Are you getting cold?"

I nod.

"Let's go," he says. I nod again and follow him to the toboggan for one last ride down the hill. When we get to the bottom, I feel like I've missed out on something. I'm very quiet now. Walking ahead, I smile. It's funny but I never once thought about Mom. I came here thinking Ross was the special person for me. Now I'm walking home with a comfortable but disturbing companion. I'm feeling so many confusing sensations. I'm so used to organizing and sorting things out in order of importance, but this job with my inner feelings — it's quite difficult. I really don't know what I am feeling right now. Silence, listen to the silence. I can hear the toboggan trailing behind us; Jere's footsteps and his breathing. I smile. Yes, I'm happy.

"Where did you get the toboggan?" I ask, when we near Mom's cabin.

"Oh, it's Ross's father's toboggan. I asked the old man if I could borrow it after Ross left with the other one!" Jere answers.

I grin and, shaking my head, I push the door open. Annie and Ken aren't here anymore. Ross's toboggan is there by the door. Jere whispers, "I'll leave this here, too. He can take it home when he comes to get his toboggan."

"Where do you think they went?" I whisper, looking at Mom fast asleep on the bed. Her shoes are still on. I automatically take her shoes off and pull the covers over her up to her chin. I put a green log in the stove and tightly shut the air vent. I blow out the lamp and grope my way to the door, expecting Jere to open the door for us.

Instead, his arms come around me in the dark. My heart leaps to my throat. I feel his lips gently brush against mine, up the side of my face; soft kisses on each eyelid. I hold my breath, as his lips softly touch mine again. I feel myself touch my lips to his, gently, softly, hesitantly. Then his arms tighten around me, crushing me to his chest and he's covering my lips with his. I push him away, yank the door open and run out.

The door closes. I hear his footsteps behind me, before he pulls me back by the arm. "What's the matter?" he asks.

I look down and murmur, "I don't know. Just leave me alone!"

He trails along behind me. "I'm sorry. I didn't mean to make you angry." he says.

I wish he'd stop apologizing.

I bound up the steps at Barbara's house and go in. Everyone's asleep. I hear footsteps walking away and I pull the curtains aside. There he goes down the path toward the store. Now I feel like crying.

For the rest of the holiday, I stay close to Barbara. I hardly go out of the house again. Anyhow, Annie isn't much fun anymore. She and Ken seem to have eyes and ears only for each other. You talk to them and no one answers. It's really quite funny. Oh, I hope I never make a fool of myself that way. Then I start imagining Ross like a comfortable old shoe. We grew up together, seeing each other every day. And Freddy, who is a little older than us, is very much grown up, more experienced; he's very commanding and rough. I think Freddy would be the type of guy who'd beat his wife. I smile. Ross is the type of guy who would let his wife beat him up. Then there's Jere. He is gentle, serious, stable, sober, fun and reliable. It's scary. He is so solid and mature that he scares me. I feel very immature, uncertain, and forever on guard when I'm around him. It's too emotionally draining to be thinking about these things. I can't wait till our summer break from school.

It's time for good-byes again. Barbara hugs me and I promise to help her out again when I come back. Allan has gone already. I just have time to squeeze Mom's hand before I hurry after Annie. A hand shoots out from the door of the old station and I find myself in Ross's arms. He gives me a crushing kiss on the mouth. I hear him whisper in my ear, "I love you. I always have!"

I hurry out amongst the pressing crowd, till I spot Annie's back. I tug Annie's sleeve, asking, "Isn't Ross coming?"

She yells back, "No. He's going to try to go to work with Ken."

"Is it just the two of us going back now?" I yell, boarding the train.

"Well, Jere went back home to his parents a couple of days ago. He didn't know if he was going back either, or whether to start working now." I follow her to a seat.

It's going to be another while before summertime, when we'll all be back home again.

26

MY LAST SUMMER HOME

Summer 1966

It's such a beautiful morning. The dew is heavy on the ground. I swish the mop around in the water several more times. I squeeze the mop dry on the pebbly beach where I'm standing ankle deep in the water. Cora's footsteps come pounding down the path from the house and she stops at the edge of the water. Her hair is combed and gathered in one braid down her back. Her eyes are twinkling and her smiling face is scrubbed and shiny. I laugh, "I've got an idea you're going to be running everyone ragged today!"

"Look, the sun is coming over the hill now," she says. We watch the lake, the seagulls and other birds, in total silence.

"Your grandma used to tell us each morning to honour the Sun that it may shine on you again tomorrow, with its blessing." I say softly.

She looks up at me with a puzzled look. "What does that mean?"

I grin, "I don't know, except she used to make us wash our faces and comb our hair and stand by the window to watch the sun come up. Well, come on. Let's see if John has decided to dump another sinkful of water on his chest." Laughing, we race up the hill.

Barbara glances up when we enter. She's nursing the baby by the window. She shakes her head at me. "You've never gotten out of the habit of running around barefoot, have you? You're going to cut your foot or step on a nail one of these days."

I grin at her and say, "Let's just say, I never got into the habit of wearing shoes. I saw Mom coming in from the lake when I was down there. I recognized the canoe before I saw it was her. She must have checked her fishnet so she'll be eating fresh fish today." I sigh.

Barbara smiles. "Yeah, she'll probably cook one over the open fire for breakfast."

I laugh, looking at her. "Why don't you just take a walk over there and see what kind of fish she's cooking?"

She grins and nods, "Yeah, I will!"

I take the baby and hold it over my shoulder while Barbara slips her shoes on. In a minute, she and Cora are off down the path. I sigh in the sudden quiet. Allan has taken John over to the big dock. I can see them there watching the old man fishing. That old guy just sits there day after day. I wonder if he's ever caught anything?

Someone is passing by the open window, whistling. It's Jere! I turn to the door when I hear him bound up the steps. "Gee, everyone's chipper this morning. It's a perfect morning." I smile.

Chuckling, he stops in front of me. "It's great to see you, too!"

I feel my face burn. I didn't mean it like that. He runs a finger around my chin to my cheek. I quickly turn my head away. I'm getting very uncomfortable. "Here, let me take the baby," he says. "Hi there, little girl? How are you?" The baby cracks a wide toothless smile. Jere gently slides an arm around my waist and pulls me to him. "Why don't you give your aunty a smile, too, eh?"

Suddenly, a voice speaks behind us, "Well, don't you two look cozy? Why, you look like you were just made for each other!" I spin around. Allan's standing there grinning. With a flushed face, I reach for the baby and escape to the kids' room. I hear them talking.

Allan says, "I saw you come into the house. Did you just get into town?"

Jere laughs, "Just for the day. I just came from Greg's place for the weekend. They're doing fine. I usually stay with Daniel whenever I come here but he's gone to town to stay with his daughter, hasn't he?"

Allan answers, "Yes, I don't think he'll be coming back either. Actually, I don't really know who's taking care of whom! But listen, we have a bed for you right here if you want to stay for as long as you like. We'll just put it in this corner. I'm sure the young lady in the other corner won't mind." They laugh.

I stand there by the crib out of their view, hands on my hips. Well, this lady does mind. What makes you think I will share the living room with him? Then my hands drop; it's not my house, is it? He can invite anyone he wants. I know Barbara won't object, She's always said the more the merrier. I guess it's okay. Maybe I can put him to work drying the dishes for me or throwing the slop pail out. See how he likes that. I march out ready for battle. They're gone. I can hear them talking on their way to the lake. I think maybe Allan's the one that's dying for company.

"Allan! Where's John?" I yell.

Allan glances back. "Oh, he saw his mother going to Grandma's. He took off after them long before they got there!" he laughs.

I watch them head down to the lake. You know? I'd kind of enjoy having Jere around. If only he'd quit touching me. I can't ever trust anyone... not even myself. I wish he'd stop making me feel uncomfortable.

"Is Annie here?" I poke my head in at Mom's place. She looks up from the lamplight. "They were just here looking for you. Where did you come from?" Mom asks.

"I was at Ross's house. His mother called me there and I never did figure out what she wanted."

Mom looks at me from the corner of her eye. "They said they'd be at the station. Just be sure you go home when your sister does!"

I grin, "Yes, Mom, I will!" I jump off the porch, ready to run for the station, when I stop. Bobby. I can see him coming down the path. I don't know how many times I've told myself to listen. Listen first. But I still manage to blunder. I turn quickly and run back into the cabin. "Bobby. Bobby's coming down the path. He's drunk. He had his head down; I don't think he saw me!"

Mom glances at me, then points to the back room. I push the blanket aside and scramble under the old, abandoned couch that was pushed in the corner. I just barely fit under there. I kick some boxes and junk out of the way to make room for my feet and there I lay flat against the wall. I hear Bobby, breathing and stomping toward the bed where Mom sits.

"Where's your daughter? And don't ask me which one. You know the one I'm talking about! Where is she? She's not at Barbara's! She's got to be here. Where is she? And you'd better not lie to me! She won't listen to me, so maybe I'll just shoot her if she doesn't stop running away from me!" His voice vibrates throughout the wooden structure of the cabin.

He's gotten very violent and I'm terrified. When I'm helpless or terrified, I pray. Oh, God. I hope he doesn't hurt Mom because, if he does, I'll be out of here and I'll kill him myself. I know I will. I would kill him, if he hurts Mom. There is absolutely no doubt, I would kill him.

He yells, "Bring the lamp. Go in there! If you are lying to me, you're going to get it!"

I can see the wavering light shine into the room as Mom pushes the drapes back. Her voice is very calm and quiet when she finally speaks, "As you can see, she is not here at all. Annie came looking for her just a few minutes ago. Said they'd wait for her at the station. But you know, if you go carting that gun around, she'll never come close to you. Would you go to someone who's threatening to shoot you? That's a .22, isn't it? Where did you get that from? They don't make those anymore."

Then Bobby yells, "Don't try to sidetrack me! If she's not here, then where is she? This was my father's gun. But I'll still use it, if I see that daughter of yours!"

I hear a sudden clatter all over the floor. Bullets. Bullets are falling all over the floor, rolling under the couch, where I lie. He's still arguing with Mom, getting madder by the minute. I see his knee as he kneels on the floor. Then a hand, groping all around, picks up the bullets. His hand just about touches my nose. I start pushing the bullets away from me as quietly as I can. I shut my eyes… he pulls my shirt, then pushes it aside as another bullet rolls under his hand. I am holding my breath and shaking so bad. He finally satisfies himself that he got all the bullets. Meanwhile, Mom has been constantly talking to him. Thank goodness, I hear the door close behind him. I relax and feel tears biting my eyes. I am so relieved as I roll out and stand up

Mom comes in. "Better leave now before he comes back to check."

I nod, then stop beside her. Somewhere along the way, we came to understand each other. I give her a swift hug and say, "Thanks!" I hurry out the door. I run toward Barbara's place. When I enter, there sit Jere, Ross, Annie, Ken and Sarah!

"Where you been?" Jere is the first at my side.

"I was at Mom's," I say shakily. I wish I had someone to lean on.

The train will be here soon. We all parade down to the train station to see who is going to get off or on the train. Ross is really making an effort to stay beside me, but his place is taken by Jere or Freddy. I wish they'd just knock it off. But then I have to admit, I rather enjoy it when I have all three of them making my day more exciting.

"Hi Hanna! Haven't seen you in awhile! Come here, join us!" yells Sarah, "Rita! Come here!"

Gee, now we're all together again. In the winters, everyone goes trapping or away to school, but summers are ours. We make room for each other to sit on the platform of the storage shed, with each wooden step holding at least three people. That kid, Little Tommy, still hangs around us, too. He's a young lad now but he's still the baby of our group and he gets to sit with us.

Ross whispers a message in my ear, "Hanna wants to see you out back."

I lean back and discover Hanna's seat is empty. She was here a minute ago, sitting between Jed and Annie. I slide off my seat beside Ross and walk around the corner of the building and there I meet Freddy. He plants his hands against the building wall on each side of my head and looks down at me. "Why do you do this to me?" he whispers as his face comes closer.

I struggle to turn my face away, but his lips come down on mine hard, bruising. I put my arms against his chest and push him back hard, "I've never done anything to you! You're the one that keeps bothering me this way!" I whisper angrily.

His arms fall to his sides, just as a shadow falls across us. It's Jere.

"Are you okay?" he asks me, looking at Freddy. He takes my arm.

What's with these guys? I yank my arm free. "Yes. I'm fine! Just fine!" I hiss at Jere, then rush by him and stomp around the comer back to the crowd. I return to my seat and Ross reaches an arm down and pulls me back up. I lean against him when he pulls me close beside him. I can almost feel his heart beating. Everyone has burst out laughing at one of Ted's jokes. The train is coming. Hand in hand, Ross and I follow behind everyone to the train station. We watch an old couple get off but Jere makes no move to get on the train. Apprehension settles over me at the thought of Jere in the same room. The train is gone and we're walking back to the store saying good night to each other. Jere is beside me taking my arm, saying "Come on, let's go home!"

Ross stands, uncertain for a moment. I lean over and whisper, "I'll see you tomorrow. I guess he's my bodyguard." Indicating Jere, I giggle, "Maybe they even paid him!" Ross breaks into a grin.

Jere pulls me away and asks, "What's so funny?"

I shake his hand off. "Nothing." Annie and Ken are way ahead of us already, arm in arm, walking toward Mom's cabin.

The lamp is turned down low, shining through the window curtains when we near the house. At the door, Jere turns to me and closes his arms around me. I stand leaning against him. I'm tired, very tired. I put my head up to say something. Instead I find my lips, throat, ears, devoured with such intense passion and I feel him tremble against me. Jere has never acted like this before and the panic is rising inside me. Why is he always making me feel this way? I push him back roughly. "Don't! Please don't do that ever again!" I whisper, whirling around to go inside.

Acting like nothing happened, I proceed to fix his bed. He'll be in the furthest corner from mine. He's there helping me from the other side of the bed. Suddenly, he grabs my hand, stopping me. I look up and he says, "I'm sorry."

I continue spreading the blanket. "I thought you were getting on the train tonight." I say.

He grins. "I decided to take Allan's offer and stay the weekend."

I decide then and there to stay away from all three of them!

Jere ends up staying a couple of weeks, leaving me constantly on guard. But that doesn't stop him from planting kisses on my neck or hand whenever he's close enough.

One night, while we're all sitting around the storage shed as usual, Jere gets a great idea to blindfold each other and try to find a specific place. Whoever gets there first wins all our cigarettes. Great idea.

The night is dark and clear and only the northern lights are in constant motion above us. We all stand around Bobby. Yes, Bobby. He's always had the biggest and brightest flashlight in the community since the ice-skating days. So now, we've nominated him to be overseer of the contest. He is tightly blindfolded by Jere and Ken, his flashlight is turned off, and among claps and shouts, he is spun around to a count of ten. Then he staggers around the circle we've made around him. His left hand touches Hanna and his right touches Jed. In this way, Annie is paired with Rita; Ross with Ken; Jere with Little Tommy; Sarah with Ben; and Freddy's with me.

He yells in a loud voice, "Everyone, two by two, blindfolded and together! First couple to the big dock wins! No yelling! No screaming! No laughing! No noise! Or else you give your positions away! Swing each other around and no peeking! Make sure your blindfolds are in place! I'll be waiting there for the first couple!"

The blindfolds are tied on everyone. I feel Freddy beside me, breathing softly. I listen; there's no noise. "Let's go," he whispers.

Five steps, then suddenly there's a grating of loose gravel to our right, followed by curses. I giggle. That was Jed. Well, that must be where the tracks are, so we have to go this way. Freddy is laughing under his breath when we take a sharp turn to the left. Oh, there's the path. I feel quite confident, as we stroll hand in hand, my other arm outstretched to ward off any sudden obstacles.

Suddenly, I feel something squish and pop under my foot. I pull Freddy to a stop. "Oh God! I think I just squashed a frog!" I gasp. I can feel him shaking again. I hiss at him in a whisper, "What are you laughing at?"

He pulls me forward again. "Hurry! Come on, let's go!"

I feel a smooth road under my feet, "I know where we are! Hurry!" I say. We're half running when an object hits our clasped hands and whips us back. We collide with full force; my head against his jaw. We both yell, "Ouch!" Then we realize it was a poplar tree that blocked our path.

He moans, "I can just see myself trying to explain this bruise to Mom tomorrow!"

With a giggle, I reach up. "I'm sorry." I put my hand against his jaw. I've never touched his face before. Suddenly, he grabs my hand, then slowly kisses my palm. I reach to free my hand, "Listen!" I whisper.

We can hear Hanna and Jed laughing and falling over cans and bottles in the garbage pile. It must be the teacher's garbage. I know where we are. On impulse I reach up on my tiptoes, pull Freddy's head down and kiss him full on his lips. Before he can react, I pull him forward. "Let's go! We'll get there before they do!" We practically run down to the lake and to the dock. I'm thinking, why did I do that? Boy, I'm really asking for trouble.

As soon as we hear the swishing water and the giggles, I know others got there before us. We've no sooner sat down when Jere appears beside us, yanking his blindfold off. Ross and Ken don't show up for the longest time; they really got lost. They come in rather sheepishly, twirling their blindfolds.

All too soon, the train is coming and it's time to go home. This time, Ross walks me safely home, right behind Jere. I really have to put a stop to this, but how?

I wake up to see Jere very close, his eyes just inches from my face. I feel the panic rise inside me again. I jump out of bed and run outside the door barefoot in the early morning light. I kneel by the water and splash fresh clear water on my face. I have a very strong urge to dive in and scrub myself clean all over. I don't like this feeling.

Today was very nice. We had a party at the far island. We had two boats full of people and we played records and went swimming with our usual group, but Jere is beginning to worry me.

Do I like him? I'm not even quite sure what love is. But he's beginning to crowd me.

I'm very comfortable with Ross. I know he won't put me in uncomfortable situations and I know he can't hurt me. Then there's Freddy; he's very rough and possessive and I can't trust him. He's capable of forcing me. And Jere is the perfect gentleman. He would listen to whatever I told him; he would stop when I told him to, but he is so serious.

If I decided to be his girlfriend, it would have to be for real, for good. I'm just having fun right now. No, I don't want that. The only way to keep him at arm's length, is to make sure that someone else is always with us.

One evening, Jere comes through the door at Barbara's house while she and Allan are in the next room, talking. Cora and John are already asleep. I have the baby in my arms on the bed. Jere reaches for the baby and pulls her out of my arms. "I'm leaving tonight, you know. And you haven't said anything," He says, his eyes searching mine.

I grin. "Thank God! I'm getting pretty tired of bumping into you everytime I turn around!" I say in mock seriousness. Or is it?

He laughs and kneels beside me. "I may not be able to visit again before school starts."

Just then, Annie drops by to visit. Interrupted in what he wanted to say, Jere goes out. After awhile, Annie also leaves. Putting the baby to bed, I decide to run after Annie to walk her home. Just as I close the gate behind me, Jere clamps a hand around my arm. "I have to talk to you! Come back before the train comes! Please?" I look straight at him. He looks at me grinning. "If you don't come back before the train comes, then I'll come and talk to you right in front of your mother!"

I feel my face burn and yank my sleeve free to run after Annie. Things are coming to a head and I don't like it. I don't have to decide on anything. I don't want to.

I'm at Mom's, waiting for the train to come. Annie has gone to sleep and finally, Mom sends me home to bed. Why does the train have to be late tonight, of all nights? A flood of relief flows through me as I near the house. The lights are out. Barbara and Allan must be asleep. Then, in the moonlight, I see a tall lean shadow detach away from the building. I stop. My heart is pounding in my ears. He comes towards me and I can't move. He stops very close to me. I feel his hands brush my cheeks and he pushes my head up. His hands are trembling. I can feel his heart pounding against mine. Then the familiar rise of panic is flooding my chest again. I push him away. I hear him say, "I love you! I've been waiting, wanting to tell you that I love you very much!" I feel his arms slide around my back again, pulling me against him. I pull away so violently, he jumps back.

I hiss at him, "No! No! Leave me alone! You are always making me miserable! Why don't you just leave me alone? I hate you! I hate you!" I hear his sharp gasp of breath and a moan escape his throat as he turns away. I listen to the sound of his running steps fade down the path in the darkness. I hear the train coming now. Trembling, I barely make it to the steps where I sit down.

Slowly at first, tears roll down my cheeks. Then, like a flood, they wash over my face. Deep wrenching sobs shake me as I cry my heart out. Finally exhausted, I lean back against the door frame. I wish I was just a little kid again. Why does life have to be so complicated? I'm tired, so very tired. I haven't cried like that since I was a kid. I stand up and softly go inside and lock the door. I grab the quilt from the bed in the corner and lay down on Jere's bed. I smell Jere when I turn my head on the pillow. I whisper in the dark, "I'm very sorry, Jere. Please know that I'm so sorry I hurt you like that! I'm very sorry!"

Shoving my hand under his pillow, I feel something. It's a cigarette box. I pull it open and feel one cigarette in it. He never smokes the last cigarette from a package. "Bad luck," he'd say. I grin and trail my finger along the window sill above the bed till I feel a match where Jere always kept them. I strike the match, light the cigarette, and slowly watch the match burn out thinking about what kids used to say. "Where the burnt out end points is the direction of the person who is thinking about you." It pointed to where the train had gone. I smile in the dark and puff on the cigarette, thinking that perhaps growing up wouldn't be so bad after all.

I love Jere. It has always been Jere who I've liked, isn't it? Yes, since the first time he pushed me on the swing, I've liked him. Now he's gone and I've told him...

Suddenly, I become aware that it's hot. My side is very hot. Then I'm wide awake! Noticing a huge, wide, round glow of embers on top of me! I jump up, out of bed with a pounding heart and dash across the room towards Barbara's door. Then I stop. I run back to the bed, roll up the quilt into a ball and run outside with it, dropping it on the ground. I dash back into the house again and open all the windows. The kids' door is closed so I softly open it. There is no smoke. I close their door again and run outside picking up the quilt from the ground, heading down to the lake to throw it into the water. I splash in knee deep after it and unfold it in the water. There's a big hole, two feet across, right in the middle of the quilt. A faint dawn in the eastern sky means it's just getting daylight. It must be four o'clock in the morning. What am I going to do with the quilt? I drag it to the shore and wring it out as well as I can. Spreading it on the ground, I sit down, studying the damage. It starts in a long drawn-out giggle deep in my throat, then comes out through my nose and I clamp both hands over my mouth. I gather the front of my shirt and hold it against my face as I lean forward taking a deep breath. I am laughing so hard I'm shaking all over. Then I become aware that I'm being watched. Through my tears of laughter, I see a dog silently watching me. That only makes me laugh harder. Finally, I decide to just leave the quilt there in a pile. If they ask me, then I will have to tell them. If no one asks anything, then I won't have to tell them anything. I kick it into a pile under some bushes and walk back to the house.

I sniff when I enter the room. There's a faint smell of burnt material but otherwise, the smoke is all gone. I pull off the rest of the sheets from Jere's bed and throw them in the laundry basket on the porch. Then I lay down on my bed and pull the blanket over me. I grin as a sudden thought comes to me. You're right, Jere. The last cigarette is bad luck.

27

LAST ENTRY

Summer 1968

The stillness is broken only by the occasional chirp of a bird somewhere in the bushes beside the path. It's very quiet. I always find myself going up this path when I'm feeling lonely or sorry for myself.

A breeze gently rustles the leaves of the poplar trees as I near the cemetery. The cool morning air is still present here under the tall pine trees. I stop beside my father's grave. The ribbons are faded and some have rotted off the cross. Mom used to change those fluttering ribbons every spring. Now they look like she hasn't been here in a couple of years. My gaze settles on another grave further over. I'm a coward; I haven't been able to bring myself to come here earlier. I never did get a chance to say how sorry I was to Jere. That was two years ago and I never saw him again. About five yards away is Jere's grave. He left behind a wife and a new baby. I see a fresh grave beside it, which I know is little Tony's. As I look around at the crosses, I recall most of them. The old graves at the corner are all but forgotten now. I don't know any of those. The thought slowly comes to me that only one or two older people could have died a "natural death". The railway line and alcohol-related accidents take so many lives. I think dully that I should straighten the cross on Tony's grave; it's tilted a little to the side, but my feet won't move me forward. Tony died trying to jump on a moving freight train last year. I want to run.

The sand cascades down the hill as I run blindly down the path. Gradually, I calm down as I slowly walk past the soft flowing creek. A dragonfly hovers unsuspectingly above a frog. As my foot lifts again, the frog leaps and with flying legs, disappears into the murky pond. I pause to wipe the tears off my face and take a deep breath. It's peaceful here. The frog popped up among the weeds and I continue down the trail; my feet lead me down to our cabin by the lake.

I love this community. I know every hill and hollow, stump and tree. This poplar on my right has my initials carved on it. The overgrown bushes brush me on both sides, obscuring the path.

I've come to the cabin now and stand there surveying the tall grass and weeds that have grown all around. The windows are all boarded up. Someone's chopping wood by the bay.

The sun has just emerged from the morning's layer of haze spread across the horizon. The sky is a clear blue; it'll be a hot day. Suddenly, something catches my attention. My gaze rests on a man sitting on the rock by the lake where our woodpile used to be. I know him. I smile. I slowly approach him, taking in his neatly-combed, thin, white hair, the blue jacket and pants hanging over his small frame. A blue-checkered shirt is buttoned up to his neck. He sits knees crossed with a smile on his face. He doesn't move. His eyes twinkle, I remember them so well. I stop in front of the Medicine Man. He pats the rock at his side motioning me to sit beside him. In silence, we sit there together. He is as he always was. I feel his calming presence flood my soul, a rushing warmth of completeness, of knowledge undefined, then calming peace settles over me. I feel like I have just completed a circle; I glance at him thinking that here the medicine man is one person in total harmony with his world.

Finally, in his peculiar accent, he says, "Your family has moved."

It was more a statement than a question. We sit there looking at the cabin. I answer, "Yes, everyone's gone, scattered everywhere, all over the place..." My voice trails away. I'm wishing at the same time that we were all here together again. I can hear dogs fighting somewhere by the train tracks.

"Your mother?" he asks.

I glance at him, he looks so frail. "Mom got married last year and moved across the tracks with her husband. I don't like him, so I better move too."

I ask, "Did you just get off the train this morning?"

He doesn't answer. There is a long silence, then he says, "Where will you go?"

Sighing, I answer, "I'm going to live in the city with Vera and Greg. Brian is at Barbara's place on the train line where Allan works." I snatch at a circling buzzing horse fly — got it.

He looks at me, "Don't you like the city?"

I smile, "Yes, I like the city but summers are for holidays with family, lakes, camping,... I'll miss this place very much."

His eyes crinkle at the corners when he smiles and he asks, "How old are you now?"

I answer, "I'm sixteen, but I feel like ninety-four sometimes."

We look at the cabin again in silence. Then he says, "Yes, I got off the train this morning. I have a person to see so I thought I'd stop by for a visit and found... '' he indicates the cabin, then continues, "I'm sitting down for a rest — that's what being old is!" He smiles.

A dog races by at full speed, thundering down the path. I say, "But even with four legs, an old dog goes just as slow as an old man."

He looks at me and laughs. We continue to sit, looking at the cabin. "It looks so cold and lonely." I say.

He leans forward with his elbows on his knees and says, "Even its logs get warmed by the sun and who's to say that your voices don't still echo deep within. The cabin is only a reflection of what you're feeling right now."

Thinking about that, I say, "But sometimes it's hard to remember the sun on cloudy days when you can't see it, or hear the stillness when you're surrounded by too much noise."

He studies my face for a moment, then says, "One thing you know for certain without a doubt is that the sun comes up every morning and sets again in the evening. Does it care about the clouds? The stillness itself lasts forever but the noise can be silenced."

I smile and nod, "Yes." I understand. The sun is always up there even when you can't see it and silence is always within you.

"Owl, tell me how you got your name." he says, looking at me.

I laugh, thinking I haven't heard that name since I was a kid! "An owl hooted several nights in a row outside our cabin before I was born. My brother threatened to go out and shoot it because it kept everyone awake. It went away when I was born but I was a night baby with big round eyes and I made such an awful noise crying all night long, that no one in the cabin could get any sleep." I giggle, "I don't think my brother was too happy about me, either!"

He laughs and stands up, brushing the seat of his pants. "Tell your mother that I'll come to visit this evening."

I nod and I hear him chuckle as he slowly walks around the corner of the cabin. I wish there was something I could do for him; I've nothing to give him, yet he's given me so much. I get up and notice how the weeds have overgrown the many paths our feet have worn along the shoreline. I jump down to my rock and stand there looking out onto the lake. How many times have I stood on this exact spot as a child? It seems so very long ago.

My boxes are all packed. I'm leaving on the train tonight. I take a deep breath of the clean, fresh air and watch the sun's rays dance on the water's surface and think, "The sun will keep coming up till the end of time but the people it shines on are here, then gone. Is that what Mom meant? What was it she used to say? "Honour the Sun, child, just as it comes over the horizon, Honour the Sun, that it may bless you come another day…".

SMCL
3 5151 00143 2756